Falcons on the Floor

Falcons on the Floor

Justin Sirois

Publishing Genius Press 2012

PUBLISHING
GENIUS PRESS

1818 East Lafayette Avenue
Baltimore, MD 21213

publishinggenius.com

falconsonthefloor.info

ISBN 13: 9780083170648

Copyright © Justin Sirois 2012

Book and cover design by Justin Sirois
Typeset in Garamond Pro, Minion, Prestige Elite Std
secondarysound.blogspot.com

Promotional illustration by Connor Willumsen

This novel would not exist without the editorial support of Haneen Alshujairy. Haneen and her family fled Baghdad in the summer of 2003 as Iraq succumbed to sectarian violence. After spending two years in Jordan, the Alshujairy family moved to Cairo, Egypt where they currently live.

Haneen consulted on *MLKNG SCKLS* and *Falcons on the Floor*, providing an authenticity that would have otherwise been impossible. Haneen also plays a vital part in the Understanding Campaign, an international Middle East awareness project that continues to grow.

This book is dedicated to Haneen and her family.

Deleted scenes from *Falcons on the Floor* previously appeared in the book of short stories, *MLKNG SCKLS* (Publishing Genius, 2009).

The author would like to thank Christy Whipple, Lauren Bender, Michael Kimball, Joseph Young, Aaron Cohick, Adam Robinson, Jamie Gaughran-Perez, Dahr Jamail, Joseph Cashiola, Tim Johnson, Gregg Wilhelm, Tai Turner, P.H. Madore, William H. Macy, Felicity Huffman, and Yoko Ono as well as all the people who blogged, interviewed and recorded *MLKNG SCKLS*: Matt Bell, John Dermot Woods, Ginny Dermot Woods, Bret McCabe, Blake Butler, Brian Allen Carr, Aaron Henkin, Gina Myers, Matthew Simmons, Amelia Gray, Spencer Drew, Michael FitzGerald, Seth Amos, Gene Kwak, and John Madera.

Excerpts from *Falcons on the Floor* and *MLKNG SCKLS* have appeared in *Lamination Colony, JMWW, Nano Fiction, Consequence Magazine, Dark Sky, The Stamp Stories Anthology, The Signal* (WYPR Baltimore), *The Marc Steiner Show* (WEAA 88.9 Baltimore), *Gutter Magazine* and *Big Lucks*.

I cry out to the Gulf: "O Gulf,
Giver of pears, shells, and death!"
And the echo replies, as if lamenting:
"O Gulf: Giver of shells and death."

Rain Song
Badr Shakir al-Sayyab

Before the war

I walked with my hood down. The ice-sharp wind slicing hairlines in my shin bones. That late Maine November. Never thought I'd miss the snow.

My brother, five years older, had joined the military too, but only after college. He was more patient than me. With two useless degrees in Medieval Literature and American History, he joined the Marines, became an expert marksman. He met a woman in Germany. Lovely. He excelled as a Ranger, saved every extra dime, returned from the Gulf War with only a missing big toe, early onset carpel tunnel and a big smile. He married the German. He bought lakefront property. Now he lives in Vermont, far enough from my parents to keep them from visiting every other month.

His life is perfect, 'cept for missing that toe.

The week he left for boot camp he pulled me into his bedroom before dinner. I was almost seventeen. Mom seemed unable to climb stairs wearing an apron and Dad, not home yet, sat furi-

ously in traffic. So this was the safe hour. It was the hour we per-
fected our butterfly knife opening, added footnotes to the *Anar-
chist's Cookbook* with the intensity of PhD candidates and schemed
perverse revenges on homeroom rivals: light bulb bombs, Bouncing Betties, pipe grenades, zip guns, shotgun shell traps – scribbled
diagrams for instruments we only daydreamed about. We'd heard
kids lost fingers trying that shit. We liked our fingers the way they
were.

His room was always dimly apocalyptic, lit from a single
red bulb in the center of the ceiling. My brother leaned on the
banister, making sure Mom was occupied, and pushed me inside.
Locking the door, ceremoniously punching me in the shoulder –
the sure bet something exciting was about to happen. He walked
to the corner of the room. His bass guitar leaned against the wall.

He pulled his dresser back and reached down. He pulled out
a lockbox. Handed me the key once it was open. He pulled out a
pistol, a semi-auto silver and expensive pistol, and cocked it back
to show me it was unloaded – waited for my wide eyes to blink.

"Dad gave it to me. Early Christmas because I ship out next
week."

"No shit," I said.

"I can't take it with me."

And I understood.

We marveled at the gun. Released the magazine and stripped
out the bullets and cocked it and practice-fired. He put the pistol
back and said, "You hold onto that key."

And as he knuckled me again in the top of the shoulder, the
boney part, it felt like he was offering access to his bedroom, too.
It was a weird honor, standing there with plates of macaroni and
cheese partly devoured and petrified on stereo speakers, lacrosse
sticks and posters of Kathy Ireland on the wall. It felt like another

world. He was offering his room as a sanctuary from the unfettered parental attention I was about to endure.

"Cool," I said.

Then he left for Boot Camp, and I was alone.

* * * * *

All the time I spent in there, Mom thought I just missed him. She might've been right.

Weeks later, during Thanksgiving break, I sat in his old room, on his old bed, perfectly made and warm. The baseboard heat rose around the skirt of the comforter. I held the cordless phone in my hand, pulling the retractable antenna in and out.

I knew Katie's number.

I could dial it without looking.

A plate of food steamed next to me on the bed.

Saturday leftovers – Dad's favorite and my favorite: turkey sandwich with a slice of cranberry sauce as thick as a hockey puck, gravy and mashed potatoes – both sweet and white – billowing from its seams.

I couldn't take a bite. I let it congeal like my brother had let his old plates mummify on his bureau, on the stereo.

Dad had the volume turned too loud. TNT was playing *The Wizard of Oz*. Monkeys flew from the living room TV.

I dialed half of Katie's number and turned off the phone. I wanted to mash the phone face-down in my turkey sandwich.

Early in the week, we had blinding snow squalls. They lasted only half an hour, but that was long enough to slick the roads. Our school bus driver had taken his time navigating the un-plowed surfaces. We passed stuck cars unfit for winter and everyone on the bus kept unusually quiet, peeping out the white-washed windows.

The temperature plummeted. And I remember it was windy because all the Christmas figurines that had been prematurely planted were strewn across lawns and driveways like mass suicides – a plastic reindeer dangled off a neighbor's roof by a string of flashing lights. Wise Men and Mary toppled like bowling pins.

I went right home, immediately sucked into whatever video game I was obsessing over at the time.

Sometime that night, Katie's mother had been hurrying home from her weekly book club. She hit a patch of black ice and slid. The van careened over a little bridge and flipped, crushing like a tissue box. Snow banks cushioned the blow, and she hung suspended in her seatbelt, pinned for hours, semiconscious and praying between nods. The horn honked for a minute but no one heard.

Two kids carrying toboggans spotted her brake lights from the guardrails. The kids took turns holding her hand through the busted glass. The ten o'clock news called that a "miracle."

Paramedics arrived.

Snow mobiles and ATV's were the only vehicles able to access the wreck. A helicopter medivacked her to Maine Medical Center where she lost a leg from the knee down – barely saved the other. I heard all of this the next day at lunch from Kevin, whose mother was a nurse.

"Lost a leg," Kevin kept repeating.

The Wednesday before Thanksgiving, Katie's family surrounded a hospital bed, heads lowered, and, instead of saying grace, they begged for the morphine to keep the razors of pain at bay. I suppose they were lucky. Of course they were. Though miracles are never without suffering of some sort.

I could've called, but what to say?

I dialed half her number, buttons illuminated in the dark,

and hung up. There was nothing to say. She probably wasn't even home. The phone glowed like a little office building in my hands. The buttons were lit windows. Somehow I thought my brother's room would give me the courage to call, because I knew he'd call. No matter if Katie knew about any undisclosed and longstanding crush – he'd call.

I stuck my finger in the mashed potatoes oozing out the side of my sandwich. I licked it. It was all I could eat.

The door was cracked.

Only a spade of hallway light shined through.

Sometimes I'd sit in his room with the Sega Genesis playing loudly through the stereo. I'd just stare at the big pixelated heroes on the screen and listen to the music. My brother always had a better TV than me. He played *Rambo* the video game better than the real Rambo could be Rambo.

From the living room, the Wicked Witch melted into smoke. Mom laughed and laughed, snorting a little, making Dad and my uncle laugh too. That was her favorite part, the melting witch.

Snow came.

Flurries outside the window made everything quieter than normal, like the world had been sprayed thick with fixative, and we were waiting for it to dry.

Waiting for everyone to pass out, I lay on my brother's bed with the dial tone in my ear, as if by listening hard enough I might hear Katie crying, too.

I knew I'd have to walk it.

* * * * *

Sneaking out wasn't hard.

We'd been good at it, my brother and I, making practice runs even when we had no secret rendezvous with a girl or plans to smoke-out the old club house tucked a few acres back in the woods. In hindsight, Dad probably knew the whole time, probably thought it good for the behind-the-line reconnaissance missions he fantasized us performing in the future – extended crawling through pinecones and rotted logs, socks clogged with mud-like pastry bags. His liberal policies with knives and BB guns were all part of some elaborate military doctrine.

As long as at least one of us signed up. We were both happy to.

I checked the hallway, making sure my parents' room was blackened – no late night aura from their television.

Combat boots would be enough. Even with a fresh ankle-deep snow, the trails were compacted by snowmobile and cross-country skiers. My boots laced high, sealing most of the dampness out. I got my best gloves and hat from the bathroom, drying by the tub, and laid them on the bed next to my jackknife and a flashlight.

I crept downstairs. I stepped light-footed on the kitchen tile. I planted one foot right as the ice maker crashed a fresh round into the bin. Uncle James turned over, snoring and gasping in his semiconscious gravy-coma. The sofa bed squeaked. Someone farted, asleep.

I covered my mouth, vinyl gloves snuffing out a laugh.

Then everything was frozen again.

The clear sky radiated moonlight off the snowfields. From the kitchen window, the tree line – maybe a quarter mile away – looked like a handsaw sticking up at the stars, each treetop a tooth.

Leftovers lined the counter. I opened a bottled water and

ate two oatmeal cookies, washing them down before pocketing the bottle.

Dad never replaced his Golden Retriever, Xavier, after he died. He only used the burglar alarm during vacations or when Mom got spooked by her crime shows. Dad had other means of protection — methods of protecting his property that I'm sure he fantasized about as often as he read the paper.

That night, the system was disarmed.

This made covert operations out the deck and down our backyard slope as easy as sliding down a water slide.

Four miles wasn't a difficult hike in fair weather.

That night was different.

Against the white-washed gales and with the open pastures encouraging the wind to rip open my hood, sandblasting my ears, I walked — hands in my pockets, down and down and across the black. Fault lines in the sky split clouds like weightless rock.

I hugged myself the way I wanted to hug Katie.

* * * * *

Clear roads wound between pure white snow plowed high from earlier storms. I remember missing school twice in one week before Thanksgiving that year, and people quoted the Farmer's Almanac like the Bible: *Gonna be a chilly one, once in a decade cold, Holy Moses! You feel that?*

State utility trucks kept the trails under the power lines free of boulders and fallen trees, and in some un-drivable lengths, hikers and ATV enthusiasts maintained wide and crooked pathways. Off the road I turned east, following the steel supports that suspended the power lines like giant crucifixes. The gusts increased. My nose burned cold. Up those hills the wind roared through the trough dug into the forest – the wide clearing like a trail blindly scratched into the earth.

An old truck rusted, tires stripped and seats pillaged, chin-deep in the accumulating drifts. Other kids had mangled it years before we'd explored its rotten seats and found places to bang new dents. So many initials were chiseled into its panels it was hard to tell what color the original paint had been.

Fresh snowmobile tracks lead me up craggy accents.

My boots crunched deep. Great craters staggered behind me. Snow painted my legs knee-high, crusting layer on layer, and I beat the snow off my jeans just to see it grow back.

"God, it's cold."

I must've said that a dozen times.

Slipping down hills, I kept close to the margins of the trail, strangling saplings for support. The light of the moon cast no shadows. There, in the wide trails where the wind pushed on the high-voltage lines – their welded skeletons groaning like frigates floating in the sky – I tripped on snow-buried stones and hiked with frozen shins past the rock we used to call *Turtle Rock*. Those were the days when we found it necessary to name things.

I climbed, grabbing roots and fangs of jutting rock to summit where ice sheets made it nearly impossible to pass. I re-laced my boots. The strings were packed white. Sweat soaked the lining of my gloves. I took them off, wiped them on my thighs, and slid them back on.

I drank some of the bottled water.

Sitting on a bare rock, I wiped my nose with the rough vinyl glove and sniffed back shivering drips that threatened to freeze over my lip. The wind died down. The pines lining the trail relaxed.

Sprawling rooftops dotted the western grassland where old suburbs cluttered and new subdivisions bricked off what farmland remained. And like thermometers slid into the prairies, television and radio antennas blinked red, white, red. It snowed and snowed. The relentless blankness wanted to erase me, too. I leaned forward, blowing heat into my palms, bouncing it back to my cheeks and nose. Powdery ice peppered the stripe of skin on my lower back.

Stay still – freeze solid, I thought.

My knees bent. I was up.

Where the power lines veered south with the main trail, I entered the woods through a path hacked into thickets and naked blueberry bushes, abandoning the reliable order of the wide trail. This was the quickest way to Katie's neighborhood. And in the safety of clustered trees, the wind died further, replaced by a stilted cold and forest sounds – ghostly shuffles like shaking horses, popping branches sulked by frozen weight. Icicles toasted each other in the canopy.

I kept on through the skittish light.

I held my flashlight, clicked it on, waved the light back and forth but it wasn't needed. I pulled back my hood. The crisp air stung my earlobes. I sipped panting breaths, my mouth like a smokestack, before pulling the hood back tight around my head.

I wondered if I'd forgotten to turn off the portable phone.

I scrunched my toes inside my boot, keeping them warm, and tried not to think.

I tried not to think about anything. Two miles of nothing.

Glimpses of streetlight teased me through the darkness. Trees shimmered and vibrated. I exited the woods where a brook tunneled under the street. Traffic beyond the chimneys and ridges sounded like plywood dragged over cement, long steady scrapes fading in and away.

Almost there. Katie's house was visible from the top of the hill.

There, the snow was deeper.

Over a clearing and through rolling farmland, I kept my face down, hood puckered and shoulders pinched to my chest.

Around Petty Lake – which was more of a pond but fishable, a good swimming hole too – I re-entered the woods that overlooked Katie's neighborhood. Along the low ridge I came to another lookout besieged by teenage debris. I sat on the rock I'd sat on maybe a hundred times before and stared at the dark window – Katie's bedroom – where drawn curtains kept my imagination firing.

Two cars were in the driveway. Her father's and an uncle's. And, on the house, where Christmas lights usually shined brightly, only wet icicles grew. The family's lawn figurines moped motionless, elves and Santa frozen in mid-cheer. No plumes from the chimney, either.

I rubbed my aching legs. Overlooking the house, all I wanted to do was let Katie cry on my chest 'cept I'd only ever hugged her once and that was at a party where everyone was drunk and you were one hug away from getting puked on. My shirt smelled like her perfume for days. I must've smelled that flannel shirt a dozen times before it just smelled like a regular old shirt.

Salt trucks crisscrossed the neighborhood, doing doughnuts in the cul-de-sac. The bill of a plow ground across the cement like an ax blade over a grindstone. Someone honked and honked.

I would've been smart to write a note, using Mom's good stationery and even an envelope. Katie would'a known I'd walked all that way or begged for a ride just to deliver it, but there was nothing to say. Maybe she'd smell that letter like the way I smelled my shirt, but I doubt it.

Keeping still for as long as my body could handle it, I shivered and stood and hopped in place to keep warm. I sat back down, sniffing and wiping my face with the back of my hand.

Just knock on her door, I told myself, if she's home, just offer her a hug and leave. Just do it. Jackass. Coward-ass-jackass.

But I couldn't.

After taking one last look at Katie's window, where I always imagined the top of her brown head would rest, by the window, hair pulled up in a rubber band like at school, the pony tail I could spot from across the gym out of a thousand swarming perms and bobs and calm shell bangs, I trudged back home the way I came — the longest way to a lesson I'm still walking.

Iraq

Erbil

Ninevah

Ta'min   Suleimaniyah

Salahuddin

Euphrates River   Diyala

Fallujah

Ramadi   ®Baghdad

Anbar

Babil   Wasit

Karbala

Misan

Qadisiyah

Dhi-Qar

Najaf

Basrah

Muthanna

```
0        100       200      300 km
0            100          200 mi
```

Half Fallujah

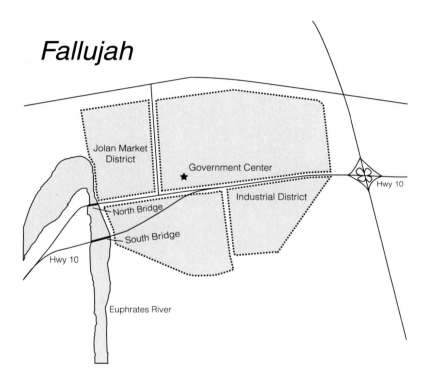

Fallujah

Jolan Market District

Government Center

Industrial District

North Bridge

South Bridge

Hwy 10

Hwy 10

Euphrates River

1

Beyond the desert, the road extended into blackness. No street-lights or sounds. The ground, cold as a corpse.

Khalil Hammadi wished the Digging Man would just explode. He figured if the Digging Man happened to detonate, he could just go home.

That would be that.

Khalil could live without the money.

He knew he was supposed to be standing, alert and ready. He sat and then squatted, bouncing in the dirt. It was impossible not to fidget in the dust. Sand choked his sneakers. It blew into his tracksuit's waistband, itching. He sat when his knees felt like dry rubber and the man he was watching was too busy digging to care if Khalil, his Spotter, was squatting or sitting or watching the roadway.

Somehow, squatting illustrated the Spotter's alertness. Sitting was too close to sleep. In the arid blackness where the moon couldn't see, sleep came easily. Chances were, if the Spotter wasn't alert, both the Digger and the Spotter would wake up bound on a concrete floor in a locked room – or worse.

Khalil squatted and thought about that – being captured, being questioned. He stomped it down in the corner of his brain to be forgotten. Looked around him. No noise troubled the night. No traffic or aircraft.

Khalil hadn't spotted one approaching car or suspicious form crawling along the horizon, and the chilly night air was dampened by afternoon rain. Quick gunfire knocked kilometers away like woodpeckers. Flashing mortars made a flipbook of the cityscape. Some explosions were closer than others, thunder cracking seconds after the flash. He didn't care.

Telephone poles lined the roadside and vanished into starlit dunes. Khalil in his black track suit. He like the invisibility.

Before he could stand, the Digging Man was back with his shovel slung over his shoulder. His oily nose glistened.

"No sitting. No sleeping. Understand?" He knocked Khalil's face with the shovel's dark and oily handle, rapping its steel against cheekbone. Then the Digging Man trotted off to work. Khalil's cheek pulsed. Eyes watered.

The road and the dirt underneath it grumbled. Kilometers in the distance he saw the last few seconds of artificial sun and then rising smoke where it had shone, billowing like crumpled carbon paper.

Oil fire maybe, between here and Ramadi, Khalil judged, *probably off the highway.* Now the night was wide awake.

* * * * *

2

The Digging Man, lanky and hunched, looked twice in each direction, surveying the highway for headlights or movement. He carried the shovel like a dead limb against his leg to mask his intentions. Khalil waited for him to vanish before rubbing the hinge of his jaw. *Bastard. Tall bastard.*

Why would such a tall man take such a dangerous job, he thought? Anyone could see him. He should just leave the tall bastard to be shot. Khalil slid his back against the tree, careful not to snag the jacket's nylon. Around him there was no life except a herd of goats grazing against the cobalt backdrop, clustered and slow.

The explosion carried on the wind. It smelled like someone had sliced open a battery and held it under his nose. Khalil took out his cell phone.

The man's shovel made occasional sparks in the blackness and rang a rare *clang* when its steel struck crumbs of concrete. He dug furiously, grunting and huffing.

Cloud cover made the moonlight marble dull, its ruffled gray sheets tossed haphazardly above.

No one could know what the Digging Man had buried once the digging and the burying was done.

But people were looking.

It was their job.

* * * * *

Watching the Digging Man, following him from the pickup point to the blast sight, paid 50,000 dinar. Easy for half an hour's work. It required a cell phone and patience, but – most of all – trust between two men who might have met that evening over tea. This was the lowest risk job, the job of recruits and people too feeble to dig quickly. Khalil, as able-bodied and trusted as he was, preferred this assignment. It was safer. Less stress. No touching the thing that goes in the hole. Easy and painless and detached.

He'd only seen one digger vanish – his body dropping as if he'd been thrown off a building, cracking on the asphalt with a sound that no human should make.

Digging the hole for the thing, with the thing sitting millimeters from your ankles, its white tape like a bandaged foot and wire intricately woven into red and green and black braids, paid 100,000 dinar. It was a considerable amount. It meant exposure to night-vision goggles, soldiers skirmishing in small teams across overpasses and creeping peep sights of rifles leveled at distant green figures, lone men with shovels lingering along roadsides for too long. Most of the digging men did it once and never again.

Some digging men enjoyed the adrenaline-sped danger, the accomplishment, the exhilaration of hitting the switch.

He'd transplant the thing with trembling fingers, resting it in the hole and, using his feet like trowels, cover it quickly before arousing suspicion. Dust coated shoes ran in the night. Then the thing would be ignored, buried like a pet in the far corner of a yard.

Every shopkeeper and crocked policeman eyed it, told their loved ones to keep clear.

Detonating the thing earned 200,000 dinar.

Too much for some to decline. The risk was high. Capture meant torturous death. But, if ignited accurately, if the explosion was precisely timed and the vehicle close enough to the roadside, escape was assured by the roaring confusion. All the trigger man had to do was run and never look back.

Lying in the brush a few hundred meters away, head invisible from the road, he'd hold copper wires in each hand like two incandescent hairs. They'd be so thin it'd be impossible to imagine their potential. The wispy strands would beg to be wrapped

4

around the battery trembling in his other hand.

He'd wait and wait.

Buses would pass, filled with workers. Men crammed in sedans returning home. People with gas canisters might stroll by. Dogs. Always dogs limping or dogs running. The target would approach. Wires would be wound. They'd send the spark, the blasting cap igniting a fiery plume, sand erasing the sky. The concussion would hit people in the chest like a giant fist. A chassis flipping in black plumes of wrinkled smoke with the column of traffic backing into each other while vehicles scrambled over curbs. Sand would cloud the roadway. Truck doors and tires would litter and burn.

That was murder, Khalil knew. It was murder no matter which way the *Fedayeen* branded or renamed it, and he couldn't and hadn't and probably never would *murder*, and in the stagnant April evening he stretched his legs and yawned as the Digging Man grunted, heavy and transfixed. Tiny headlights winked and disappeared. The Digging Man stopped digging.

He wiped his hands on his pants.

Panting, he set the thing in the hole.

* * * * *

In the cradle of an emaciated palm tree where no patrols could see, Khalil used the light of his cell phone to view the photograph torn from a newspaper days before. Though the open phone's bright screen might attract unwanted attention to him and the Digging Man, he sat against the tree's thick scaled stalk and squinted, gawked – thinking, *me for all the world to see.*

Al Jezeera and *Arabiya* Television flashed the photo hundreds, maybe thousands, of times. People worldwide, he knew, saw his face. Behind his face was the bridge and on the bridge hung the charred silhouettes swaying like ruined food. But it was his face in the center of the photo and his face everyone knew.

Everything had changed since.

In the streets, men looked at him longer. They tilted their necks up or, squinting from plastic lawn chairs under awnings, nudged their friends as he passed. Boys pointed, some yelling his name with dirty cupped hands, *Khalil! Khalil!* He waved back at them the same way they'd seen on TV. He'd signed three autographs; one of them on the back of a jacket because the admirer had no copy of the photo.

It was a simple photograph. A strategic photograph.

Two massacred silhouettes silently begged people to shout, to scream, to find something to wave – and if the closest thing was your hand, they waved that with as much fervor as the afternoon's fever allowed.

Two burned men – tied and hung – abstract hunks hinting at a greater whole; their previous suffering was increasingly apparent in the excitement of the onlookers, their indignity as plain as livestock, otherworldly and abysmal. And before it all stood Khalil.

Hundreds of photos were taken that day, but someone at the Associated Press chose Khalil's pleasantly anguished expression, his outstretched arm, only him. Khalil knew exactly why.

* * * * *

The deed was done.

After brushing dirt over the closed roadside hole, the Digging Man jogged back to the palm tree where Khalil stood with cell phone folded into his black track suit pocket. The man propped the shovel against the tree. The roadway was silent except for his heavy panting. He sopped sweat from his large forehead with the unbuttoned wings of his open shirt, leaning an elbow against the palm's terracotta stalk and breathing in deep, wheezing inhales.

A kestrel flew overhead.

Neither spoke.

In the dark of the moonless sky, eyes closed, the man craned his chin heavenward with his lips tightly bloodless, and Khalil, searching for something to say, thought the man was trying to see where the bird had flown.

Everything was still. The man stood in the pitiless air.

They walked on.

* * * * *

The Digging Man abandoned his shovel in the shadow of the first building they approached, planting it silently in the dark. Pressing the pad of his thumb into a fresh blister on his palm, the man opened its tender white cap where his wedding ring met his joint, wincing as they walked east into the drowsy city. Khalil tried not to watch.

From his breast pocket, the man pinched 25,000 dinar, discretely slid them across the bench. He waited for Khalil's fingers so the notes wouldn't take to the wind. The man leaned back. One leg crossed.

Khalil counted and said, "This is half," with as much nonchalance as he could muster. "Where's the rest?"

"So. This is what you earned," he explained.

"50,000's what. That's what I get," Khalil hissed. He made a movement to stand, but stayed seated as the man jerked his weight toward him in preparation – a fair warning. Sipping his water with a tight grip, he was ready to cock back and hit, the bottle crushed in his fist. Khalil added, "That's what was agreed."

Bringing the bottle down, the man reached to his back one more time and produced a cheese and cracker Handi Snack. Buckled in the middle from his pocket, the crackers were intact and the cheese glowed orange in the dark as if the manufacturer decided to mix in florescent liquid. The man peeled off the plastic top and set it on the breeze. Khalil would have licked any speck of cheese from the plastic.

He lifted the packet to his nose, red glasses reflecting two giant Handi Snacks in their greasy lenses. He dipped the crackers, like tiny ceiling tiles, into the cheese, dunking generous gobs and chewing slowly.

His grin infuriated Khalil.

"We agreed you would watch. The whole time," he said through his chews. "You played with your cell phone half the time, so you get half your money."

Part of a cracker, apparently unfit for consumption, fell from the man's fingers. He smashed it into the dirt.

Khalil turned the ground with his sneaker so hard, rocks sanded his toes through the hole in the rubber sole.

"I was not *playing*," he nearly screamed.

"And you were not sitting either, huh?" Snapping the crackers each time he dipped, the man started using the little red applicator to spread the cheese in delicate waves, setting the package on his knee. The water bottle had only a splash left, so he let the rest dribble over his dirty hands, each fingertip dripping beads in the gray soil, instantly disappearing.

"I wasn't playing with my phone."

With his hands in his pockets, he crumpled the corner of his photograph and it was almost impossible not to flip it open like a badge for the man and maybe, maybe he *hadn't* seen the photo in the papers or on satellite news. The tall bastard was so busy drinking bottled water and nibbling Handi Snacks and planting bombs for Mr. Hassnawi that he'd somehow missed the most important day in Khalil's life.

Khalil mashed the dinars in his jacket pocket with the photo. He wanted to toss them at the man's flaking nose. Who was *he*? A cattle farmer or an unemployed welder? Another nationalist with nothing left?

"It doesn't matter anymore. Go home," the man said with a dismissive hand flick, as if he knew what was in Khalil's pocket and what little it meant. "There'll be more work anyway. Always."

"Mr. Hassnawi won't be happy with this," Khalil threatened, immediately regretting it, sucking in as if he could vacuum the word back out of the air. The man would either knock him out or walk away. Either would bring consequences other than pain.

"Yeah?" the man laughed. "Hassnawi has more important problems to take care of, Khalil." Using his name for the first time, using it like a teacher, like he had some authority at all. "He'll make me give the money back to *him,* all of it, and he'll have one of his men beat you, or worse. What *then*?"

Khalil curled his lips. "At least *you* won't have my money," he answered, sliding down the bench, away from the man's reach.

Licking the red stick from the Handi Snack, carefully scouring its plastic for every particle of pasteurized cheese, the man refused to dignify Khalil's comment and, instead, flicked the little implement at Khalil's feet.

Goosebumps rose like tiny rivets on Khalil's arms.

He shivered.

People moved behind them, singing loudly. Two older boys walked a dog on a chain. The dog stopped to sniff something and the boys paused a few feet behind Khalil and the man.

One sang:

"Yeah … gimme some new sheet."

The other:

"Yeah … gimme some new shit."

"Yeah … gimme some new sheeeet."

Then again. And again, until they turned down an alley with the sniffing dog sniffing everything and the chain jangling angrily.

The man tugged on the bottom of his shirt, trying to shrink the creases and wrinkles, with no success. He flipped up his collar, swatted away the sand snuggled around his neckline. With his fingers he combed out the grit in his hair, scalp and eyebrows, and when he felt fully shaken out, he popped his collar down. Bent, he swabbed the trenches between sock and shoe, snapping the elastic off his socks where too much ankle exposed itself from the rising hem of his ill-fitting pants. Groomed, satisfied, he sucked his teeth and faced Khalil.

Khalil braced for a fist or a kick.

He said, "You're clever, Khalil Hammadi. I knew your father. He was too smart to be driving trucks day and night for a shit salary – for a life of *shit*." With a clenched jaw he said, "He'd be proud of you. Standing for something now." The man never looked toward Khalil, his eyes hovering above the cityscape as if looking for Khalil's father to hover down from the heavens. "*Inshallah*, he is."

Khalil said nothing. He ground the rocky sand and felt pebbles gluing themselves into the hole in his shoe.

"But you can't be lazy, not for a second. We are fighting for the future of our country. People are counting on you – not just me, you know?"

Balling a dinar in his fist, Khalil let the Diggin Man vent while he squeezed the bills harder and harder, compressing them into a little ball.

"I'll tell Hassnawi you did a perfect job, I will, but this means next time," turning toward Khalil, "you do it perfectly. No sitting or playing around – even if some other guy is digging the fucking hole."

This was too much.

Squeezing the money into a sweaty gob of fiber and filth, Khalil wanted to cave in the man's cratered nose, lodging broken glasses into cheek with the hammer of his heel.

The Diggin Man stood.

In the shadow of a passing cloud, the man picked at his blister. He spoke to his hand.

"Be patient. Soon. This world will turn, Khalil," he said flatly, the blister like an amphibian eyelid embedded in his palm. "It will turn its head toward the righteous and never look back."

Khalil pulled his fists from his windbreaker's pockets like two rocks tied to rope. He raised them toward the back of the man's head.

"The world will turn and see *me*," Khalil hissed through his teeth, not exactly sure what he meant, and stepped forward with a fist cocked, ready to swing.

Still talking into his palm, unaware of Khalil's fist, the Digging Man urged, "Go home. Be happy with half your pay. It's half more than most people have."

Behind them, the sky spread black. In the deafening dark, the man's thick eyeglasses tilted to the side as if leading him in the direction he would turn. Finally, he loped away, disappearing as another helicopter swooped from the North, motivating him to gallop. Then he was gone.

Sand and paper scraps practiced their waltz in the wind. Khalil squeezed his fist so hard he thought the dinar in his hand might compress into a diamond. When he unclenched the fist, it was the photograph of the Blackwater mercenaries that he had balled and crushed, not the dinar.

Khalil peeled it open and scrutinized the ruined photo. With the light from his open cell phone, the little screen casting a sickly neon glow. He rubbed his thumb along the perimeter of his photographic head, ears, up the extended arm to the bridge – the bodies – those bodies.

He cycled through the saved numbers in his phone out of habit before flipping it shut. No one to call. No reception anyway. Screw this dumb waste of a night.

It didn't matter if this clipping was ruined. Dozens of newspapers were stacked under his bed. An infinite number on the Internet and networks. Salim probably had a copy saved on his computer, too.

He hated sun up.

Thirst beyond thirst, his mouth felt flecked with lint. It'd be twenty minutes until he'd tiptoe into the back door, a soda in his hand, sleeping on the couch where he always slept.

Behind him, beyond the dunes and the sulfite smoke muddled in the breeze, the two boys led the chained dog and sauntered back, one singing, "Go."

The other, "Go."

Then, "Go."

And together,

"Go, getcha getcha getcha getcha freak on –"

2

Salim knew if he stayed in Fallujah he would die. He would be forced to fight in the uprising. Already, two nights in a row, *Fedayeen* – Saddam loyalists and militants, some of them ex-military – had knocked on his door looking for him. Salim's father told them his son wasn't there. "He's been missing for days. The Americans have him." And when they were gone he locked the door and told Salim it was just one of his tenants. "Don't worry son, it's nothing."

"What did they want?"

"Nothing. Go back to bed."

But they both knew what was coming.

If Khalil wanted to stay and fight, that was his decision. That's what his crazy ass wanted. But Salim had to leave.

Ramadi would be safer. About 60 kilometers up the river, where the Blackwater mercenaries hadn't been lynched, hung from that bridge. Where no one knew him. It wouldn't be an easy hike, but he could do it. Word was – at least for now – the fighting had stopped there.

Salim stood, turning on his laptop. Its internal fan hummed to life. Dust whirled in little slices of sunlight from his bedroom window. In the distance, the diesel engines of bulldozers gasped and rattled like dying livestock, their oil-sweat smearing the wind as they crept closer and closer.

For days the Coalition Forces bulldozed a collar of sand around three sides of the city, sculpting a half-moon to strangle the Euphrates. There would be no way to leave. That was the idea. And everyone in Fallujah knew this because they'd seen it so many times before, in so many different forms – containment, suppression, control.

Both bridges to the west were blocked with concrete barriers which busses and tired sedans slowly zigzagged. Helmeted men in sweat-stained fatigues made Highway 10 unusable. Slowed, the city ground on with men tight-lipped and their wives' suspicious feet scrambling home, cautious as birds in the road.

Salim waited for the laptop. With a blank disc inserted, he began burning the design files for the propaganda leaflets Mr. Hassnawi had hired him to create.

* * * * *

Salim was relieved to see his alarm clock flashing. The power was on. He wouldn't have to fire up the generators – worrying his father and calling attention to what he might be doing.

He brushed sand off his keyboard.

He couldn't even look at his laptop without thinking of Rana. Her daily emails. Her uploaded photos. It was the only reliable way they used to communicate – until the Coalition discon-

14

nected the city's Internet, darkening the cafés where he used to sit for hours chatting with her about Syria and how she felt to be one of millions of displaced Iraqis there. *I've never even met you Salim and I miss you so much.* It was obvious now that the oncoming siege would mean no electricity, and no Internet, for a very long time.

He wondered how all the bootleg DVDs of Hollywood movies would be created if there was no way to download. With the economy destroyed by war and everyone out of a job, bootlegging seemed like the only honest profession.

Salim clicked to check his Internet connectivity, but he knew it was pointless.

Once all the discs were burned, Salim erased the files from his laptop in case he might be captured and searched. He wondered what reaction his new leaflet would get. "*The Americans Will Crumble like Awat,*" they read – the slogan written by Mr. Hassnawi himself. This was the silly phrase he wanted on every postcard and poster, every piece of propaganda – that the Americans would crumble like cake.

Ridiculous.

Salim slid the printouts of the leaflets and the discs into a manila envelope before packing his backpack. With the laptop folded and its charger wound tight, there was room for roughly two weeks of rations: wrapped flat bread and sweet chutney in a little jar, a cluster of unripe bananas, dates, cans of beans and coconut milk. There were even a few *Awat* cakes nestled by his folded underwear.

All the money Salim had saved from working with the *Fedayeen* was rolled into a knot and tucked into a hidden pocket, in case he needed it for a bribe.

One spare shirt and one pair of pants barely fit among the provisions, but he didn't care about sweating through his clothes.

He crammed his old Russian rifle scope between his folded cloths to cushion it. Water would have to be borrowed from the Euphrates, hopefully pure enough to drink. The laptop charger and cord took up a considerable amount of room, but they were necessary. He knew the battery would be dead before he reached Ramadi.

The elusive moon would provide the only light. Salim didn't have a flashlight. Campfires were out of the question. He had no weapons, only a pocketknife to defend against thieves or wild dogs. Salim knew a rifle would attract unwanted attention from patrol boats and convoys policing the banks of the river. He would leave their one Kalashnikov in the living room closet where his father hid it, unloaded and locked away.

Salim forced the pack's zippers closed.

* * * * *

It was safe to leave with his father, Yasir, out checking on his tenants, seeing what they needed before the city's invasion, fortifying what apartments were left empty by fleeing residents.

But Salim worried about Khalil. Only he knew where Mr. Hassnawi lived. So only he could help deliver the propaganda files that might prove to the *Fedayeen* that the coward Salim Abid, son of the coward Yasir Abid, though too scared to stay and fight for the one true God, would be worth sparing because of his devotion to the uprising. Only Khalil was close enough to the network of insurgents to know where to find them.

Salim's trick with Khalil was if he wanted him to show up at noon, he would tell him eleven. If he needed two ink cartridges for his printer, Salim would write down three or four. Looking at his watch, heaving his backpack on, Salim noted that Khalil was right-on-time late.

* * * * *

"Sal!" Khalil yelled from outside.

Salim stuck his head out his bedroom window. "Be *quiet*."

After double-checking his backpack, Salim ran downstairs and grabbed a roll of paper towels from the kitchen, noticing it only had a little paper left, thinking they were probably the only house in the neighborhood with paper towels. One of the many luxuries Khalil had brought them.

There were so many secrets he'd kept from his father. The leaflets. The *Fedayeen* money. All the time he spent with Khalil. And now this.

On a pad of paper on the kitchen table Salim wrote:

Dad,

I know you'll understand that I had to leave, but I don't expect you to forgive me. I'll be back in a few weeks, or until all of this is over. Please be safe. Stay inside.

Wadaa'an,

Salim

* * * * *

In the backyard patio, among the date palms and sunflowers, Khalil leaned against their stone wall, a leg up and a wrinkled wax paper package in his hand which he held out to Salim. "Kahi?" he offered. "Your favorite."

Salim smiled at Khalil's English, which had gotten better over the years. He wondered if he was the only English speaking person in Fallujah that Khalil knew – if that's why they'd become friends so long ago. Growing up, Salim realized it was the first thing Khalil envied about him. That was okay.

Salim opened the wax paper and took the flaky dough, licking off the cheese and sweet syrup from his fingers. "What, no *gemar?*" he asked, "I only eat *Kahi* with cream."

Salim tore off a paper towel for his friend.

Khalil snickered. He wiped his sticky hands on his track suit pants and followed Salim through the gate and into the street.

* * * * *

Salim hurried against the surging crowd.

Eastward, people shuffled with crates balanced on their heads. Babies and extra blankets stacked on anything with wheels. For every family there was a donkey pulling a wagon, it seemed, and for every donkey there was another family parked on the side of the road as they readjusted photo albums tied to the swaying summits of suitcases, dining room chairs, television sets, barrels of bedding and boxes and boxes of dry goods. A man shouldered a bulging pillowcase. His wife shouldered a newborn. Children lay on sacks of rice that lay on trucks, overburdened with end tables and rugs and clanging alloy bowls like bells tolling. The somber exodus meandered through dust and stood still when the human traffic could not continue. A truck puttered out of gas. Its riders slapping doors and hoods and roofs. Children hovered like cherubs above the crowd on the blackened clouds of their mother's shoulders, their weary bodies shrouded.

Overburdened, a packhorse collapsed on the roadside. A man and a woman soothed it with damp towels.

Few spoke. Talking was toilsome.

Coiled concertina wire, pulled like giant phone cords, herded the refugees out of the city, many of them not knowing where. As long as it was out of harm's way, no one cared. Salim wanted to touch the spiraling razor wire, but knew to stay away. Bursts of rifle fire rattled, and in the distance, the more unnerving and occasional crack of a single shot – a sniper, Salim reasoned. The sound made everyone but the hardest men hunch in a synchronized recoil. Two men rushed past them – the only others – besides Salim and Khalil – heading west.

Police sirens pinched the air.

They walked side by side, hurrying out of the neighborhood. Noon approached.

They inched against the crowd, wondering if they too should turn around and follow the people out of the city.

Past the vendors at the edge of the neighborhood, Salim took his backpack from Khalil. He had waited until they were blocks from his house. He slipped it on his shoulders, worried about it weighing him down for the next few days of walking. Secure enough, he thought. Wouldn't be a burden.

Salim stopped. In the shade of an awning he removed cans and clothes from his backpack to make room for the paper towels.

"Toilet paper," he said, expecting Khalil to crack a joke, but he said nothing.

They moved on through *Nazzal*, the old city, under the recessing shadows of buildings, and stepped over toppled crumbles of wall, some of them burnt black. Drying puddles looked like age spots in the dirt. Avoiding them, Salim took the long way around, careful not to muddy his sandals.

A woman hung jeans out to dry – unaffected by the ruckus – her clothesline flapping like rows of damp flags. It was the only color amid brown and ochre brick and the thick mortar slathered between them. She waved as they passed. She knew Khalil.

Everyone knew Khalil.

Ahead, Route 10 was backed up with traffic.

A green street light had fallen over the road, run over by tank treads, calligraphy drawn in the street by its long-dead wires. A man and two boys corralled stray sheep through the dust. Herds skipped over the downed wires, little billy goats and larger adult goats with gray beards.

They passed a Red Crescent ambulance parked at a stand where a vendor weighed furry piles of tobacco. The driver of the ambulance, his face somber and gray, pointed to the horizon beyond the marching people. Salim turned to see the great masses marching away. The driver puffed on his pipe and squeezed a soapy sponge in one hand, a froth of suds foaming at his knuckles. The muscles in his arms looked like taffy pulled over bone. Ponds of water spotted his pants and shirt. He returned to his chore, drawing foamy moons in the splattered blood on the hood, erasing the day's evidence with a sponge and the heels of his hands.

Then Salim realized the ambulance had no windshield. Shattered glass salted the ground where the jagged edges had been smashed and cleared. The man dipped his sponge for more soap. At his feet, a shoeless boy played in a hubcap filled with the same soiled water. Some of the runoff was pinkish-brown. The boy stared at Khalil, and Khalil winked at the boy.

If the water couldn't be drunk, Salim thought, *why not wash an ambulance in it?*

They continued west.

* * * * *

A family of five – two daughters and a younger son – shuffled past them. "Excuse me, excuse me." Each of them said.

"Excuse us," the father said, trailing behind like a desperate shepherd. He pushed a baby stroller crammed with food, covered by a blanket.

Salim glanced over his shoulder, watching the family shrink away.

Reaching the end of the block where an overturned car sat crumpled and charred, its doors twisted like burnt paper, they passed a resistance checkpoint. Three *Fedayeen* guarded the street. Sitting on sandbags, they ate steaming rice and red curried potatoes on dinner plates recently delivered, and a woman, her *abaya* flowing, served them tea from a kettle. Khalil nodded at them. One returned the gesture.

Swerving potholes punched into the road from mortars, a young boy passed on a bicycle heading in the direction of the crowd.

Khalil skipped ahead.

Salim grumbled, "Quit fooling around."

But Khalil chose not to hear, jogging backwards in place, jabbing at shadows like a boxer. "So, where you going, Sal?" he asked.

"Dropping off this CD to Mr. Hassnawi. This is the last job I'm doing for him."

Khalil jumped in place, swinging his arms, uppercutting phantom enemies as he landed. His black vinyl jacket shimmered like oil. "No. Where're you going with that bag of junk?" he asked and spun forward.

"You still have those friends in Ramadi?"

"What, my cousin? Sure."

Salim didn't say anything.

"C'mon, man. What're you doing? Leaving before the fight?" He put his arm around his friend's shoulder and rubbed his own short hair into Salim's bearded cheek.

"Stop," Salim said, pushing him away

Approaching the city's congested center, the stream of refugees tapered off, while the people who decided to stay were closing fruit stands and tea shops. Two old men stacked a sandbag wall around their house. Their sons filled bags using cut water jugs and bent scrap metal, and smells coming from inside suggested the women in the home were baking bread. One mother and two daughters carried trays of warm loaves, too many for one meal. A squad of *Fedayeen*, some lumbering with rockets over their backs, scrambled into an apartment building and closed the door. Someone sneezed a few times.

Waiting for the *Fedayeen* to reappear at the door, Khalil said, "You leave now, they'll never let you come back."

And accepting this as truth, Salim knew he'd be labeled a coward – maybe even a collaborator with the Americans – something more terrifying than having to fight.

They'd never forgive him and they'd forget all the work he had done for the resistance, the propaganda designs and the stupid slogans painted on cinderblock barriers, distributing leaflets at night when death could come with a quick whistle and a thud. They'd forget the time he ducked under the meager ledge of a curbside from a sniper for three hours and crawled backwards, his ear filled with dirt, through gas saturated streets and litter strewn alleys. His head still rang days later.

He would be a traitor to them and to his friends and eventually, when word spread throughout town, to his father too.

"I've got something to do," Salim said.

"More important than defending the city, Sal? Whatever."

"You think your cousin, in Ramadi, still has the Internet?" Salim asked, embarrassed to bring up such a seemingly petty thing at a time like this.

Khalil paused for a second. "I guess so. Things might be a little better there now. It's stable at least."

"They good people?" Salim said, knowing his definition of "good" varied from his friend's. Scratching his chin through his beard, he looked at his overgrown fingernails and wondered if he'd packed a clipper – if there was anything else he had forgotten. Only one nail clipper in the house anyway, would have been rude to take it.

"You're going all the way to Ramadi to see the Internet?"

"Log on, yeah," Salim corrected.

"Yeah, whatever. Can't you do that here?" Khalil asked. "What about the cafés?"

"Shut down. Or seized. It's been weeks." Salim stopped, lowering his gaze to the dirt road where sprigs of dry weed sprouted like hairy moles, and let his backpack slide off. He pulled his sweatshirt over his head. "Hot," he said.

"Yeah."

Though he checked it once before, Salim made sure the laptop was turned off and then crammed the sweatshirt into his pack, squeezing it shut with his knees, forcing the zipper together. He couldn't wait to ditch at least a few cans of food once they were eaten. He smoothed what wrinkles ruffled his t-shirt and aired his armpits with pinched fingers. "Really, really, really hot."

"Yeah."

* * * * *

Double lanes opened to the main road.

Mountains of white brick piled along the roadside where buildings sagged like ziggurats smashed by a lost civilization, and the random explosions had no philosophy in what was spared and what went demolished. Flattened bakeries leveled next to preserved warehouses, maimed offices collapsed into the entrances of untouched apartments. Light poles leaned dangerously low. The downtown mosques hung over them like opal tears dropped out of the sky – the tops of their tiled domes shined, celestial – the only guiding light.

Walking on, they rubbed sand out of their hair and the canals of their ears. Salim shook out his short beard with frantic fingers.

"It's that *girl*," Khalil said, punching mock jabs at Salim's stomach then pinching the loose skin of his elbow, twisting it.

"So?"

"So," Khalil nagged, pulling, twisting, "*so*, it's that *girl*."

"Yeah. So? *Stop* that shit, man." Salim yanked his elbow away. "You're always doing that shit."

They walked and walked, the shadows turned away from their direction. Their shins already ached, and it was only the beginning.

"*A girl*," Khalil groaned.

"*So what?*"

* * * * *

Through two more checkpoints, each one more heavily fortified and better staffed than the one before. They approached the *Jolan's* tight streets and narrow alleys where people hurried – shopping for cabbage and raisins, discretely exchanging CDs and baby clothes – ignorant of the imminent siege or confident that the encroaching forces knew better than to assault the *Jolan*. A man gestured for them to approach. He stood behind a table lined with leather belts and second-hand shoes. Khalil rolled his eyes. "I bought a belt from that guy a year ago and it lasted two months. Complete crap."

"I have to buy a blanket after we drop off this disc," Salim said, reminding himself, but there were no vendors for that in sight.

Khalil said. "This way."

They took a side street. Deeper into the market, the crowd's roar drowned out every nerve-stripping sound of the war.

Vendors barbequed kebabs, *tikka* and marinated goat, and the grease-smoke seared the air sweet, so that when they passed they couldn't help but pause and suck it in. Grinning, Khalil bought two sticks of chicken and handed one to Salim.

"*Fim' Allah*," the vendor said. Old men sipped tea from short glasses. A group of them pointed at Khalil, mumbling and nodding. The youngest slumped in a plastic lawn chair fashioned into a wheelchair, bicycle parts bolted to the frame and wire wrapped where screws and nuts would not hold.

"You see those old guys. They know who I am," Khalil said.

Salim would not dignify him with a reply.

He nibbled his chicken, navigating the marketplace cautiously. Someone stepped on his toe and didn't apologize. Khalil was still turning, walking backwards, tripping over curbs and chewing open-mouthed.

"You have to do it now? You can't wait?" he said, finishing his snack and flipping the stick over his shoulder. Picking his teeth, "I bet the Internet will be back soon. Give it a few days."

"No."

"You can't drive, you'll be spotted. You'll be spotted by the Americans and shot. Even if you pay someone – *not* one of the *Fedayeen* – to drive you, you'll get killed, no matter how fast they drive. It's crazy."

"I'm walking," Salim mumbled. "I'm just going to walk."

"To Ramadi – "

"Yeah."

"To get the Internet."

Salim groaned and handed the rest of his *tikka* to a skinny boy standing alone with a Power Ranger's knapsack hanging unzipped from his back. Tearing into the cubed chicken, his wide eyes said *thank you* and Khalil patted him on the head as he passed. Khalil pointed down an alley before they missed their turn. Mr. Hassnawi's house wasn't easy to find.

"I know. It's stupid," Salim said.

"Stupid for such a smart guy, Sal. Weird too. You've done some weird things, but this is the weirdest."

"She's gonna think I'm dead if she doesn't hear from me soon."

"What does that matter?"

"Matters to me," Salim admitted, except they both understood there was a lot more to it, more than a crush and more than an email, and the closer they got to Mr. Hassnawi's house the more obvious it got.

"You can't call her?"

"No number."

"Can't you look her up?"

"She's fled to Syria – is there a special directory for displaced people? I've never talked to her, anyway."

Khalil threw his arms over his head. "You've *never* talked to her?"

Salim sighed through his nose.

"I can't believe you."

Further west, the neighborhood grew more affluent. Apartment buildings became two-unit dwellings, and when they passed a busy restaurant, men were jammed into every table. Bisected houses became larger single family homes, some of them surrounded by cinderblock walls and intricate gates. Washed Nissans and Toyotas were parked inside fortified perimeters. Their owners, returning from work, carrying groceries and briefcases and children, locked up their cars and hurried inside.

"This way," Khalil said, pointing to another alley.

"Okay."

Khalil lifted a small plywood door hidden at the end of the alley, looking back to make sure they weren't followed, and let Salim crawl through. He pushed his pack when it snagged on a nail. Salim propped the door open, allowing his friend to scurry to the other side – let him continue leading. They both jogged to the main road.

Mr. Hassnawi's house was ahead.

They approached a locked gate.

High walls formed an enclosed courtyard lush with palms and groomed shrubs. Mr. Hassnawi's arrogantly large villa rested in the shade of the palms, its freshly cleaned windows so clear they could have been missing their panes. No bars were needed for security. Glasses and a full decanter of tea sat on a wrought iron table with matching chairs where a young girl swung her feet, headphones covering her ears. Someone practiced the *oud* from inside.

Khalil stooped, head low, his back along the wall.

Salim would let him talk first.

Two *Fedayeen* fighters stood on either side of the shining brass gate, both holding Kalashnikovs with folded stocks and thickly wrapped *keffiyehs* around their heads, brown eyes tired in the sun. Their fatigues were assemblages of surplus Russian and stolen Iraqi police uniforms. One of them puffed a pipe through a slit in his red and white headwrap. Prayer beads dangled from their belt loops like little strung cherries. Red diamonds, sewn to their shoulders, confirmed their alliance.

Salim admired their boots. If he could have afforded anything but sandals, he would have bought them for the trip.

"Why are you sneaking?" Salim said.

"Hassnawi's guards," Khalil whispered, not answering.

"I know," Salim said. "Who else would they be?"

Posturing, one of the guards released his rifle's magazine and racked it against a boot heel, rattling the rounds inside like coins. Re-engaging the banana-shaped clip, he cycled a fresh bullet into the chamber with a machined *snap*.

"Khalil!" the guard without the pipe yelled. "Come here!"

Khalil straightened.

"He knows you?" Salim asked.

"Of course he *knows* me," walking and rubbing his hands together.

The guard raised his hand to chest level, gesturing for Khalil to stop. Salim trailed, his eyes on their boots and their rifles.

Gunfire popped in the distance, east of the city, where most of the people were fleeing. Salim ducked at the thought of bullets ricocheting, jagged and fiery, off brick and through pant leg into thigh, muscle, bone. Small concussions rumbled kilometers away, random rockets corkscrewing into truck convoys, the convoys jumping curbs to flank and reform. Louder reports followed – turret-mounted cannons – and Salim knew fighters were increasingly returning shots before sunset.

Night-vision goggles and scopes destroyed their pop-shot advantage.

The guards craned their heads as if they could see over the

buildings, but were satisfied by the concussions echoing off plateaus and temples. Mortars were keeping the city secure, at least for now.

One guard kept watch of the westward byway, his pipe creating thin flags of smoke left – right – left and he tapped his trigger nervously.

"Hey," Khalil smirked, brushing off his windbreaker's sleeves, straightening his approach, chin high.

The one with the pipe kept tapping his trigger.

"You're Khalil, right?" the other one said.

"Yeah man."

"Been looking for you," he said, swatting a fly away from the places where his *keffiyeh* exposed his face.

"You?" Khalil asked. "Okay. What do you need?"

Shooting smoke through his nose, the tapping guard stepped between Salim and Khalil.

"No. The Project Manager," he answered.

"Who?" Khalil chuckled, unfamiliar with the term, his hands in his tracksuit's pockets, arms flapping.

Munitions whistled overhead, close enough to make them cower. All four leaned against the gray wall.

The *oud* player stopped.

Someone in the house clapped and stopped.

The guards cocked their heads at a jet slicing high through the clouds. The smoking guard pointed south, moving his finger along the horizon – Salim's palms were wet with nervous sweat – and they braced for an earth rattling detonation that never came. No one had seen the aircraft. Shrugging, the guard puffed his sweet tobacco, made white streams with his nostrils that snarled over beard and uniform collar. Salim wondered if he could speak.

The *oud* started again.

"When will he stop?" the piped guard finally said. "I love the man, but he cannot play the *oud*."

"*Insh' Allah*, he will, *habibi*," the first guard said, continuing, "The Project Manager, go see him. Take your friend around back of the house. He's been asking about you, celebrity."

"Hardly famous," his pipe bobbing with each syllable. "All this mess for four men, not even Army, just private contractors."

Khalil chewed his cheeks to keep his mouth shut.

"Would've happened anyway, *shel* or not. We're on an *accelerated schedule*, that's all," the first guard explained, adjusting his grip on the rifle and pulling his *keffiyeh* over his brow. "Go," he said again. "Around back."

Khalil snorted, "For what?"

"For your *assignment*."

Salim looked at Khalil as if they'd been told to shoot each other. His face looked white as a corpse under the black strap of beard, his eyes about to tear. "I'm just here to drop off a disc," he stuttered.

There was a silence long enough for Salim to think he hadn't spoken Arabic, that he'd accidentally said those words in English. Now that the words had evaporated in the air he couldn't tell what language he'd spoken, or if he'd said the words at all.

"Huh?" both guards huffed, the tapping, puffing guard stepping forward again.

"A disc. To Mr. Hassnawi. Leaflets," Salim struggled to say through quivering lips, considering this new assignment and how hard, if not impossible, it might be to avoid: rifle raids on heavily armed platoons, mortar duty on the outskirts of the *Jolan*, rocket deliveries to undersupplied bunkers – suicide missions all of them. He'd never fired a gun in his life.

"On a disc?"

Coughing into his hand, Salim said, "Computer disc."

The piped guard swirled his index finger at Salim, searching for words. His long fingernail circled Salim's face. "Okay! Yeah, yeah, yeah!"

"A disc for a computer," Salim kept explaining.

"Okay. You're the *Awat guy!*" he said, putting his hand on Salim's shoulder, patting with great whaps. "You're good, man. I like that stuff. Really."

"What guy?" the other guard asked.

"The *Awat* guy – the leaflets."

"Yeah," the guard nodded and went for his pocket. Salim thought he might take out a pistol, but he was only searching for a leaflet that wasn't there, pulling out lint and a few dinar. "Not bad. Not bad. It's everywhere. Crumble like *Awat!* I thought I had one right here."

"Crumble!" both guards yelled, lifting their Kalashnikovs over their head in celebration.

"Well, I don't think they'll crumble, really," the first guard reasoned.

"No. They're tough bastards. Tougher than we thought."

"Crinkle?" the first guard offered, nodding at Salim.

"Crumple!"

"Like paper? Really?"

"Yeah, man, you don't have any easy job, *Awat* guy."

"I wish I were creative," the first guard sulked.

"*Ee wallah*, me too." Still patting Salim's shoulder, the guard pulled down his headwrap, revealing his face. Khalil kicked the dirt and looked into the courtyard for signs of Mr. Hassnawi and lifted his sneaker to inspect the tear in the sole at the ball of his foot. Sand was getting in it again. The guard continued, "What's your name?"

"Salim. Salim Abid."

"You do t-shirts?" one asked, taking his hand away from Salim's shoulder.

"Uhh – I could," Salim said. "I've always wanted to, I mean."

"*Nice*," the other guard said excitedly.

"Okay, man." The guard knocked charred tobacco from his pipe against his free wrist, ash and shredded leaves falling like confetti. "When this revolution's over, I'm going to hire you to make shirts. Okay?"

Salim smiled, "*Khosh* deal."

"Me and my sister, we've been drawing these characters for years, and they're perfect for shirts. People would love it." He rummaged his back pocket and then both side compartments of his jacket, loose ammunition jingling. "I thought I had a sketch in here – "

"Man, don't bother them with that," the first guard said.

On the other side of the house, ambulance sirens blared, a rush of voices began yelling. Someone punched a car horn over and over. A crowd gathered.

"C'mon, Sal. We've got to go," Khalil interrupted, punching his friend's shoulder. "Our *assignments*."

"Hold on!" the first guard demanded, gripping Salim's arm, his entire hand circling the bicep as if he were holding onto a bus's handrail. "What's in the bag?"

A joke, Salim thought, *a joke between new friends*. Looking at them with a dopey open mouth, his lips were numb, his legs felt dead.

Khalil froze – arms and legs instantly petrified like a mannequin, and it seemed like his body had given up its entire natural reserves in order to fuel his brain with a spontaneously generated lie – the more absurd, the more believable. His lips moved. Salim heard the words in slow monotone.

"Sal's art supplies. His laptop. They're too valuable to leave at home, might be seized, used against him – against *us*." Khalil's fingers addressed them like an orchestra conductor, typing on an invisible keyboard and he nodded cartoonishly at Salim.

Salim nodded with the same ridiculous fervor.

"Paint cans weigh a ton. He wanted *me* to carry it. Ha! Me? Ha!" Khalil said.

"Yeah," Salim added, his bloodless cheeks leeched of life.

"I was like, you see *this face*. Everyone in the world knows me. You should be making leaflets that say *Khalil Will Crumble the Americans like Awat!*" Making a rifle out of the air, he tap danced and shot pretend rounds down the street. "*Sht-t-t-t.*"

Both guards laughed.

The one packed another pipe and said, "You guys are crazy."

"Yeah," Salim said. "Heh." He rubbed his arm where the guard had squeezed and let Khalil pull him by his shirtsleeve. He started to say *thank you*, but thought it might be a stupid idea as he tripped down the block.

Like men already dead and men who had readied for death all their lives, the two guards, unblinking, still as storks, lifted their muzzles skyward, watching Salim and Khalil shrink down the street as if they were dead, too.

One called, "Around the back, in the office. Hassnawi isn't seeing visitors. See the Project Manager."

And the other called, "Remember, t-shirts, Salim!"

And now they knew him by name.

3

The Digging Man was no longer the Digging Man because he had put down his shovel that night, after burying the bomb along the roadside, and hadn't touched it again except to pick up some dog shit outside the mosque last Thursday.

Now there were dogs everywhere. Their shit was everywhere too.

To most people, The Digging Man had always been the Tall Man ever since he reached full-grown, in ninth grade, far sooner than most all the other kids in Fallujah, and his father had been a tall man, but not *this* tall. He liked shorter women because they were all shorter than him, but the woman he married was taller than he ever thought a woman should be. He loved her very much. He felt she deserved more, but he knew this was a common notion among men both short and tall so he didn't feel so bad.

The Tall Man hadn't seen his bomb explode, and he never knew who made the bomb. But weeks later he heard the stories of the convoy it hit and the ensuing ambush, how the damage had been severe enough for *Al Jazeera* to cover the scene. Photos were published internationally.

The Tall Man circled his new office.

He had yet to sit.

Hassnawi had finally noticed him for something other than digging holes or being tall.

Cacti lined the windowsill in clay pots, which he loved very much too. His predecessor hadn't had the opportunity to clean out his desk, something he loved even more. In the steel drawers he found vintage atlases the size of prayer rugs, paper clips of every size, unused journals and paper weights and empty picture frames and an American revolver with a cedar handle, its stainless frame as polished as a silver spoon. He'd spent an hour carrying it around the office, sniffing the barrel, cocking the hammer, pointing it at the door. It had no bullets and there were none in the office. He had looked behind every book and file cabinet.

There were things he'd never buy for himself like hard candies and licorice. Even if the cigars he inherited were dry as autumn leaves, the Tall Man would carefully remove them from his new desk and clip their ends with a razorblade, savoring them down to nubs. Even the wide open windows couldn't clear out the choking smoke. It would be glorious.

People had been coming in all day.

Hassnawi expected excellence and he would receive nothing less. The situation was dire.

Resources like medical supplies, drinkable water, electricity, and food were nearly as scarce as the talented people who knew how to administer and distribute such things in a fair manner – without prejudice or favoritism, without expectation or praise. Some people with these responsibilities were doing a shameful job

– what Hassnawi called an *immoral catastrophe* – and he, forever wise and observant and just, removed these people and assigned other, more diligent followers to take their place. After years of dedication and hard work, not privileged by advanced education or family connections, the Tall Man was proud to be one of these people.

Hassnawi took the Tall Man aside and said, "You've worked hard, and we trust you. You'll be an honest and dedicated manager of our projects."

"Like a Project Manager?" Tall Man asked, humbly.

"You are now a Project Manager," Hassnawi said.

And Project Manager bowed. "Thank you. Thank you."

* * * * *

Two men stood outside to meet with the Project Manager.

After waiting twenty minutes, one of them trembled as he walked away. A bib of blood stained the front of his shirt, blood that wasn't his. The other man held his cell phone toward the sky, turning, trying to get reception.

Khalil and Salim waited for their turn to see the Project Manager, sitting next to each other in the ochre dirt.

The back of the house faced one of the busiest streets in the *Jolan*. It lead to a mosque appropriated by the resistance as a medical center. Coalition forces had raided Fallujah General Hospital days before the siege, and few public buildings remained to support the influx of injured or dying. Disabled and elderly people huddled in small patches of shade. Neighborhood stewards brought them water and bread.

Ambulances screamed in and out of the main entrance. Frantic drivers opened their doors to carry limp passengers through ornate archways, then ran back to their idling vehicles, screeching away. Volunteers set up stations for blood donation wherever they could and took every healthy arm willing, some of them far too young or malnourished.

Salim watched the wounded being carried on stretchers fashioned from wood planks and plastic sheeting. Most of them were men either gripping gnarled limbs or burned torsos.

It was hard to breath in the nagging heat. More bodies arrived, dragged by rope-slung sleds. Collapsed heads soaked through *dishdashs* and limp hands raked trails in the dirt.

Salim tried to steady himself.

Khalil blocked his view. "Those guards, they would've shot you back there," he said.

"I doubt it," Salim said, swallowing hard.

"Shoot you or cut your head off, whatever. Me too, probably."

"Shut up," Salim said, letting his backpack relax on the ground.

"I'm saying, they would've ended you – and me. The one without the pipe, whoever he was, he would've brought us both down that alley and killed us right there if I hadn't lied like that. I can't believe this."

"Okay, thank you," Salim interrupted. "You're slick. You're brilliant. Is that what you want to hear?"

Khalil rolled his eyes.

More people gathered by the mosque's entrance. Afternoon prayers began. Loudspeakers mounted high from minarets repeated verses despite the cracking of rifles in the distance.

"They would've taken everything you have."

"Yeah."

A bus roared around the corner, tipping on two wheels before righting its course. Dust erased the road, and, as the clouds settled, the bus was gone. A truck followed behind it. *Fedayeen.*

The office opened and the man with the cell phone disappeared inside, not bothering to shut the door, reemerging minutes later with some typed agenda in his hands. He jogged away.

Khalil slapped both knees and helped Salim up. Salim's stomach churned. His face, his whole body burned.

* * * * *

"Khalil!" the Project Manager said, mockingly lighthearted. He sat behind his desk with open arms. "Khalil Atallah Hammadi, I knew you'd come to see me!"

"Oh, *Allah*," Khalil muttered, clearing his throat.

"What?" Salim whispered, shrinking behind his friend.

"I *knew* you'd be coming. I told everyone, 'if you see Khalil, if you see the boy from the photograph', and I had a copy to show them," he waved that exact copy in the air, "'tell him to come *right here*. To *my* office'."

Grinning, the Project Manager planted a stiff index finger onto his desk like marking a location on a map.

"You know him?" Salim whispered.

"Sort of."

"*Everyone* knows you, right?" Salim said. The nervous swamp inside his stomach gurgled loud enough for everyone to hear.

"Come in, come in!" the Project Manager urged, his palms thudding on the stainless desktop.

Salim studied the tidy office, keeping his thumbs hooked in his straps to keep his fingers from raking his beard.

An ambulance peeled out in the street with the same urgency as the bus and the truck filled with resistance fighters.

They watched it from the large office window.

The Project Manager leaned forward, resting his elbows on the metal desk, and fluttered two fingers at them to sit down in the chairs set before him. "Sit, sit. This is important. *Sit*." The same two fingers pushed his red glasses back to the bridge of his nose, exaggeratingly slow.

"Okay," Khalil said. They slumped into the old metal chairs, Salim's big bag forcing him to hang on the end of the seat. "How did you get *this* position, Haji?"

"Sssssss – " the Project Manager hissed, shaking, his glasses sloping down his greasy nose. "Sit. I'll ask the questions, you dog. You and your friend don't say anything."

"Just curious," Khalil said, knowing the man would want to talk about himself if pushed.

"I *earned* it. With hard *work*. And scrupulous attention to the intricate relationships of our, and don't repeat this to anyone," he said, taking off his glasses to gesture with them, "poorly run organization. Hassnawi wants me to correct this ... *immoral catastrophe!*" he yelled, rapping his knuckles on the desktop calendar, "quickly and without the bias executed by previous authorities."

"Okay," Khalil agreed, confused. "Okay. We can help you with that."

Rotating the two rings on his middle finger, the Project Manager expanded, "Corruption and greed are the very *compulsions* we're fighting in this war – how can people undermine the fundamental goals of the uprising even before it succeeds? *Mkhabbal!*"

"Absolutely right, sir. Yes," Khalil agreed.

"And you?" the Project Manager's eyes penetrated Salim's skull through his scuffed lenses. His brow tensed, yanking his mangy eyebrows. "It's crucial we're in agreement. Otherwise, you're part of the *problem* and not the *solution*. Okay?"

Both Salim and Khalil nodded.

"So you're not part of the problem?" he taunted.

"No," they said in unison.

"Good, good."

Nodding and smirking, The Project Manager twisted his two rings, one silver band, the other copper, and he twisted them and peeled back his lips to reveal the moldy tombstones of his teeth. "Who is this, anyway? Who did you bring in my office, Khalil, you dog?"

"Sal," Khalil said grimly, "Salim Abid. Mr. Hassnawi's artist."

"Designer," Salim corrected, adding, "graphic designer."

"Computer guy!" the Project Manager said. "Good with computers!"

"Designing stuff," Salim said, "not the hardware part."

"*Khosh* job. I like that."

Reclining, the Project Manager reached for a pitcher of water and poured himself a glass.

Salim watched the man drink.

He hadn't seen ice in months.

Speaking through the crushed ice, the Project Manager said, "You have something for him?"

"Uh. Yeah." Salim took off his bag and slipped out the folder, making sure it hadn't creased. He frantically flipped through the printouts to be sure he hadn't forgotten anything. "They're the leaflets he asked for and a few, uh, more designs in case he wants different messages, I guess. And the disc, too. For the printer."

"Perfect!" the Project Manager said. "You're the *Awat* guy. I see that stuff everywhere. I found one taped on the men's room mirror once in Baghdad of all places, at a restaurant. *You get around.*"

Salim wanted to believe him, but couldn't. He wondered if he'd be the *Awat* Guy for the rest of his life. Watching the streak of water on the desk, he slid the folder next to a statuette of an armadillo, nudging it.

"That's one ugly paperweight, huh?" the Project Manager noted, sneering at the armadillo. "Eh."

"There should be enough new material there for a few weeks, maybe a month. There's even a poster if they need it. I scanned some photos of – "

"Excellent, excellent!" the Project Manager shouted, snatching the folder and opening a desk drawer. He tossed it in without looking and slammed it shut. "I'm sure Hassnawi's dying to see them, Salim, I bet he's been up all night thinking about it. He's probably pacing his room right now in anticipation." He jumped to his feet, sending his chair wheeling backwards, and strolled around the desk.

"I think he's playing the *oud*," Khalil chimed.

Salim cupped his chin with trembling hands.

"Sssss –" the Project Manager hissed, circling them like some bird inspecting carrion. He wore a sport coat that mismatched his pants. Salim could tell he wasn't comfortable in it, the way he carried his shoulders, his inability to raise his arms too high. The Project Manager continued, "What we *need* to know, and when I say *we* I mean the entire uprising, every member of the *Fedayeen* and every citizen of this besieged and suffocating city, is if you can shoot a rifle."

Lifting the lid of the Xerox machine, he peered into its opaqueness as if it were displaying footage of Salim and Khalil, and he lowered his face to the black window. "Patiently and accurately take aim, squeeze the trigger, make whatever you're aiming at fall down. Bang! Simple!"

Releasing his hands, the lid slapped shut.

Salim snapped out of his seat. He sat back down.

"You can do that, right?"

Neither answered.

The Project Manager sashayed behind them, knowing they wouldn't answer. Salim rocked in his chair. Khalil carved tight, bloodless fists. They heard the Project Manager rummaging for keys, trying three before finally unlocking the door behind them. He removed two old Kalashnikovs from a closet. Using a barrel to slam the door, he came around and dropped them on the desk like logs of firewood and crossed his arms.

The rifles' wooden stocks were chipped and their spotted bodies rusted from exposure. One had a personalized sling that a previous owner had hand-woven.

"Pick them up, pick them up!" the Project Manager yelled, punching the desk.

Salim popped up, grabbed his weapon.

Khalil lingered, leaned forward in his chair and dragged the rifle by its frayed sling, opening the chamber half way to find it already loaded. "Careful, Salim," he warned.

"That's right – *careful*," the Project Manager mocked. "You wouldn't want to blow your finger off, your *computer* finger." Salim's rifle stock chattered in his shaking hands.

Opening a desk drawer, the Project Manager pulled out a thick brown cigar. Searching for something sharp enough to cut it with, he settled on the ballpoint pen. With the tip, he punched a small hole in the end of the rolled tobacco, and clinching the cigar in his teeth, pulled a matchbook from his blazer pocket. Salim fumbled with his rifle's rickety components. He tried, with all his effort, to mimic Khalil's confidence, watching his friend take thorough inventory of his rifle the way someone would check the components of an engine. All Salim could do was shake.

Salim watched the man twist and puff the cigar until it was

sufficiently lit. The man said, "With all things in life, you must be *careful.*"

"That doesn't *mean anything*," Khalil snickered, aiming out the window at a streetlight already shot out.

"Don't get him *more* mad," Salim whispered.

From the same drawer, the Project Manager pulled an ignition key and tossed it on the table. "This is your chance to prove yourself, Khalil. Make up for your negligence. Right?"

Khalil said nothing, lowering his barrel, a finger hovering outside the trigger guard. His face was stiff and dead. Bad decisions always followed after making that face.

Salim felt nauseous. His palms were so sweaty he had to squeeze his rifle to make sure he didn't drop it. He expected Khalil to distract the man with a poorly composed rebuttal and casually, as if gesturing to accentuate his point, level the weapon to the man's chest and break him open like a tangerine. The windows might shatter. Tissue chunks and muscle pureed across bookshelves. They'd be traitors before they'd stepped out of Fallujah.

When confronted by indignities, this wasn't beyond Khalil's range of violence. Salim prayed that whatever negligence the Project Manager spoke of wouldn't inspire his friend to prove himself through means more savage than the situation required.

The room dimmed behind Salim's eyelids.

If Khalil took the shot, he didn't want to witness it.

The crowd had grown outside the mosque.

The room was frozen against the panic outside. Small-arms fire rattled closer. A car spun out in the street, the driver leaning hard on the horn as passengers poured out of open doors.

Salim swallowed back the saliva building in his mouth and caught sweat beads gathering on the shelf of his lip. He focused on the legend hand-painted in red and green on the wall behind the desk – *City of Mosques - City of Heroes.* Cigar smoke reduced the room's air to gray glaze that obscured the Arabic on the wall. Salim blinked to keep from passing out.

Honking, the car backed out the way it had entered.

"Your friend doesn't look so good, Khalil."

"He was up all night finishing Mr. Hassnawi's work. Maybe he shouldn't be fighting."

The Project Manager let out a cackle. "We're all exhausted, *none* of us have slept." He shook his head and puckered his lips, cigar in his teeth, crooked glasses and dirt beneath the lenses. "Think of all the children and women who do not have the option of waking up, Salim. They have left us forever. This will invigorate you in battle!"

Salim moved his head in what could have been interpreted as a nod.

"There's a truck parked outside," the Project Manager explained, sliding the ignition key across the desk. "The ambulances are adequate, but they're easy targets. Take the truck east to the fighting, but avoid Highway 10 – won't make it far that way. One of you can shuttle the wounded back here, the other can fight."

Searching for an ashtray, he settled for the empty water glass and flicked a fat ash where it fizzled like a little gray sponge. Salim listened to the hiss. He felt like his mouth was stuffed full with tape.

"Whoever's the better driver, you decide," the Project Manager said.

"How do we know where to go?" Khalil asked, taking the key with the Kalashnikov lying on his lap and he tickled the trigger's cold crescent with his index finger.

"Follow the fucking explosions!" the Project Manager laughed, inhaling a thick plume of cigar smoke the color of old meat. He steadied himself with the back of his chair, waving at them. "Excuse me," coughing into his fist. "It's been a while. Not used to these things."

Khalil stood. Salim too.

"Out front?" Khalil asked, slinging the rifle over his shoulder with a naturalness that Salim feared and admired.

"Yes. Out there."

"Tank full?"

"Ha! Good, Khalil. You keep that attitude. Funny," he chuckled. "Don't use your cell phone while you drive. Very distracting."

"C'mon, Sal."

Khalil let his friend leave first, making a wall between Salim and the Project Manager, and, stepping backward, his finger teasing the trigger, he made sure Salim cleared the door. "Go," he whispered. "Don't worry, man."

Worry was all there was. Worry and the heavy rifle slipping out of Salim's hands, worry in each bullet eager to misfire. Salim thanked *Allah* they escaped that office without compounding whatever problems they already faced. He collapsed on the sidewalk, letting his sinking pride displace the tears he'd somehow been able to suppress.

Salim knew if he had cried in front of the Project Manager, there'd be more than water dripping from his eyes. If he'd begun to cry, Khalil would have ended it. There would've been no choice. Either they or the Project Manager would be dead.

Salim doubted the rifles even worked. He laid his down on the sidewalk, aiming the barrel away from him. Khalil stomped into the street.

"Call *me* a dog? That tall bastard," Khalil said.

With the office door shut, they could still hear the Project Manager shout, "The Americans! They say they're *pacifying* this city!" Another crackling cough. "*Ha!*"

* * * * *

Salim handed Khalil his rifle and hid his face under his arm, sucking back tears. They stepped away from the gray office windows where they wouldn't be seen, tripping down the block toward the truck. Khalil worked the action of Salim's Kalashnikov until the useless lever snapped backward and locked there, jammed. Ejecting the magazine, he tossed the rifle into the truck's bed and spit.

"Chinese junk," he cursed.

In the short time they'd been in the office the streets had filled with even more wanderers. Every class of person was lost in the confusion: men in wrinkled slacks, foundry workers and carpenters still in their uniforms, all of them wondering if they should evacuate their families.

The wounded who had tried to flee only found the journey too miserable. They staggered like zombies, stunned by the velocity of encroaching forces. They had walked back to the marketplace and the mosque-turned-hospital. The *Jolan*, with its crammed storefronts and tenements stacked high, was the safest district in the city. Rugs lined the sidewalks at the margins of the mosque. The injured lay or sat shirtless with water jugs and bandages.

Peering from under his arm, Salim could assume the relationships of the people – mothers and sisters and wives – by the way they swarmed loved ones, fanning exposed shoulders and removing shoes, swabbing foreheads boiling in the hot sun.

People knelt and prayed, bowing and kneeling with fingers to lips. They rocked forward in unison with their cousins beside them and their aunts behind them in the powdery light. They sipped the sour wind and the chemical soot within it.

Khalil slapped the truck's roof.

"I should'a killed that *khibil* fuck right there. Bang!" he yelled, punching the jaundiced metal of the truck until his knuckles were ready to split. Sitting on the bumper, Khalil looked at the paint and realized it was a captured police vehicle. Someone had spray-painted an identification number on the back. One of the doors was blue but the rest of it was white.

"Man, this truck is a mess," Khalil said.

Nodding, Salim turned and marveled at its smashed window and web-cracked windshield – three bullet holes the size of walnuts on the driver's side with larger holes punched in the passenger's door. Through the one remaining window, he could see a pair of blood-soaked sweatpants balled on the bench seat. Dark red swirls smeared the vinyl upholstery like mashed date juice.

Salim turned his head away from the reeking mess. The truck must have been sitting in the sun for hours.

Sliding off the bumper, Khalil found his door unlocked. "Get in the truck, Sal."

"No way."

"*Just get in,*" Khalil said, using the muzzle on his rifle to hook the pants and fling them into the street. "Don't worry."

Flies blended in the stench. He swatted them and used a rag on the floor to clean Salim's side and wipe down the steering wheel, clutch, and door handles. Flecks on the ceiling would have to be ignored. When the rag was drenched, he found a t-shirt crammed in the glove box and sponged the vinyl seats.

"I'm not getting in there," Salim said through the glass.

"I'll get you to the river. This'll be faster. We have to move it anyway or he'll know we ditched."

"No."

"It's really not that bad. I've seen worse, believe me." Khalil said.

"I'll just walk. You take the truck."

"This will be safer."

Huffing, Salim opened the door and stood with his arm braced on the frame. "Ach, it smells like piss!"

"Because someone died in here. Get in."

"It looks like fifteen people died in here."

Jumping in, Khalil bounced on the worn seat, popped the shift to park, and cranked the key. Surprise flushed his face when the engine hiccupped and turned. "C'mon, when was the last time we drove around together?"

"We *never* have."

"And in a *war zone*, we'll never have this opportunity again! It's an *adventure*," he said with a smile so wide it hid his eyes. "How quickly do you want to find the Internet?"

"I'm not *finding* the Internet." Salim coughed into his bent arm, snorting in cleaner air over his shoulder. He wasn't sure if Khalil was impervious to the stench or if he was trying to be tough.

"Sal. Let's get out of here." Khalil smacked the dashboard.

"This is gross, man."

"Yeah," Khalil admitted, uncurling his tongue, scrunching his nose. Unidentifiable wetness clogged the heating vents. "It's pretty gross."

People with carts walked past them carrying more battle-weary and slain fighters, stopping at the entrance of the mosque where the archways began to resemble frowning mouths. Also, Salim hadn't seen so many dogs in his life, rib-bare and curious hounds scrounging with noses low.

Two helicopters circled the marketplace then hurried away, toward the explosions erupting steadily from the east. Their cleaving propellers left the square swirling with sand like powdered leaves in tea water. People scrambled to shield their half-naked loved ones susceptible to infection.

Night would be worse.

The poor would be blind in the blanket black and powerless against infrared scope.

Salim knew it was coming. They were wasting too much time.

"Seat's not going to get any cleaner," Khalil admitted. "Time to go."

"Ugh." Salim slid in, holding his backpack, so overfull that it touched the glove box. A raggedy pelt stretched across the dashboard like a gutted teddy bear. Clumps of its brown fur were matted with blood and an air freshener was caught in one of the coagulated pools.

"C'mon," Khalil said, wrapping his fingers around the tacky steering wheel, the break pedal slippery with each tap. He opened his door and, pinching a dry patch of the pelt, flung it into the road. Salim closed his eyes. He leaned and vomited out of the window. He tried to curse through the spasms, but he was overcome with heaving.

"Man! You carsick, Sal?" Khalil laughed. "We haven't even started moving yet!"

Salim waved Khalil away and vomited again, hugging his backpack like a flotation device. He cleared his throat, pointing his free finger forward, rasping, "Go."

"Sure? You okay?" Khalil looked behind them to see if the Project Manager had come out of his office.

"Yeah. Drive."

"Right," Khalil said, shifting to drive. The transmission ached to shift. Headed westward, he knew to take the back streets.

Burping, Salim swabbed puke from his beard.

"Whoo! You think we should smash the rest of the windshield to air this thing out?" Khalil asked, screeching around the corner to avoid a checkpoint, swerving around potholes.

"No."

"Okay."

The engine rattled and steamed and they were gone.

4

The truck's internal combustion clunked and gasped as it struggled west. It pissed and jerked. Without consulting the temperature gauge, Salim knew it was overheating – dying along with the rest of the city.

The engine block was finished. In the evening heat, it would only sputter so long before rigor mortis set and the steaming hulk farted to a stop. It made everything seem even dumber. To Salim, the plan and its shit execution was dumb. The Project Manager's suicide missions were the dumbest wastes ever. The libraries and schoolyards were dumb because they didn't know what was coming. Magpies and gulls all dumb like hurried flies, and Khalil was a dumbshit, too.

Khalil pushed the accelerator hard. "We're only going to make it a few kilometers."

The streets were abandoned. Steady gunfire snapped between crackling explosions like a blown speaker bass heavy in the sky.

"Sounds like they're starting early!" Khalil shouted.

No shit, Salim thought.

"Sounds like real hell," he added.

Hoarse explosions thundered from somewhere impossible to gauge – the center of the city and then North of it, too. Three and four clustered at a time, heaping powdery contagions into the breeze. Each explosion cracking the clouds collapsed Salim's confidence that he'd escape at all.

Tan buildings zipped by. Their balconies were decorated with planters and deck furniture and Khalil swerved the truck like a war-torn chariot whose horses were too spooked and exhausted to comply. Salim held steady to door handles.

A tipped over car smoldered on the sidewalk.

Khalil slowed to an idle and scrutinized the backstreets. He sped on. The truck coughed and sputtered. He coasted through puddles and accelerated whenever a concussion vibrated the asphalt. Smoke chugged from under the truck's hood. Thin wisps of gray streamed through the bullet holes in the windshield. The accelerator produced throaty rattles from the engine that shook the frame. "Gonna have to ditch it."

Salim covered his face. "Okay."

Salim leaned out the window and puked again. All water this time. Draped out the window, he let his arms dangle like pendulums independent of time. Riding through each diaphragm spasm, he was careful not to scratch his wristwatch on the door. He didn't care if some blood stained his t-shirt. Sand could permanently color his black hair gray, as long as the watch was okay.

"You alright, man?"

Salim flipped a thumbs up behind his back.

Swallowing, he rubbed his temples with his fingers, elbows resting on the backpack. His sandals propped on the dash. He cleared his throat of phlegm, asked, "What should I tell your cousin when I see him?"

"Nothing," Khalil said plainly, studying the temperature gauge. "I'm gonna pull over."

"I need the address – of his place."

"Why?"

"So I know where it is," Salim said, taking out a pen from his pocket, rummaging for a piece of paper in his bag.

"I'm taking you there, man. We're going." The pickup wheezed and idled until it settled into dystrophy. "Good girl, good girl," Khalil soothed, patting the steering wheel and kissing the bloody rubber where he patted it.

Spitting, he said, "That was probably a bad idea."

"What about the fight?" Salim asked, panicked. "I thought you were staying."

"I would," he explained, opening his door and grabbing the Kalashnikov, "but I can't let you go alone. Too dangerous. Way too dangerous, man. And look. I'd have to walk all the way back now."

"I'll be fine. Stay here," Salim said, yanking on his door handle to no effect. He shimmied across to the driver's side. His backpack snagged on the truck's shifter.

"You'll need me," Khalil said, reaching into the truck to un-hook the pack. Salim swatted him away. "You know, moral support, your wing man, your black guy in *Dead Hard*."

Salim freed himself, the gear shift smearing bloody syrup in his arm hair. "Die *Hard*," he corrected, scanning the area for trouble. Men sat cross-legged on rugs under a pillared entrance across the street, aware of their presence; they made curious gestures at the wrecked police vehicle. One of the men wouldn't stop pointing.

"No. This is something I have to do myself."

"What does that mean?"

"Like, just me."

"Why? You're only walking. It's like 60 kilometers. Maybe more. You're going to get bored, man. Really, really bored. Okay?"

"I *like* being alone, Khalil," Salim said, walking away from him and the truck and whatever the men across the street might think.

Khalil hopped in place. "Maybe, but it'll be more fun with me. You know, you might get to Ramadi and maybe my cousin isn't there. What'll you do?"

"Improvise. Ask around," Salim said, walking faster, trying to orient himself. "Where's the bridge?"

"This way," Khalil said, leading them northwest through an open lot. Between terraced apartment buildings, a large group of children rode bikes and took turns launching off a ramp fashioned from concrete and scrap plywood. The oldest, the daredevil, circled around for another jump and Khalil hooted as he landed, peeling out in the sand. Salim shook his head.

"Khalil. I'm going alone. I have to," Salim said sternly, taking the lead. The Highway 10 bridge – the one made famous by Khalil's photograph – grew larger in the distance. He knew he'd have to go around it. Barriers fortified both sides and no one other than coalition and Iraqi police could cross. It was evident that no lynching would happen there again.

"I'll protect you, man. We'll protect each other."

"Believe me. I'll be fine."

"Why are you being a dick?"

"I'm not being a dick."

"Okay. Okay."

Salim walked on.

Khalil followed. He kicked a flattened can, skidding peddles where it landed, spinning.

Salim ignored him, secretly fuming. *Should've known this would happen*, he thought, *should've just left by myself.* He wished Khalil would ditch his rifle, because it only made his black outfit more of a target, and if he was a target so was Salim. It was impossible to tell how far they'd gone in the truck. They weren't nearly as close as he thought they were to the river's north bend, the wide stretch of water bordering the city, and he wanted to ask Khalil if he knew where they were exactly. But why start relying on him now?

Keeping to the street, but avoiding the main traffic, he planned to flank right around the river's elbow and exit the city's northwestern limits. *The most inconspicuous route*, he reasoned.

Khalil punted the can into a doorway. He was attracting even more attention.

Russet and ochre structures obscured their bearings, confusing landform and manmade squares. Squinting through the setting sun, Salim found it hard to see where the sky started and ended. The land began to open. Large stretches of sand expanded where rugs of wheat met the horizon, and the route seemed safe enough. Salim pointed at the terrain like a conquistador with no compass, and he hiked his backpack higher.

His throat felt like a rusted tailpipe.

Isolated from the oncoming siege, the *Jolan's* usually frantic outskirts were unusually quiet. People were preparing, hoarding water and whatever nonperishables they could barter. Some hauled tins and jugs in dragged sleeping bags. A woman used her *abaya* like a kangaroo to carry amber ribbons of jerky. Stray dogs jittered everywhere, scavenging for carcasses or scraps, but it was the stray cats that seemed to have the best luck, leaping freely into open windows.

As much as Salim wanted to run, he knew he couldn't draw

attention their way. Walking in the direction of the water, blending in groups of other asylum seekers with their necks exposed like heads out a bus window, Salim and Khalil went – and so went the others carrying children, some two at a time like conjoined twins hobbling along, little elbows and scalps flapping. A great diaspora, without destination or real purpose. *There's no sanctuary from themselves*, Salim thought, rubbing his neck, *like there'll be none from the sun once I've committed to the river.*

There's no heading back. Everyone who drinks from the Euphrates returns to Baghdad.

Khalil said something inaudible.

Salim said nothing.

Khalil found another can to kick.

* * * * *

The sun descended into a slot in the earth. It tanned their cheeks and arms. Blocks away, the river expanded like a bright ribbon draped across the dunes where bulrush swayed, and they could feel slight temperature shifts across the valley. Salim welcomed the April night, but the cold might be as harsh as day and he remembered the blanket he forgot to buy in the *Jolan*. It might not be too late.

"Crap," he whispered to himself.

Maybe they had walked an hour or more – Salim didn't know. Khalil didn't care. Their bickering had slowed them down; the Project Manager slowed them even more.

"You'll have no one to talk to," Khalil said.

Exactly, Salim thought.

"What if you get hurt?"

Khalil lagged farther behind. He let his Kalashnikov droop

lower and lower on his shoulder. Finally, he let the rifle hit the ground and stopped. Salim knew the sound of a rifle clanging on asphalt.

He turned to see his friend with his chin to his chest, the same way he had done as a kid. But it was for far more trivial reasons then – a stolen ball or a fight with his father.

"Are you kidding me?" Salim yelled. "Go back and fight like you're always bragging about."

Salim was glad they were far enough from the tenements for anyone to hear.

"Or stand here and sulk. I don't give a shit!"

But Khalil didn't answer.

He turned away, head down like a decapitated statue in the street. Salim expected him to run, but he just stood with the backdrop of Fallujah beginning to burn away, gray plumes crawling Eastward on the wind.

"Go! You'll be a *famous martyr!*" Salim yelled with cupped hands. "Pick up your gun, man!"

Khalil didn't budge.

He shoved his hands into his pockets.

Apache helicopters buzzed over the east end of the *Jolan*. One sprayed neon tracers and dove before retreating back to an occupied Baathist palace outside the city. The braver Apache swiveled to hose a rooftop with its machine gun and sank, circling to avoid rockets that fizzled from windows.

With a glass of tea in his hands, an old man shuffled by Salim, oblivious to the dazzle behind him. He was humming.

"I'll be fine! I'll be back in a few weeks," Salim said.

No response from Khalil.

Huffing, he backtracked and waited for his friend to recompose himself. "You've been waiting for this for months. It's all you fucking talk about."

"I can't go back," Khalil mumbled, his eyes on the dirt.

"Huh?"

Louder, "I *can't* go."

"Why?" Salim asked, wanting to hear a real reason, wanting him to admit he was scared. "You're all set. You got your 'uniform'. You got a gun. What else do you need, man?"

Khalil looked at the ground.

"I just *can't*," he repeated.

Salim and Khalil shifted their gaze to the helicopter dodging rocket-propelled grenades. It flew closer, blades purring, nose tilted down. A rocket tube smoked like a spent Roman candle, tracing the gunship's path.

Sporadic burps of cannon fire crackled from side-mounted barrels; brass shells twinkled down. *Sounds like a stampede*, Salim thought, the bullets thumping dirt and gnarled road. He was hypnotized.

People panicked, hands over their heads and ears.

"Are you afraid you won't be as brave as your photo?" Salim said, surprised at himself, but hoping it pressured Khalil to go back to town.

"Fuck you," Khalil said.

Other families noticed Khalil's all black track suit and chose to cross the street. Salim saw them. A mother covered her daughter's eyes.

"Yeah," Salim said, scratching his beard. "Okay."

A jet tore through the fading sunset. A slower plane trailed behind, growling low. The real siege had begun.

Salim waited for Khalil to pivot around. He never did.

They both faced Fallujah and the escalating barrage until an earth-cracking concussion thunderclapped and sucked up all sustenance, backlighting the silhouetted palm trees like black and frozen fireworks in the sky. Embers sparkled, perishing in the wind. The rancid tang of phosphorus chlorinated their tongues until it was all they could taste. Khalil turned. He didn't lean down to retrieve the rifle. Hands at his waist, he kept his cheek to Salim – looking off at some nothing. He greeted Salim with a wrinkled grin.

It would be impossible to say *no* now. "Sorry." Salim said, "Sorry for saying that."

"Okay."

A bus rushed by, filled to capacity. Several cars followed close, their roofs stacked with suitcases bound by twine and power cords.

"I only brought enough food for me," Salim said.

"Then I won't eat."

"You *can* go back, you know. And you don't *have* to fight."

Hands hidden in his tracksuit pockets, Khalil's brow hardened. Maybe for the first time in his life, he expressed more than he ever wanted to with no words at all. Stiff jawed, he nodded, considering his few options. He rubbed his hands, his knuckles, and thumbs.

Khalil named his friends. "Saad's fighting. Right now, I know it. With his brothers and his father, probably," he said, focused on a sign swinging over a mechanic's shop. Saad, the mechanic since birth like half the men in Fallujah – Saad who saved for years for a motorcycle and crashed it a month later. "Falah. He's got a crippled hand, you know? He can shoot better than me." Khalil held up his right hand, mangling it into a claw. "Fucking claw boy is a crack-shot."

"Doesn't matter, Khalil."

"It does. Sure it does," he answered, unblinking and grinding the ball of his foot in the pavement. "Their fathers and uncles were taken – now they fight."

Salim breathed in hard. When the air came out it sputtered, and his chest felt like someone was sitting on it. "I know."

Cars darted in front of them, honking *good luck* and *good-bye*.

"Can't." Khalil shrugged, working his tongue between his lower gum and cheek like he was sculpting words that wouldn't form. "Can't, man."

"Huh?"

"I can't," he said again.

There was little to say. Salim was sure Khalil would just keep following no matter what was said or done. He knew that if he returned to Fallujah and Khalil was dead, he would never forgive himself.

Salim cleared his throat, prompting Khalil to smile one of his thousands of smiles that could be interpreted a thousand different ways, but Salim knew this was his *I'm going to get what I want* smile.

Salim turned his cheek, cleared his throat again.

"You can't take the rifle," he said, his voice hoarse. "We'll look like resistance fighters."

Khalil's face beamed. "It could save us, Sal," he said, already reaching down.

"Anyone sees you with that, they're going to kill us. You already look like *Fedayeen*."

"Yeah," Khalil admitted, letting the Kalashnikov's strap slacken and drop. Salim knew it was hard for him – couldn't believe he was giving in.

"You can't look like that. We'll have to swap shirts."

"I guess," Khalil huffed. "Okay."

They traded shirts. Salim held Khalil's black t-shirt up, knowing it would fit tight around his stomach, but it would have to do "You can wear your windbreaker at night, that doesn't matter."

"Okay."

"It'll be dark enough."

"Okay."

Salim stretched the shirt down, sucking in his gut, then relaxing. He shouldered his backpack.

They continued west.

* * * * *

When Salim was tired of looking at the line of cars, he looked to the sky.

The battle had stirred every type of bird from its roost. Gulls, cranes, and hawks swept westward. Skulking people overloaded into taxis and crammed into creaking sedans envied their graceful freedom, but the birds were only temporarily escaping the siege. "Maybe we can get a ride," Khalil suggested.

"No."

The street was already blocked by bottlenecking traffic. Checkpoints stalled families, keeping certain roads clear in case coalition forces struck. Salim took a right, Khalil on his heels.

"We need a blanket."

"Okay."

"All the shops are closed."

"There." Khalil jabbed his chin at a clothesline stretched between two columns. He took out his 20,000 dinar and jogged away. Salim ran alongside him. The straps of the pack wrenched his shoulders back, the stuffed lump pulling down like a boulder. Slowing, they looked for homeowners or patrolling *Fedayeen*. There was no sign of anyone. Khalil hugged a high wall, spying the yard and the patio and the shuttered windows. Standing on a flipped flowerpot, he popped his head up twice, ducking behind the bricks. They ran together, heads low.

Four clothespins clamped a thick cotton sheet like a truce flag. The closer they got, the larger it appeared. Khalil gave a thumbs-up.

"You can't just take it," Salim protested.

Huffing, he said, "We'll pay for it. 10,000 dinar. More than enough."

"*That's not cool.*"

"It's not a big deal. We need it."

"Pay who?" Salim asked, looking around nervously, thinking he saw someone along the upper terraces.

"We can pay for it, return it later," Khalil justified, making sure no one watched him un-pin the sheet. He balled it quickly, stuffing it in his jacket before clipping the dinars to the close line. He unclipped and folded them so they wouldn't flap in the wind. "Man, there's one over there too," he said, gesturing to another line where a thick blanket draped.

"This is stupid, Khalil. I'm not taking it," Salim refused, already stepping away. Someone sat in a parked car across the street. His nose stuck above the base of the open window. Maybe he wasn't sleeping. Holding his stomach, Khalil snatched the blanket and folded it under his arm as he followed, tripping on a rake laid flat in the dirt.

"Shit, man. We'll bring them back," Khalil said. "I bet no one's even home there. They probably fled, too."

Salim remained silent, sticking to the adjacent streets. He kept Khalil close.

Finally, the river appeared – a strip of brilliant twinkling blue between two riverside buildings, the final minutes of sunshine illuminating what bit of water they could see. *Can't get too close*, Salim thought. *Not dark enough yet.*

Flanking the bridge, they could make out Humvees parked around the entrance.

Turrets rotated on their armored roofs, but none fired a shot. Soldiers sat in neat platoons and fanned themselves with magazines, shared cigarettes and readied for the dead. A sniper nested on a vehicle's hood while his partner, as meticulous as an owl, scoped mortar teams and pillboxes on rooftops.

Across the Euphrates, at the other end of the bridge, tanks positioned themselves with cannons as long as telephone poles. More men stood in staggered regiments – infantry, radiomen, a chaplain, lieutenants, and medics all witnessing the prelude of hail-fire before the first push into Fallujah. Salim wondered if he was visible to them. Probably not.

He wondered how old they were and where they were from. He thought of states whose names had curious origins – Iowa, Ohio, Kansas, Arkansas; and towns with similar folklore – Amarillo, Decatur, Saginaw, Walla Walla, Alliance, and Selma – the vast plains of the Midwest and mountain ranges he'd researched on the Internet, and whose images he had saved to use in his designs and drawings. He remembered the countless hours he'd dozed at his computer screen, staring at the impossibly green lawns. He wondered who they'd left back home – their wives and fiancées and brothers.

Then he thought of Rana and if the media was covering the siege, and if she hoped he was okay.

Out of breath, Salim and Khalil used every wall and abandoned car as cover, hustling from each scant sanctuary to the next.

Wide stretches left them exposed to night vision and scope. Salim hoped they weren't spotted before they reached the city limits.

"What do you think they're waiting for?" Khalil asked.

Salim ignored him and cursed the road and everything that had ever ridden on it.

"All them, just standing there," Khalil said.

"Quiet."

The building smoke choked the dusk to early dark. Quick artillery strobes flashed like heat lightening. They crept the scratchy streets and continued up the river until the road abstracted into sand and apartment complexes simplified into mud huts. No foot or wheeled traffic came or went. Thick grass shielded them from view, and Salim could see that they were rounding the topmost bend of the Euphrates that bordered the city. If the map in his mind was correct, they had walked southwest, keeping the water on their left.

Squatting along the shore, a woman washed dishes and stacked her clean plates in a tub. She ignored Salim. She used an old rag lathered with liquid soap. A basin bobbed and clinked and bubbles swirled. They were embarrassed to come upon her. Salim pulled Khalil closer to the road. The woman's daughters played downstream, splashing ankle-deep in the water. The war could've been countries away.

Chiming across the cement, the wind scraped two empty soda cans attached by six-pack rings. Khalil jumped over it.

White brick shelters lined the water where thick brambles made it impossible to walk.

They saw a family sitting at a table outside. They ate roast chicken and flatbread. The father flipped more meat on the grill. His boys waited with eager hands. The mother sat with her hands pressed between her thighs in the same manner.

"Smells good," Khalil said.

Dust spread over the blackening asphalt.

* * * * *

Narrowing, the river turned south, giving liberty to wildflower and hardy ferns. They traveled onto drier soil, avoiding river slime and sticky muck and the random fish littering the shore. In the mischievous light of the evening, they went as if they themselves were shadows. Khalil, in his tracksuit, was the real thing; he grew harder and harder to see.

Salim felt, even without his backpack weighing him down, that he always made too much noise when he walked. He tried to step more carefully, avoiding rocks and garbage. Walking slower, he let Khalil take the lead. He focused on his breathing and relaxed and let the river overcome him. In some spots, the surface was varnish. Brassy tinges and gold fleck mixed in the brine. Gulls skidded on the water, admired their reflection, and swooped away. Downriver, a paddle boat bobbed and rotated as slowly as a sundial. No passengers or cargo floated in the coming night.

Stepping over a junked air conditioner, they scaled a large drainage pipe sticking out of the riverbank. City trash sank in the muck: Coke bottles, spray cans, bullet shells, a doll's leg, a purple sock. Bird feathers decorated a rusted monkey wrench sticking out of the beach. Whenever they could, they stuck to drier land, but away from the road patrols and away from anyone who might mistake them for resistance fighters.

They climbed up eroded embankments and when they got to a barrier or house, they crept so that no one heard – even though it was impossible to hear anything other than firefights as the siege matured into war.

Every few minutes, one of them would stop and listen.

"Man," Khalil would say.

Thunderous drums thudded deep and offbeat, barreled in the stony peeks of cloud. The horizon lit up – the flashes splashed the river with light like a glowing crack in the planet as bombardments above Babylon decimated history. Mosques shook. Brittle ruins dissolved into dust.

They kept their backs to the battle as much as they could.

Khalil took out the bed sheet and folded both it and the blanket into a cape that flapped behind him. The more Salim stared at the waving cape, the more he resented Khalil for tagging along.

It would be a miracle if no one spotted that white sheet, Salim thought.

Coming to a concrete wall where irrigation pumps fed a system of troughs, they veered right where two homes met the simple road. A one-lane byway ran parallel to the water. No pedestrians or cars could be seen. Khalil led, his cape the only fabric not black on his body.

Huts lined the road. Plastic chairs collected dust under sun-bleached awnings. It was the last stop before open desert and kilometers of unforgiving terrain. There was no access to the river. Barren and limitless ochre stretched onward as foreboding as a burned orchard, yet they hid their fear and said their private goodbyes to the city.

"I just want a soda," Khalil said.

"If you're going to start that already, just go home."

They kept their distance from the homes. One-room hovels with makeshift doors looked brittle enough to be claimed by the next strong gust of wind. Inside, families snuggled close enough to smell each other's hair, trade breaths. All of them prayed. Each home was fortified by faith and their prayer.

The brightly lit homes doused their lamps as Salim and Khalil's presence became known.

"We'll get back to the river past these houses," Salim whispered.

"Okay."

Khalil wrapped his head in the white sheet.

Donkeys brayed.

A goat on a rope leash jerked, butting phantoms. Under a lean-to made of welded car hoods, a man sat with a cane or a rifle in his lap and his long beard reached for his shoulder in the wind. He made no movement. He crossed his legs, gloved hands tucked in his armpits, and watched the sky.

"Make a left after these here," Salim said, referring to the last of the homes.

Not listening, Khalil started to ask, "How far do we – " and then he squatted, jerked toward the city limits. "*Shit.*"

"What?" Salim asked, ducking too. "What?"

"Hear that?"

"No," he said, stooped, knuckles in the dirt.

They waited a second.

Faint rumbles followed flashes over the city.

"Trucks."

"Naw. That's over there," Salim answered, referring to the battle and the avalanching clouds.

"Behind us," Khalil gasped, squinting to see.

"Right," Salim said. "In the city."

The man under the lean-to dipped into his hut and slammed the door. The goat made circles in the dirt.

"*There.*" Khalil spit and pointed down the road. "Trucks." He pointed to a black column, headlights dulled in the blinding dust.

An SUV and two smaller pickups fanned out across the road, erratic. Maneuvering for position, the second pickup turned and drifted, slammed its bed into the porch of a house. A passenger flipped overboard like a gymnast, arms and legs somersaulting. The remaining passenger slid a rocket into its launcher but couldn't align the round, and he clung to the doorframe as his *keffiyeh* swam up his face. Another truck packed with *Fedayeen* fell into step, swerving so as not to hit the man thrown from the accident. It roared to catch the leading SUV.

"Go!" Khalil yelled, ripping at Salim's sweatshirt.

"Shit, shit, shit!" Salim screamed, running.

"Go, go, go!"

Salim's pack punched his back as he ran. Scrambling, they broke formation and Khalil sprinted ahead. Salim heaved, eyes scrambling for a place to duck. His toes were numb and his shins hammered, and even if the trucks intended them no harm, Salim screamed as if the screaming would scare off the coming stampede.

"C'mon, Sal! C'mon!" Khalil cried back, arms open, "Toss your bag."

Untangling himself, Salim threw the bag, and they both bolted with the roaring pickups accelerating louder. The *Fedayeen* in the truck's bed fired the rocket. It arced in the exhaust like an egg on a string, but failed to explode.

"Here!" Khalil gripped the backpack to his chest, the blanket and sheet wrapping it like a baby. They skidded down an embankment to the end of the shanty village where the limits opened up to the shore. Khalil helped Salim steady himself. They broke for the wheatgrass. The trucks drove on. The strained engines faded away.

"Okay," Khalil panted, patting Salim's back. "Okay." Salim heaved, lowering to his knees. In the naked brush, they waited until the night's silence overshadowed their fatigue, and, looking around at the open land, felt more exposed than ever before.

A few villagers came to the roadside and eyed the two – losing interest when the thick, riverine growth disguised their form. In the dark, they looked like shivering stones.

"Not okay," Salim quivered, sitting in the matted grass. "Could've – could have been killed."

"Naw," Khalil said, sitting, too. "Weren't after us." He aired his collar out. It shot heat like an opened flue. He took the shirt off to flap it cool. "Probably not. Not us."

"Whatever," Salim said, bending his knees and stooping his head, sniffling quietly, face hidden. He knew Khalil hadn't seen him cry. That was good, he thought. Tears dropped on his toes.

The wheatgrass recomposed to the wind's will.

The sky burned with white raining light.

"*Shit,*" Khalil said, fixed on the barrage coming from the northern end of the city, the *Muallimin* and *Jeghaifi,* even parts of the industrial park. "I didn't think it'd be this intense."

They could barely see the bridge.

Small arms fire popped a few kilometers away, muted like distant firecrackers. Platoons traversed the bridge where Highway 10 was cordoned off. Between the men, vehicles rolled with their treads and tires pulverized rock, their weight playing the ironwork of the bridge – plucking beams, bending struts, bellowing an eerie nocturne across the water.

Khalil walked to the river's edge, held his elbows in the cooling night. He searched the shoreline for the roving squads patrolling the city's outskirts. Acquainting himself with the sloping banks and rock, he mapped the easiest escape route. It seemed that only herring and the occasional bullfrog would disturb their sleep if they decided to camp there.

Whatever safe was, this was it.

He urinated in the ferns.

Salim was still sniffling when Khalil returned.

"Man. It's not that bad. We're fine." Khalil hooked his arm around his friend's shoulders. "Those guys are idiots."

"Yeah," Salim said.

"C'mon, man."

Salim ground his teeth and nodded and tugged on the side of his beard with shaking fingers. Khalil held him while he wiped his eyes, both of them listening to the quiet gargles of the river.

Salim stared at the water and sat in a nest of patted wheat, still careful not to dampen his toes. A cool breeze skimmed the river.

Khalil made camp.

He spread out the stolen blanket and sheet, smoothing away air pockets and creases. When everything was still, a rock on each corner secured the blanket. He made himself comfortable, prying off his sneakers, burying his socks in wooly folds. The shirt and the windbreaker and the sheet barely kept him warm. He huddled close to the tall flimsy fences of grass.

Salim cleared his throat, trying to compose himself.

He could hear Khalil's stomach gurgle. Food and water were out of the question until morning. They would have to wait.

Behind them, the twinkling road opened up to more traffic. On the river, a ferryman in a *mashoof* rowed by. He dipped his pole, drew radar blips in the water that grew circular and faded. Rowing, he was transfixed by the cityscape's fever – the auroras of besiegement as they were reflected off the river.

Mashing his heel in the marsh, Salim hiccupped and looked at the munitions flowering above Fallujah. White-hot stars like welding arcs flashed before the boom.

"Get some sleep, man," Khalil whispered.

Salim opened his backpack to get his sweatshirt and took the laptop out. The screen lit up. He inspected it for damage, finding none. And though he knew Khalil might ask him annoying questions about the laptop, or why there was no Internet signal, he sat in the camp they had built and waited for it to power up. He thought of Rana in Syria, in her dorm and in her sweatpants, ready for bed. He remembered her profile, her favorite bands he had never heard of, her photo and her vacation album, and her guy friends that filled him with jealousy.

No service out here, he thought, *no way.*

He clicked on the connectivity icon anyway. It flashed like a distress beacon. He kept the glowing screen close to his body so it wouldn't signal their whereabouts. Now and then, the river bubbled. Fish kissed the surface.

The laptop's fan hummed. The square screen shielded the wind blowing off the water.

Now it was just him.

He could barely see the English letters on the keyboard.

Eyes bloodshot and teary, Salim used his baggy sleeve to wipe his face. Sand scratched his cheeks. With his hood like a cave, with his father sitting on the couch where he had left him to endure the siege alone, he opened Microsoft Word. He clicked on *New Document* – curser blinking – and typed in the language he always wanted to speak –

Going to the Dogs

Selected Word documents
from the laptop of Salim Abid

5

Fleeing blindly in the failing dusk, Khalil and I scramble free, the burning city behind us. We scale toppled walls and blown brick hovels. We run through market squares and the crippled township, to the river running west and closer.

All I can think of is Rana and how she'll assume I'm dead if I don't contact her soon. Her family was smart to flee to Syria before the real war began. Before the siege and the fire within it.

Khalil pushes my backpack from behind. We reached the stone plateau, slipping on talcum, hints of gypsum.

The night sky crashes white. We turn toward Fallujah. Empty steel drums roll under clouds. A few drop on the town, sending ripples through our teeth. Great gales of depleted uranium scatter like seed. Deltas of oil smoke leech the sky.

We breathe like dogs.

The river is at our backs.

In the quiet muck, we're alone.

Breeze off the marshland rustles high grasses. They shiver like hairs on the scalp of the Earth.

We glare past arid pastures of grain where nitroglycerine and stone resist synthesis, and smoky cones of sulfur grow – dissipate and grow. The cityscape appears in blue flashes.

We've stopped breathing.

Khalil says,

– We're OK now. No one's going to make us fight.

– Yeah, I say.

– We're safe.

Khalil rubs the corners of his eyes.

Fading sunlight brightens the gray and malnourished cinders. Khalil pulls me like a toddler. We hurry over fresh rubble and splintered wood until the city is a brilliant ruin behind us.

He's faster. He makes me faster.

We think we hear screams, but we're too far away now with the opal river approaching and we already feel like fossils buried under fire. He says,

– Keep going.

We finally push beyond the endless wheat and reach the crooked elbow of the Euphrates.

The randomized pattern of bombardment, efficient in its clumsy chorus, baffles us. We stare at the bulbous mosques backlit by flashes, waiting collapse. Fires expand over neon vales of carbon, orange tentacles stretch where municipal buildings once stood, and I shiver and pray that my home and my father somehow defy their diligence.

– OK, I say.

– OK.

Even if Rana thinks I'm alive, it will be months, maybe a year, until we might talk again. She will forget me.

Hunching low, silently following the riverbank, Khalil is only a silhouette between flashes and the rumbles hunting them. Further and further, the mud suctions and farts, and I'd trade all the water in the world for a pair of hiking boots, ones with soles as thick as bars of soap with tight laces to seal out the silt.

Blue-white clusters balloon like shattered tungsten over the city's south end, close to the industrial park. Jets slice the black above, birthing thunderous concussions. Munitions trickle down. Some burst above rooftops. Their scorched fragments burn so high in the altitude that we can't distinguish broken sound barrier from incendiary boom.

It looks imaginary. It could be television.

We finally stop and rest on flat rocks like the stoop of a childhood home that we might never return to.

* * * * *

It was my mother.

* * * * *

Most definitely, it was my mother. Fed up with the first war and the subsequent sanctions, freed by true poverty and liberated from any ambitions of prosperity – the dwindling grams of weekly coffee, her necessity – the anemic electricity – and same-old, same-old chic pea and kabob dinners – she found herself reeling and bored and unchallenged. And then, as if she'd seen a commercial for the idea, she fled. That was it. My mother. Blame her. Was – and always will be – her.

Nisreen Abid, who passed solely the genes of rebellion to

her only child, the woman cast from iron and painted to look porcelain, a totem of dissent and a Trojan horse to the establishment. Prankster. Provocateur. As aristocratic as a falcon with the talons to prove it. Blame her for the dumbly planned sedition of my dearest, dearest city and the stupendous shit we're in.

My martyr and foolhardy mother let her hair down like a painter's brush dipped in tar, and she would strut with that hair, cutting through centuries of servitude and superstition, sashaying through the markets and rec centers and libraries in ways that tested the vested institutional traditions. Men grimaced. Sheiks groaned. *Allah, here she comes.* Snide whispers from café tables. Pretentious eyebrows raising. Mostly they left her alone.

That was in a different time.

Blame her.

It's cold out here.

* * * * *

Here's a list of the three things I'd wish for if we found a lamp with one of those magic genies in it:

- a high speed Internet connection.
- headphones. I forgot my headphones.
- a hot fudge brownie ice cream sundae from TGI Fridays.

You can blame my mother for the last one, too. She took me to Cairo once. There's a TGI Fridays there. We shared this brick of a brownie with vanilla ice cream and hot fudge covering everything. I've been dreaming about it ever since.

It's colder than I thought it would be. In the city, heat settles into concrete and the packed clay. It radiates from windless crannies. Out here in the open, we're completely exposed. But the wheat helps, shielding us from the wind. Its rustle sounds like muffled rain. Stars above. There's a colander over the planet and someone's shining a spotlight, and those white pricks of concentrated energy burn silent through the incalculable nothing.

If my own inadequacies didn't already prove me puny, then these stars do.

I yawn like a camel.

Big camel lips and yarns of camel spit.

Khalil's got the right idea. He grasps for elusive warmth. Sneakers off, there are wet spots on his socks where the holes in his shoes were exposed to the soil. Cocooned, he's shivering like a newborn. His stomach sounds like a calf mooing for food. Crazy idiot is so obviously macho. Reckless. He'll get me killed if we're not careful.

No one's on the road. The people in the houses have lost interest in us.

I open my pack.

I tear off a corner of flatbread, and there's no guilt in not sharing because Khalil shouldn't be here anyway. It tastes decent without chutney. It absorbs the acid in my throat. Blood from the truck's armrest stained my shirt. I'd wash it out in the river if it wasn't so freezing. But it's not the cold that freaks me out. Scorpions and red ants populate the outer desert and brontosaurus-sized spiders with incisors like serrated razors tiptoe after dark. I know that each wind gust across my cheek will tickle me awake.

I shiver, trying to settle in. Fingers draw the string of my hood tighter. I wonder if it's the chill or my nerves that won't let me hold still. Kicking off my sandals, I rub dried mud on the blanket and exhale warm huffs into cupped hands. My knuckles are wind-licked red.

* * * * *

Everyone waited for the American election results. Four more years meant more to us than it did to the Americans, I think. There was something about Florida and voting machines or something. I searched on the Internet *Florida* – swamp land, Seminole Indians, Mickey Mouse, NASA, alligator wrestling – the place seemed like the complete opposite of our city. Every television was on in Fallujah. A week of waiting for the final results.

Then, that was that. Four more years.

Months passed. The city waited. Armed itself. And then the contracted mercenaries were killed and hung from the bridge over Highway 10 with Khalil's photograph in every newspaper around the world. I knew Fallujah was done for.

* * * * *

The ongoing soundtrack of war is nearly a cliché by now – drums roll in the stratosphere, and the hollowed core of Fallujah absorbs more and more until it contracts on itself like a rotten gourd.

My poor city. My stubborn city. We can only see some of its skyline.

With the cattle and birds, we could watch the whole place disappear, but every animal has run. Only the water is calm. The beautiful river.

Sandpipers peck for earthworms. They prance in the silt. Their thin feet emboss hundreds of tridents in the sand and one of them, jumping happily, carries a leaf in its beak like a kid with a streamer. I'd like to be a little bird right now. That'd be fine. A little bird with his head buried in a hot fudge brownie ice cream sundae – sugar-poisoned and freaking.

Fish jump for bugs, rippling the water.

There's a guy in a boat coasting downriver.

He looks like the most peaceful Arab in the country. Can't blame him for it. Once in a while he lights up when a bomb-burst disturbs the black, and I want to tell Khalil we should keep walking away from the sledgehammers and high-sounding mis-siles – while the dark cloaks us safe – but I can't. Can't move or talk. My legs are Twizzlers.

Blame my mother for bringing me Twizzlers back from a college reunion – Amman, 1987 – they tasted like strawberry candles and glued solid to my molars.

* * * * *

In the morning, we'll succumb to the river, the slow study of the Martian desert with its weirdness and tricky rock. We will have to move slowly. We'll make it – I know.

My typing is slow, too.

I love this computer.

Its battery won't last long. Maybe I should have bought a better battery. In the control menu, I dim the screen and think it will conserve what energy I have left, and I'll write at night when our necks are glowing and our knees are filled with rocks. I hope Khalil doesn't get us shot.

* * * * *

I'm the first to wake.

My neck aches. I rub out the kink as the morning blinks into focus. My wristwatch says eight, and we've had enough sleep, if you'd qualify it as sleep.

All night, the clouds growled, angry, over the city.

We were camouflaged by the thick groundcover.

Everything around us seemed alive. The rustling grass and wind. Khalil murmured gibberish mid-dream. It took me an hour to drift back to sleep.

A few times I woke and saw Khalil standing in the middle of the blanket with folded arms, and his jaw gritting with only explosive spotlights pulling his face out of the dark. His eyes were black. Once in a while he'd open his mouth, saying nothing. Helpless, he stood watch over me and breathed in the carcinogens coming off the city. He never saw me watching.

After a few minutes, he'd make sure we hadn't been spotted, and he'd lie down.

* * * * *

Kicking Khalil out of his fetal position, I whisper,
- *Hey.*
He waves me away like we're at a slumber party.
Again,
- Hey man. We've gotta move.
Khalil props himself up and looks around and he's got this baffled look with one eye wide. A pirate. His hair is slicked back ridiculously.
- I'm starving, he says.
And he rotates his socks, inside out and slips on his sneakers without untying them. There's a red streak across his face from using his arm as a pillow. He rubs his eyes.
I say,
- Thought you *weren't* gonna eat.
- Yeah.
- Well?
- I dunno, he says.

He's shaking out the sheet he hogged most of the night and, using teeth to pinch the middle, he folds it into a careful square. He says,

– How 'bout I carry the backpack for a while for some breakfast?

– I don't mind carrying it.

– Sal.

– We've gotta move, I say.

I put on the pack, checking the sand for dropped stuff. I head upriver over a few flat rocks without waiting for him to finish. Fallujah is almost out of our view. Behind us, the city is reluctant to show its new scars, but lazy tornadoes of smoke grow above the southeastern districts, and a mosque is missing from the skyline as if it's been airbrushed out – *just gone.*

It's far worse than we thought it would be. Khalil keeps looking back at the smoking skyline. Tiny black specs must be Apaches hovering over the city.

Is my father OK? He wouldn't be able to run if he had to. What about the tenement house and our neighborhood? These are questions we're scared to ask out loud, ones we're both thinking, and it won't help anyone to speak them anyway.

After dusting the blanket, Khalil folds it to the same dimensions of the sheet and yells,

– I'll wear the pack and I can put these through the straps, all together. OK?

Shaking my head *no.*

I keep walking.

He runs after me with the linens under his arm like a big sagging loaf of bread. It wags with every jogging step.

– Well, when you get tired, I'll carry everything.

But there's no answer I wanna give.

He says something else that I don't remember, and we go on.

The morning opens with sun highlighting rows of healthy palms that stretch across the river as far as we can count. Green shag grasses, tall and verdant, line the adjacent shore where modest houses affirm that good people care for these properties. One's painted sienna with a roof close to pale umber. Another is flaking like old pastry. Satellite dishes, all new, angle up like dropped contact lenses, and I imagine *Arabsat* and *Nilesat* networks which would've been impossible to receive years ago, broadcasting into living rooms – grainy Hitchcock, censored American horror, and hours and hours of *Friends*.

The river continues for kilometers – an iridescent causeway – alive and moving and free.

On any other day, the brave boys of these houses would be swimming in the frigid river because they love water. They would impress the girls – diving headfirst, launching summersaults and back flips, emerging like popsicles – and, with bare feet, skip home to dry or lay out on the smooth rocks until sunset. I've been one of them.

I can tell Khalil wants to dive in.

He flings stones into the water as we walk.

Up ahead, a young boy tends livestock. Sheep and goats run amuck inside their pens and bray duets. We pass. The boy fills a feed trough from a plastic barrel. He's the only person in sight. When he sees us, he runs inside.

The sun's a comforter around our foreheads and shoulders, and it penetrates our ribs, and it's wonderful for now. It hugs our shoulders, softens cartilage and muscle. Simple obstacles of rock stick out of the terrain like broken teeth. Kilometers ahead, our path will be clear and easy with little brush and only the meekest of reeds to trample.

Most of the animals have been scared off by the war, but a few otters splash in the river. Two float on their backs as another thrashes in the overgrowth. They emerge as black as olives with their fur slicked and paws kicking. All three paddle away. It's the unpredictable candor of nature that's most splendid.

Khalil and I follow them upstream.

* * * * *

One time my mother was fishing with my grandfather, and he cast his reel and hooked a pelican. It must've eaten his lure in mid-flight, mistaking it for a giant dragonfly. My grandfather didn't see it coming. The fishing line whined, pulling from its spool, and the pelican, sped by a wind drift, zoomed out of sight. Shocked, my grandfather let go of the fishing reel and they both watched it fly away and my mother laughed and laughed and probably laughed just as hard telling the story to me. I've heard it dozens of times.

There are no pelicans today.

Crumbs of rock, stacked in a crooked line, resemble an ancient wall that I bypass through a breach blasted by centuries of relentless rain. Khalil decides to scale it, either trying to look cool or outdo me. He comes down on the other side, pulls the blankets from the rocks where he flung them. I've gone too far ahead to tell what he's saying. He hasn't stopped talking.

Sporadic huts pop up along the shoreline. The road stretches further away from the water. This makes me more comfortable – less chance of being spotted. We go and go. Always alert.

* * * * *

I swing my pack frontward and open it. Khalil's been anticipating this for an hour. Food and finally some drink. Twice we've stopped to cup our hands in the river, slurping, letting water dribble over chins and down wrists. I asked if he thinks this is healthy to drink. We both agree it's not. It should be boiled or distilled, but we've no time or equipment. He says there've been bodies dumped recently, facedown and soft like boiled potatoes, and the thought makes me gag. I stop drinking.

– You seen one? I ask.

– No.

Pulling out a jar of chutney, I pass it to him and explain how sparing we have to be. Khalil pretends to listen. I tear hunks of flatbread from the wax paper. We take turns dunking them into the gooey mango, groan because it's so good. We're only allowed a few bites before it's wrapped tightly away. I don't tell him that I'm saving the roasted garlic flatbread for later – probably days from now when it's going to taste like the best food on Earth.

– We have to eat and walk, I say.

Khalil nods.

I'm careful not to get rocks in my sandals.

Dry grasses expand into the endless desert. They look like combed hair.

We could be walking on the back of some huge hyena, but no hyena would have a river for a spine. We see no people. We hear no trucks. I pause, letting the breeze cool the sweat on my forehead – letting my body slow to the mighty tempo of the planet, though there's little solace there. Khalil keeps walking. I take out the rifle scope from my pack and, with its crosshair aimed at the back of his head, I follow him until that gets boring. Then I scan the Euphrates.

Nothing.

Crosshairs scribble over the steep line of the shore. Thick grasses grow where they're allowed to drink. Across the water there's just a wall of palm trees hiding more desert.

If we're about eight kilometers from Fallujah, the small town of Saqlawiya will sit along the banks. But we won't stop. No reason to. Khalil says we should, but we won't. I bet we're not even that far.

Random poplars twist out of the sand. Each one invites us to sit under their shade, but we can't. A ramshackle stockade looks over the river. Its decimated walls hint at the structure it once was. A crumbling smokestack juts out of the one remaining wall, making the whole thing look like a spatula shoved in the land.

I take my time catching up to Khalil.

– So, like, how long have you known this girl? he asks, having waited all morning to bring it up.

It's the type of question that's good for coaxing incriminating information that he's going to use against me later. I look away.

– Doesn't matter, I say.

– She cool?

And I want to say, *no, we're walking sixty kilometers to email a complete dork*, but I say,

– I don't know.

We follow our feet, kicking aimlessly, kicking at the rice pudding wetland and patches of dry gravel that spray when our toes catch. A few minutes later he says,

– Just asking.

He pauses and says,

– Can I see that?

Referring to my scope.

– No, I say.

I keep glancing behind us. No one is there.

The sand is more gravel than powder. We stick to the most level terrain except when acacia trees appear like enormous mushrooms near the waterway. We suck as much of their shade as we can. Sometimes we stop and, stooped over, rub our knees under their branches, but we don't linger. Little rocks lodge themselves in my sandals – between toes and burrowed in the leather straps. They chew into my feet.

– *Well*, how did you meet her? Khalil asks.

– What do you mean?

– Is her mother a friend of your mother's?

– What do you mean by that? I say.

– Friends, Khalil says.

I'm not sure what he's implying.

He knows not to bring up my mother. We haven't heard from her in years, but Khalil knows about as much about her disappearance as I do.

I stop to pull a rock out from my heel. A blister's already growing. I kneel and cover my mouth with my hand, rubbing the length of my index against my mustache. I should have shaved my beard before we left.

Khalil begins again,

– Where did you meet, I mean. I'm not making fun of you. I promise. It's only fair that I know.

Flicking the rock, I watch ants busied with foraging. An entire troop marches in a line, practically running over each other. I wonder how they know exactly where to go and what invisible river they follow.

– On the Internet, I finally say.

– Huh?

– *Online.*

– On the computer?

– Yes, Khalil. On the computer.

– Oh, he says, like that's clarified anything, and he looks a little puzzled but drops the subject. He nods, hastily calculating something he doesn't want to share, and I think he's going to say something like *she could be a guy,* or *how do you know that's really her,* but he doesn't. Then he looks ahead of us, ahead and beyond that, at the nondescript and constant flatness, waiting for me to lead.

I do.

* * * * *

Things were different when we were younger.

Before Khalil stole the teacher's school bell, I really never paid attention to him. We were in the same middle school class. We said hi. Maybe we had a few friends in common. I never paid attention to troublemakers or liars, the boys who snatched up marbles during games, who loved the sound of smashing windows, the anxious smells of burning plastic. They boxed for blood when adults weren't looking. They kicked dogs because they themselves were the sons of dogs. Maybe that's why Khalil stole the teacher's bell to begin with. So he could ring louder than anyone else.

That was the day I vowed never to talk to Khalil again.

I was ten. He was twelve, but we were in the same grade.

One day, at the end of school, Khalil waited until the last kid shuffled out. He crouched inside our classroom, patient and oily against the plaster wall. Pencil shavings fluttered against chalkboard erasers. The day's lesson wiped down to cloud on the green slate board.

No one saw him.

Our teacher collected her bag, straightened her *hijab* until her face became a perfect full moon. Eyes as light as hen's eggs. Nearly no lips. I wondered when a man would take her as his wife. Dust in the light. Khalil listened for her slippers against the cement, disappearing.

He tucked his head down. The brass bell, as big as a coconut, sat on her desk. Khalil pulled off his sweaty shirt, stuffed it inside the bell to silence its ringer, and zipped it all up inside his backpack. He walked home. It stayed in there all night. Then all morning.

And it wasn't until the next day of school that he realized the impact of what he'd done. Children shouted, scattered around in hallways, whereas the teacher's hand bell used to ring them to order. Teachers who weren't yelling had their arms folded with their eyes skyward, looking for answers.

Our teacher shouted,

– Has anyone seen the bell? Anyone?

We shook our heads *no*. Khalil's head shook as much as anyone else's.

They searched the school, looked in every closet and cabinet, the principle almost called an assembly on account of the mystery, but there was no bell to call everyone together. Khalil, face as blank as a brick, sat and chatted normally, flicked pencil nubs at the wall with that bell stuffed into his backpack like a bomb between his knees.

Eventually, the adults gave up.

Our teacher assigned extra homework.

I don't remember who saw him. It doesn't matter to anyone now.

He knew the train schedule because there was little TV schedule to remember. He unwrapped the hand bell, shaking sand and a chewed piece of gum from his t-shirt. The bell flipped free, clanged in the dirt.

Looking behind him – vanishing city, rusty washed dusk – Khalil felt the rails, warm and vibrating. He put his cheek on the hot metal. His teeth. Hundreds of kilometers of steel. The train.

I always wondered, once the train's iron wheel struck, if it was the sound or the smashed shape of the bell Khalil was most interested in. It would ring like *Allah* kicking the moon, rocketing up, nearly taking Khalil's head off his shoulders, the crimped brass dimpled by the sparkling screech. And once it stopped rolling he'd run to it to see the bell's crushed face and wonder, if a man were to put his cheek and teeth on the rail, what those iron wheels would do.

* * * * *

A boat bobs, capsized in the water. It looks like a big almond punched with bullet holes. Khalil squints at it, his toes at the waterline. A ball cap floats away from the upturned hull.

* * * * *

Noon operates its cruel caldron. I take off my sweatshirt and Khalil goes naked to the waist, wearing his shirt as a headwrap. The sun roils. My mother's old *keffiyeh* is in my pack. I find it, put it on. Only around my neck and shoulders. Even though the white and brown fabric caps the hearth of my shirt, it feels better. For a second I can smell my mother – cardamom and lilac and butter; traces of latex from the rubber gloves she wore at work – and dates, always, her fingertips stained from relishing dates out on the patio – but the odors aren't really there. Just some phantoms lingering in our common molecules.

My beard itches. Trying not to scratch it.

Four days, I calculate. We'll reach Ramadi in four days and with the food we've got and the money I've stashed we'll get there without trouble. At some point, kilometers before the city, we'll have to cross the river, by bridge or by water taxi. Somehow.

* * * * *

Khalil keeps shifting the folded and rolled blankets from arm to arm. They must be getting annoying. He's humming a pop song by Alaa Sa'ad that's vaguely familiar, repeating the chorus that eats at my nerves. He asks,

– You wanna switch? Or you know, I can take everything if you want.

– I'm fine. You want to stop for a second? I ask.

– OK, Khalil says.

He tosses the blankets into a makeshift cushion that we sit on. We face the shimmering waves that ripple like scales on a blue snake burrowed in the earth. Khalil unlaces his Adedas, takes them off, and shakes out the grit. He's worn generic Adedas all his life, it seems. He says,

– Damn things.

And he clacks them together.

– You should get a new pair, I say.

I take out the tin cup from the pack, dip it in the river,

careful not to lift silt or slime. I sip. The water's cool, looks deceptively clean.

– I was going to, but I got robbed, Khalil says with an annoying nonchalance.

He slips off his socks, tucks them in his sneakers and buries his feet in the sand.

– You know that Project Manager, back at Mr. Hassnawi's?

Khalil cocks his head. He's speaking into my knees, looking straight at the water.

– Yeah, course I do, I say.

– We did a job together last week. Nothing major.

– What do you mean *nothing major*?

My words echo in the cup.

Khalil follows the current, searching the water for what to say.

– I was a spotter, that's all.

He sifts sand through his toes. He focuses on lifting both feet at once, so that equal amounts stream down before he scoops again. Wispy vales measure the strength of the breeze. The grains flutter away.

He adds,

– 50,000 dinar.

– 50,000? What did you do with it all?

I hand him the cup as if I'm exchanging it for more information. Khalil gulps the last of it, clasping in both hands, drums his fingers over the cylinder.

– He only gave me half. Said I didn't do the job right. *Asshole.*

– What do you mean?

I sit beside him and dig my feet in the loose grains. The warm powder is far more medicinal than I would have thought.

We burrow deeper to the colder layers, toes like worms searching for the elusive moisture of the desert. They shimmy up for air before digging deeper.

– He said I was using my cell phone too much, or something.

I laugh,

– Why would you talk on your phone when you're spotting for someone stealing a car? That's ridiculous.

Khalil laughs too,

– We weren't stealing a *car*. What are you talking about?

– Huh?

– A bomb, Sal.

– What?

I stand up with my feet ankle deep in the sand. I trip to the side, knocking the tin cup out of his hands.

– *What the fuck,* Khalil?

– It's not a big deal. *He* buried it. *He's* the one who did all of it, Khalil defends, snatching the cup and cleaning it.

– *Right,* not a big deal at all.

– The other jobs I've done for the *Fedayeen* were too minor. They weren't paying anything. I had to step up.

My body turns away and deflects what he's just said and what he's going to say. He's admitting things I probably already knew, but didn't want to. He's impossible to look at. He follows no code, and if he does, it's so corrupt it would be unreadable to the most sophisticated infidel in all Fallujah. No morals, no nothing.

I turn around, look at the road. Turn around again to the river.

– Is that what he meant by *proving yourself,* Khalil, make up for your negligence? Is that why he sent us on that suicide mission?

– Whatever.

– Yeah? Whatever? You helped bury a *bomb*, man! Something that's gonna *kill* people, fucking *burn* people. Innocent people.

– Yeah. And you make pamphlets, Sal. Same thing.

He brushes sand off his feet because he knows I'll walk away at any moment. Then he adds,

– Same *cause*.

– Paper doesn't blow people in half. I did that crap because I had to, I needed the money. We did.

– And we didn't? Me and my sisters and my mother? We didn't?

– Not the same. Not even close.

I'm already back to our invisible trail, river on the left, north facing desert. The far-expanding plains to our right. I almost want to run, let him go back to town where he belongs. But Khalil follows, keeping close. His shirt around his head looks like a lion's mane. His eyes squint harder in the sunlight and he says,

– You're right, man. I know.

– Don't talk to me, I say.

– I thought, you know, it wouldn't be a big deal. It's the only job they had.

Carrying the rolled blanket and sheet over his shoulder, he blows puffs of air at the corners of his eyes, removing grit, says,

– I didn't *want* to do it.

– Sure.

– Really.

* * * * *

We try to avoid the frying sand.

We slog over marsh and when it gets too soggy, I steer around, bringing us closer to the road where painted farm houses butt against fields of unidentifiable crops. Rocky grades curve high. We're careful not to come storming over them like unfortunate soldiers taking a hill, but there aren't many to climb and the shallow slopes are only little hindrances compared to the heat. No one comes and I'm the only one paying any mind. I can almost hear the words forming in Khalil's head. There's nothing he can say to me.

Wherever there's shade we cling to it, taking detours that slow our progress, but I figure the cooler we are, the faster we'll walk. Over-ambition will be our biggest weakness. With the heat comes wind, and it's just a tease at first, lightly tickling our necks. I mistake a loose thread on my collar for a fly a few times before I yank it out.

Airborne sand sticks to our sweaty faces. It collects like sediment in couch cushions, and no matter how diligent we are, the desert spreads into ears and eyes and ass cracks. My beard feels ant-infested. I take off my *keffiyeh* and beat it against my leg and retie it with little relief. Every available shelf of our bodies – shoulders, foreheads, scalps, and the spaces without names – becomes a resting place for desert silt. Khalil starts again,

– You know, not everyone can design shit like you. We're not *all* creative.

I offer a nod. He continues,

– We'd have starved a long time ago if I hadn't done those jobs. I woulda been called a coward, Sal.

Another nod. I don't have anything to say. The day is so hot that I can't think anyway. We're all cowards. Anyone who doesn't think so is bullshitting themselves. The bullshit is outstanding. High-grade, government-approved and blessed bullshit, and Khalil's cooking up a good, sticky batch right now. He says,

– Don't be mad, man.

* * * * *

Farmland quilts the countryside with pea green and olive green, every kind of green. Squares of nearly-neon green grow from snaking tributaries that writhe out of the Euphrates. Like the gray-green of camouflage, the muted tones of military fatigues, fields expand until they can't withstand the harsh solitude of the desert.

The sight of it invigorates us. We walk a little straighter. Bedspreads of cabbage cover northern fields, inviting enough to fall asleep in. Beside a stable, a large house keeps sheep shaded, and they cram themselves into the house's generous shadow. There's a man in his front yard leaning into a car's open hood. His socket wrench winds and clicks.

* * * * *

Miserable heat. By three o'clock, it's time to stop. I lean down and let Khalil catch up, and I collapse in slow motion. The beach is cluttered with twigs and soft dirt. Soaking my *keffiyeh* in the water, I wrap my head with it and splash my beard. Khalil does the same with his shirt, which is *my* shirt. It would've been nice if he'd asked.

Playful minnows wiggle along the shore, but, otherwise, the water's crystal and aquamarine. A catfish bobs before rippling water scares it sideways. Over in the river grass, a family of ducks paddle in a line. Mother first, her babies make a string of cotton balls.

– We should go swimming, Khalil says.

– It's not that kind of trip, I say, rinsing my face.

– Huh?

– There's no time.

– How long we stopping? Fifteen minutes?

– Sure.

He pries off his sneakers and socks and tracksuit pants and charges into the water, leaping, until he's waist deep. He stops at the crotch, wiggling his arms to ward off the cold. Then he finally dives. He'll stay under for as long as his lungs allow. I check my watch. If a boat patrol surges upriver from the city, he won't have any time to flee. Maybe, if he's not exhausted already, he could float below the boat's propeller until they rush away. Knowing Khalil, he'd wave them goodbye. He'd wave them goodbye as he was shot, too.

Front-crawling, sneaking side-breaths between reaches, he's an expert swimmer – born of the river. I'd forgotten. About a minute goes by, and he's far enough out that his head's just a walnut floating over opal ripples. I can tell he's smiling. He returns just as quickly, a breast-stroke this time. Show-off.

He beckons with a wave, shoulders above the wake, and I wave *no*. He sinks suddenly – dead weight – and reappears downstream, then vanishes again.

I take my *keffiyeh* off and drape it over my head. It probably looks like a Pac-Man ghost sitting on top of a tired hiker. Watching the world become abstract through white and brown patterns, my eyes adjust to the dimness, and the Euphrates degenerates into a simple blue bar, the far shore's tan berms degrading to bolts of khaki. This reduced composition soothes my breathing. Each exhale warps the damp fabric. Keeping my breath shallow, taking as little air as possible, I keep the veil still so the composition shifts slightly – aqua and brown where palm groves quiver.

Now I have an Alaa Sa'ad song stuck in my head, but that's OK.

I'm finally tranquil. I'm the Pac-Man-headed hiker. I scratch my chin. Wonder what Rana's up to.

It's getting muggy under this headwrap.

Peeling back the *keffiyeh*, I let my pupils adjust, blinking.

I can't see Khalil. Up or downriver, there's nothing but cattle ranging at the shoreline. My watch says three minutes passed. How long was I staring under the *keffiyeh* daydreaming? How long had it been since Khalil dove under?

I get up and crane to see, but there's nothing in the water besides a tree branch or two. I take out the scope and scrutinize the surface, running the crosshair target over river rock and tamarisk. My eye zigzags the shore a kilometer away – still nothing.

The slurping cows don't care that the crosshair once meant impending death, that the thin black cross drawn over their torsos and hulking necks would have guided the patient marksman to a sure kill. I wonder how many lives this magnifying tube has seen ruined. I wonder if it will see another one today. My hand shakes. The further I look, the more unstable the picture becomes.

Seven minutes.

A kestrel rides a strong updraft, cleaving through the sky like a chevron drawn on the wind, shooting up and up without flapping and finally descends. Maybe it's locked on a muskrat. It arcs before colliding with the earth, dips and dances gracefully. Then it disappears.

– SAL!

I somehow jump and duck at the same time, holding the scope up ready to club someone and, spinning, I see Khalil in his underpants grinning like a clown,

– *Oh shit*, Sal. You're in a zone, man. Sorry.

– You're a *dick*.

– You should get in, man. The water feels great.

I lean over with my hands on my knees, using the draped *keffiyeh* to hide how much he's scared me.

– Whatever. We have to keep going, I say.

– OK.

– Why did you do that?

– Huh?

He shakes out his hair.

– Never mind.

– Yeah.

He sniffs and gets his clothes. Behind a tall embankment of reeds, he swaps his underwear for pants and brushes sand off his feet with this socks. He tugs his sneakers, jumping on one leg like he's just stubbed his toe and falls and curses,

– *Damn sneakers.*

Fully changed, he plops his underwear over a shoulder to dry.

I rinse off the *keffiyeh* in the river and re-wrap my head. It feels great even though I know it will be steaming in minutes.

Taking his time, Khalil collects the bedding.

I've set on my way. I don't care if he has to run to catch up. A few more hours of walking is all I can manage.

* * * * *

When I was little, my mother would drag down her word processor from the office, and she'd make me sit at the kitchen table and practice my typing. I loved the mechanical clicks and pounds the machine made, the speed and precision of its spherical cluster of keys. She'd marvel at my progress even though I wasn't typing very fast at all. She'd recite poems by Badr Shakir al-Sayyab, and, instead of listening, I'd be fantasizing about dragons hosing down villages with fire, knights cooked in their armor, but I'd still transcribe her words perfectly.

She called me a multitasker.

She said she's one too.

She'd show the transcripts of perfectly typed poetry to my father and he'd sit out in the patio and read them like they were pages torn from a book. Then he folded them into his shirt pocket and grin. There were copies for him and copies for me.

At night, I'd take some of the typed sheets of paper up to bed and lay my cheek on the opposite side where I thought the embossed letters made a crude Braille. I'd rub my finger across the raised characters, across the tiny paper hills and valleys and imagine the worlds inside them.

* * * * *

We sweat. From every available crevice and un-clogged pore, we sweat. It runs down our backs like a leak down a wall and collects in our salty ass-cracks. Our shoulder blades are quarries of salt. Khalil's ears gobble sweat and keeps it for later. My hair seems to be sweating too, but that's ridiculous. Our misery is obvious. At least Khalil isn't complaining. Stopping only to drink from the river, my stomach mumbles secrets to my intestines – gargled gibberish that only organs understand.

I didn't fully consider the lack of bathrooms. There's no place to crap.

The sun creeps from behind us, then overhead, then front-and-center. We finish the first flat bread and most of the chutney. Khalil digs his finger into the walls of the jar to scrape out every gooey remnant. I think about opening some chickpeas, but we'll save them for later. The thought of plain, uncooked peas sours my guts even more. Khalil stops and asks for the spare plastic wrap and uses it to line the hole in his sneaker between his sock and sole. It seems to work. He's creative even if he can't admit it, but I don't tell him because that'll be a day long conversation. He asks,

– How far do you think we've gone?

– No idea.

I should have printed out a map. It would've been easy to gauge our progress by the shape of the river as it turns north-west toward Ramadi, or maybe I'm putting too much faith in my abilities. We must have walked about ten or twelve kilometers by now and that's good enough, good enough for one day.

Khalil lugs the blanket and sheet like they're about to dis-locate his arms, says,

– You mad at me?

Shaking my head *no*, I keep my eyes forward.

He knows I am.

– 'Cause if you're mad at me you can just say and I can go back. I don't care. OK?

I almost want to take him up on the offer except he's not serious and we've traveled too far in the sun. The desert is cruel. Unfit for life. Without speaking, the land declares that it doesn't want us here adulterating its sacred and antiquated harmonies with our impurities. Even though we don't speak directly to

102

the sands, they hear our unfit bodies searing like lamb shanks, crackling and hissing on the slow spit of the planet.

To die, out here, alone – an abysmal end – the thought is death enough. The loneliness of this place is too much for one person to bear. My lips are cracked, already.

* * * * *

The heat tapers off, and we enter a valley where the river lowers. For hundreds of meters, we can see the spanning inland plains boarding stretches of barren sand. These plains are a tranquil but temporary relief to the mundane lengths of nothingness we've endured. We descend a rocky slope. The lowland air moves colder. The Euphrates flows indigo and emerald.

We stoop to drink often.

At six-thirty we stop. I kick off my sandals and walk into the shallow banks, throwing off my pack, and bend down to slap water over my shoulders, back and thighs. It's way colder than I thought it would be. Khalil rolls his pants, and it feels like a routine we've practiced for centuries – two Neanderthals digging for answers in the water. He asks,

– We stopping?

– Yeah.

– Good, he says, cupping and drinking, his oily hair slicked into a Caesar cut. He looks over and says,

– What, man?

– You need a haircut, I say, grinning.

– I *know*, I *know*.

– Seriously. It's almost like you have a bowl on your head.

– Really? Is it that bad? He asks with alarm, messing up his hair.

– It's fine, I say.

Once I'm cool enough, I go back and spread the blanket in the sand where there are no rocks sticking out. Khalil calls something from the river and I ignore him. He calls louder.

– You think we should camp by those rocks, Sal?

He points to a horseshoe-shaped group of stones sheltered from the road. Poplars cluster the rocks closer to the shore, providing cover from the water, too. The land over there looks softer.

– You know, in case someone comes.

He's right. If we camped here we'd be completely exposed to anyone riding the highway or river. Anyone could walk up as we slept.

– Sure.

Decamping what little I'd set, we push back from the bank and settle into the secure crags. It's a perfect hideaway from would-be raiders.

– Perfect, Khalil comments, fishing for praise.

And it is perfect.

We're dwarfed by the cliff once we're settled. It completely camouflages our camp from the road and clustered acacia trees give good cover riverside. No raft or car could spot us unless we lit a fire, but we can't dare do that. Soft grass acts as a mattress under the blanket. No animals have grazed here, and there's a charitable patch of shade we lounge underneath. Grateful and yawning.

Once we've stretched and reclined and popped every joint we can, we open a can of chickpeas. Stretched out on the blanket, we share our one spoon and mix some of the other jar of chutney into the peas – my suggestion – and it's a decent supper with a little bread. For dessert, an Awat cake, split between us. It's gross. I take a bite and immediately know why I hate these damn things.

There's only river water to drink.

I'd love a Sprite right now. A cold, cold Sprite in a can, because it's usually colder in a can.

Without explaining, I take out the paper towels and slide them onto a tree branch where the roll wags like a fat white tongue. Khalil gives it a nod.

– Gonna need that in a second, he says.

Me too, I think.

I say,

– Don't use too much, man.

– OK.

Khalil talks about his sore feet and aching lower back, then tells a story that has something to do with chickpeas – a hummus recipe using olives and lime juice – but he strays from the subject and keeps the spoon we're sharing for too long, and he complains about the annoying rhymes his sisters are always singing, how they used the strip of cement in the backyard as a fake fashion runway, practicing posture and step and his overbearing parents, and how they stopped speaking to him for three days after the photograph was published, but eventually forgave him. They even let him sleep inside. He goes on and on describing how many people love him now that he's some ill-fit poster child of the resistance, how he never intended for it to happen, and how, if he could, if he could go back in time he would have turned away from the camera man – the *sneaky* Western journalist – and Khalil could have been just one of the dozens of Fallujans looking on, just someone who happened to be there because that's all that he was – just *there*.

He goes on about the Project Manager and how he hopes he chokes on his giant fucking cigar. He hopes a missile collapses his office on top of him like a tomb.

I ask,

– Would you do it again?

– What? The photo?

– No. Spotting. For the bomber.

– I dunno, Khalil says, looking away.

He huffs, speaking into the blanket with his tanned elbows on his tanned knees, adds,

– I don't know, that's a tough one.

– Yeah, it is, I say.

We both look at the horizon.

Heading southeast, hovering a kilometer away, a helicopter hacks chunks out of the air, its two propellers chopping in unison. It's hard to tell how massive it is from this distance. We wait for it to vanish.

Khalil says nothing for a while and then,

– You want me to say I'll never do it again?

– Whatever.

Instead of passing him the cup I'm drinking from, I put it on the blanket and lay down.

– I will, if you want me to, Sal.

* * * * *

I think about tomorrow and how much I don't wanna walk again. It's amazing when I lie down with the shade slowly cooling my chest. I take my shirt off. We'll sleep early and wake before dawn, get as much walking in as we can while the morning's glow isn't spoiled by the sun. I use my sweatshirt as a pillow, and once he's finished eating, Khalil goes to the river to wash the spoon, but stays and swims again. He's out there for an hour.

I still want to tell him it's a bad idea.

Listening for road traffic, I stand and use the scope. There's nothing but chalky asphalt like a long strip of electrical tape, stretching the way we came and the way we're headed. I want go out to the roadside to see if passing vehicles can spot our camp, but I figure from this angle they can't, and I don't want to go out there alone.

Who knows if there are landmines out there.

I brush my teeth using as little water as I can, even though there's more than enough just meters away. I spit foamy bubbles in the sand. They crackle and disappear. They're galaxies clotting and closing in on themselves, collapsing stars and moons.

Gulls and a camel, a scorpion as long as my thumb, water buffalo loping like somber custodians of the river. I think I see a white owl, but it's only the light pulling pranks. I think about wizards, wizards with knobby staffs radiating crazy – white cloaked and gifted with wisdom – in my head they look like sheiks, but scruffy and taller for some reason. It's a good time to write.

I take out the laptop and keep one eye on Khalil while I type. Sometimes I take a break and click through the few photos of Rana I saved from her profile. Old pics of her in Baghdad from high school, and two taken during Ramadan with her parents on either side in her dining room, I think. Her father looks like a nice guy with his business suit and mustache. His arm is always around a son or daughter. Rana's mother is beautiful, hiding a strong smile under her *abaya*. There's one where Rana is wearing a tight-fitting t-shirt. I probably look at that one a bit too long.

I keep typing.

The sun melts. Crickets serenade the new night. When I can't think of what to type, I look out into the desert, over the illuminated river and the trees and watch their details fade. Shooting stars draw chalk lines in the twilight. Constellations grow out of the black, and though I can't identify them, the fact that other men far older than me have given them names is weirdly comforting.

I type as fast as I can think.

Battery life reads three more hours, and I figure that's enough juice to last through the rest of the trip. An hour a night is all I need. When we get to Ramadi I'll recharge and send all of these entries to Rana, but I'll leave out some stuff, obviously.

There's a tiny little spider crawling the edge of the screen. I leave him alone.

6

In the predawn vacancy I hear a whooshing, like the flailing feet of a break dancer pounding millimeters from my nose before I leap up to save myself. It could've been a trampling horse – *Mujahideen* or mercenaries charging from the road.

It's Khalil flipping out.

He swings the white sheet in a circle and yells, with his hands slapping his stomach and back. He does a hopping shake around the perimeter of the camp. Half asleep, I'm trying not to laugh. He yells,

– Oh shit! Oh shit!

I ask,

– Man, what is it?

– Scorpion. I dunno.

– Quiet, man!

I stand there shivering, inspecting the ground. Moonlight still above us in the sky, barely. It could have been anything. I ask,

   – You OK?

   – Yeah. *Of course I'm OK.*

He slides on his socks and shoes without sitting in the sand. He swats at his thighs with the sheet over his head like a ghost having a seizure. He mumbles, catching himself before falling over,

   – Scorpions. Can't sleep now. No way. Didn't sleep the whole night. *Shit.*

   – We could get an early start, sun'll be up soon. We'd be less hot and we can quit earlier.

Khalil mulls like it's his decision in the first place. The longer he takes to say something the more I wonder why I asked his opinion. Wrapped in the sheet, he's shivering white with the endless blackness painted behind him.

   – C'mon, man. Let's get going.

   – OK, he says.

* * * * *

Khalil never showed up at school again. Everyone said he was the one who stole the bell, but no one knew who caught him. Everyone had their own idea. I realized that day that all that mattered was your own idea about things – people decided what was true and what wasn't true.

Because there wasn't much work in Khalil's neighborhood other than leaning under a car's open hood or lying face-up under the engine, he decided to find work somewhere else. He swept hair in a barber's shop for a while. He was fired for checking himself out too often in the mirrors, recycled from old dress-ers and headboards, fired for promising free haircuts, too.

The owner yelled,

– Work! Don't just comb your hair!

Khalil just walked out one day. Quit.

There was a radio repair shop. He lasted one day. A pharmacy. Maybe a week there.

The best jobs were in the cafés. In my neighborhood, across the street from my house, men sat at small tables and drank all afternoon. Arguing teeth bared yellow from cigarettes and dark tea. After weeks of not seeing Khalil, he appeared there, a tray in his hands, a rag hanging from his back pocket.

He stared at me on my way home from school.

One day I decided to walk on the side of the street with the café instead of avoiding it. Khalil was wiping down tables outside. He looked up,

– Hey!

I tried to ignore him.

– Salim!

I stopped. Why should I have to talk to a person like that? Khalil took a partially smoked cigarette butt out of an ashtray, lit its crooked end. Men inside the café leaned out to see if Khalil was really working. Khalil sucked on his cigarette like a straw, asked,

– How're you so popular at school?

– Huh?

Smoke overpowered the smell of brewing tea.

– Everyone likes you. How is that?

I looked up to my house to make sure Dad wasn't coming.

– I like it, I guess.

Khalil stood straight with his hands on his hips like he owned the place and smiled with all his teeth.

– No, stupid. How's it possible? That everyone likes *you*?

The owner of the shop punched the counter, knuckle crunched linoleum. Yelled,

– Khalil! Stop hanging out in the street!

Khalil stood there, teeth and smoke and bulged eyes beaming. That was my chance to walk away, and I took it.

Over the next few weeks Khalil would have a glass of tea waiting for me when I passed. He'd pretend I was a real customer. Never asked for money. But he did ask about the kids at school – the ones he never got to see any more – this boy and that girl. He asked,

– What are you doing later?

I told him I was busy. Khalil was the type of quitter that never gave up.

The fourth time he wanted to hang out, I said OK.

* * * * *

Meager moonlight illuminates the river, and there is a gentle dimmer on the current, making it brighten and fade and brighten again. Clouds scroll over like raked milk. It's cold enough for blankets. We follow the gurgling brightness. I love the subtle glow, how it appears warm and cool at the same time. The eerie stillness. We must look like two grim reapers walking – me in my double hooded-costume, the thick wool blanket as big as a barrel around my face. Khalil all white-topped with black legs tripping. We feel safer. This is a good decision, starting early, and for some reason Khalil whispers, but his volume doesn't effect how *much* he's talking.

I listen to our haplessly grappling feet instead.

But Khalil is impossible to ignore.

He comments about bringing that Kalashnikov for protection and how he could have concealed it in the blankets, set up a watch post at night. He grumbles more curses toward the Project Manager and his fragrant cigars. How he didn't give a shit about his daughter who had been killed in a car accident when a Humvee accidentally pushed them off the road – she was the only one killed. The Project Manager was driving.

Everyone knew someone with the same dumb luck – women whose husbands had disappeared in the night, sons and daughters in the wrong place at the wrong time, deadly mistakes at checkpoints. All left to chance.

Khalil complains about the oncoming heat. He suggests when we should stop for food, get more provisions in Saqlawiya. I tell him we don't need anything else.

– We could use some fruit.

A crow caws.

Its hiding somewhere in a tree.

– Just a thought, he adds.

Dawn breaks, slicking smashed beets overhead. I want to stick my hands in the glowing. Mash the cloudy color. We have an hour or so of temperate warmth before the sun grows like a boil on the back of the earth, overtaking the day, overtaking everything. We walk on. We shed the blankets and outerwear, trampling the ungovernable grasses that rule riverbanks. We're sidetracked when it's too thick, heading straight north instead of westward for meters and meters. We have no choice. Khalil snags his tracksuit pants on a thorn bush and squawks about that for half an hour. I'm ready to strangle him, face down in the river.

– Man, these are my favorite pair of pants.

– They're the *only* pair you wear, I say.

– 'Cause they're my favorite.

And it's when he blabs nonstop about saving up for his makeshift uniform and how difficult it is to keep clean – carefully hand washing it in the sink during the rare moment his mother is out of the house – that I almost snap.

– Khalil.

– Yeah?

–Quiet? For a little while? Can we just walk?

– Huh?

– Just, I'm not in the mood to talk.

He snorts like I've asked him to never speak again.

– Fine.

* * * * *

My mother used to want to be a painter, but she said it was too hard. Said she always wanted to paint naturalistically, but didn't like the noxious solvents and oils and resins and decided to go to school for medicine.

I always thought medicine would be much, much harder.

She always had Band-Aids.

But she always had paint, too.

* * * * *

A stone farmhouse comes into view. It sits against the river where a dead water pump once fed irrigation canals and crops. Besides some farm equipment, it's a simple building with a tattered outhouse, that's it – open shutters and open windows, a collapsed awning sagging over the riverside door. Cautious, Khalil and I cross burned fields of what should be cabbage. We sidestep the withered remains of potatoes crushed by tanks. Tread marks trail through the dirt until the wind reclaims the true shape of the desert.

– Hello? we call.

But no one is here.

Loose goats scramble like unruly children, butting each other playfully. One's chewing on something. We can't see what. I wonder if there's milk inside the house. I wonder where they've gone.

The front door swings ajar.

Khalil pushes it.

– Hello? he says and the door swings open with a tap of his shoe. Something on the other side prevents it from opening. He stoops, eyes looming through the gap between the hinges.

– Nothin', he says.

Inside, it's like a sandstorm hit. The destruction is obvious. Kerosene sullies the air. Everything is ransacked. Broken glass speckles tabletops and sills, spreading and twinkling over smashed timber from pulled-apart furniture. The back of a chair hangs from a nail on the wall. Thrown cloths and the guts of a radio and rice are spilled on the floor. A bureau has been dumped open.

I know the humiliated occupants of this home would be ashamed for us to see it. I look outside.

– We shouldn't be in here, I say.

– I know, but –

Khalil enters anyway. So do I.

Our feet crunch. Khalil calls one last *Hello?*

No one.

Across a puddle of kerosene, a spilled box of matches look

like logs floating in a little pond. It collects by the bedroom doorframe and maybe whoever meant to ignite the little pond fled the scene instead, spooked by conscience or sidetracked by something more callous. The smell makes my head throb.

Two prayer rugs are crumpled under the window. A peanut M&Ms wrapper lies flat on the ground, flatter than the prayer rugs. Its yellow label beams bright, and those ugly peanut men are smiling on the package. They're fat and look like carp-mouthed monsters. Khalil inspects it for candy.

Empty.

We stand still. We listen for anyone outside.

– You won't believe this, Khalil says, but the electric's on.

I take out my laptop and start charging it on a table by the door. I don't bother to take it out of the backpack.

Khalil keeps looking around.

Two drawn lines on the dusty floor must have been made by dragging tips of shoes, men carrying someone unable to stand, carrying this person hooked under their arms, and we've erased some of that proof with our own steps, but we can still understand what's happened. I look to see if they continue out the door. They do.

In the bedroom, flipped beds and a chair are piled against the wall. A mirror hangs shoulder-level. Khalil wants to look at himself – he doesn't smile though. I don't want to see myself in here. I don't go into the bedroom. Neither of us speaks. I turn back to the living room and kitchen. I circle the oily puddle and worry about my father's stubbornness and pride – how he'd never leave Fallujah even if his old house was the last structure standing – and I think about going back, right now, but it'd be impossible through the new checkouts and barricades. The city's probably locked down. No way in or out. Does our house look like this now?

Khalil opens drawers. He knocks over a clock. I let him take his time so the laptop can charge a bit longer.

Ruckus outside – goats tug on dry forage and furniture. One of them gnaws a chair cushion, tweed and cotton caught in its teeth. I look outside to make sure no people are here. No people will ever be here again.

I want to touch the walls, the windows, the hanging hemp net where fruit might have been kept, but I don't. Shouldn't touch anything.

The oven is open. Rags have slithered and died around the broiler, discarded after scrubbing. Some undeniable smell demands attention. It's severely sour and mixed with the kerosene peeling off the floor, and I can't tell what it is. I cover my mouth.

– You ready? I yell into my bicep.

– One second.

Light streams in through the wall.

Several holes are punched in the kitchen where something quickened and heavy sailed through. They match three other crude holes on the opposite side. I could stick my hand through them. One could accept my entire head. Around the holes, missing chunks of plaster reveal the brickwork underneath. I want to leave. A calendar on the wall has one date marked with a simple X and I can't tell if it's a birthday or anniversary or doctor's appointment, but above the date is a mountain range – maybe the Himalayas.

I almost want to steal it.

Khalil shuffles to the kitchen corner and eyes a few oranges hiding under a table. I agree we should take them. He grabs a gallon of water, too.

Surveying the evidence of what occurred here, I'm overwhelmed with the feeling of being somehow responsible. It's an unreasonable guilt welling up from nowhere rational. We can't be in here anymore. I kick the oven closed.

– Nothing in the bedroom.

– We need to go, I say.

– There might be more, Khalil says, holding the oranges.

– That's what I'm worried about.

I turn to get my backpack and it's gone.

– Khalil! My bag!

And before I know it Khalil's dropped the oranges and he's running out the door with a broken chair leg in his hand. I run too, but he's faster – always been faster. When we turn the corner of the house we see a guy running with my bag in his arms, the heavy thing slowing him down, dust kicked up behind him. I try my best to keep up with Khalil.

It only takes twenty seconds for him to catch up. He has enough time to scoop up a rock and lob it at the guy, hitting him hard in the back. I see Khalil chuck the chair leg at the guy's ankles. I see the guy flip and roll, head first in the dirt. My bag goes in the other direction.

And when I catch up to them, Khalil is stooped over the guy, beating him around the head and shoulders with the chair leg, yelling,

– Is this your bag? Is this your house?

Panting, the guy only cries out his defense.

I know Khalil's using the narrow part of the chair leg on purpose. When the man's hands come up to protect his face, Khalil backhands them down.

– Stop! I say.

– You think you can steal from us?

I look to see if anyone is with him, if the house is still empty, if it's an ambush of some kind.

– I'm sorry, I'm sorry, the guy says.

– Stop! Khalil!

Khalil stomps hard on the guy's chest and hold's his throat and gives his legs a few more licks, then lets him turn over and belly-crawl away. One of his shoes comes off. Khalil picks it up and throws it after him.

– Peasant! Khalil yells and spits.

– C'mon, I say.

The guy finally stands and limps away as fast as he can. We watch him disappear.

Khalil smiles. Stabs the chair leg into the sand.

* * * * *

Back at the house, I get my charger and make sure nothing is missing from the backpack.

– You didn't have to beat that guy so hard, I say.

Khalil hands me an orange. He waits in the doorway like a man leaving home for work.

– You want him following us? he says.

Khalil hangs the blanket and sheet over his shoulders and tugs the gallon of water by the handle, sloshing the water, and runs the jug over a goat's back instead of petting it. The goat barely knows we're there.

We roll the bedding and stick it between the backpack and straps like he suggested earlier. Khalil wants to carry everything, but I refuse. We share the water until it's gone. I think we drank it too quickly. Khalil hangs the jug upside-down from a tree, and, as we begin to walk, he turns to see the house shrink behind us. I know what he's thinking because I'm thinking the same

thing. Who were they? And who are we to steal? The oranges
go quickly – a little overripe, but they put us in a better mood.
My stomach gurgles like there are snakes fighting each other in
there, trying to exit through my intestines, and I wonder if it's
from drinking from the river.

Another boat wanders down-current. There are no occupants or cargo.

The distance between the river and the road narrows.
We keep looking down the highway for anything speeding up
on us, but nothing comes. We can see forever. Desert and sky.
Even when the terrain is dense with concentrated high grass
and difficult rock, we hug the shore, keeping from the road's
view. We scan the horizon for foreign geometries – squares
and strange angles stationary or moving, odd colors signal-
ing trouble. The distant mountains rise like crooked teeth.

Khalil asks,

– Who do you think they were?

– Who? I say, even though I already know.

– Whoever was in that house.

– Doesn't matter.

I was going to say we shouldn't have stolen those oranges
or even that water, but why bother – it doesn't matter now. He
won't listen anyway.

– Wait, I say, my hand at Khalil's hip.

– What?

– Get down.

– What is it?

Crouching, I focus the rifle scope on a weird hump pulled
off the highway – some blackened wreck without detail or intention – an unnatural shape confusing the desert's consistency. It
could be anything. The scope's crosshairs move over the thing,

but it's only a crumb from this distance. With so little to study we can't take chances.

– What is it? Khalil says.

– Dunno. Might be a tank. Or just a car.

– Lemme see.

Khalil grabs for the scope.

– No, I say, keeping the sights aimed on the thing. We must wait.

– Why?

– To make sure.

Only the sand moves.

We use the backpack as a perch. I lean on it with the scope, relaxing as much as I can. We lie on our stomachs, and even though we'd still be seen from the road, lying lessens those chances. Khalil asks for the scope twice before I hand it over.

I track up and down the road. There are no other shapes, no military presence or opportunities for ambush. Sprigs of high weed jut like loose thread. Palm trees and little else. No movement on or around the thing, and, as far as I can tell, it's been abandoned for days. Maybe longer.

We wait and wait.

Khalil hums a song and lists what possible things the thing might be: a broken down Bradley tank, burnt out bus, farmhouse, crashed helicopter, a giant pile of shit.

– It's a giant shit, no doubt, I say.

– Yeah! Khalil smiles, hands me back the scope.

I trace the outline of the thing, one, two, three – fifty times with the scope's black crosshairs, then draw the crosshairs down the road as far as I can see and then trace it fifty more. It's the only way to keep concentrating. My mind wanders. *That would be a hell of a lot of shit*, I think. Massive mastodon shit in the middle of the desert. Archeologists have painted away the dirt with tiny brushes, their meticulous tools erasing centuries of preserving mud. Exhausted, they've taken a lunch break and left the excavation site unguarded. But maybe it's something better. The more I stare at it the more it looks like a hot fudge brownie ice cream sundae from TGI Fridays. If it were, we'd run, dive face first into its warm cake mattress and drench ourselves in melting vanilla waterslides. I'd get the cherry.

There are rocking chairs in my stomach. Khalil hears the grumbling.

– Hungry?

– A little, I say.

Khalil drums on the sand with his palms and hums over the thumping. He rants about all the restaurants he's tried in Baghdad: *samoon* the size of tea trays, goat korma, boneless, without a trace of fat, mounds of *palak* with cubes of cottage cheese the size of marshmallows. And then he even tells me he's had a slice of pizza, but I know it's all bullshit. He's only been to Baghdad once with his father to buy a car. I switch eyes, using my left through the scope. It feels weird. Almost a half hour passes and Khalil's jabbering and shuffling makes me wanna scream. I say,

– OK.

– Yeah?

With a smile, I say,

– Yeah. We can go.

* * * * *

We creep forward, like two cats staking a bird, stopping every dozen meters to look through the scope. No movement around the thing. Not a man or mutt or mercenary. Then the sounds starts.

– You hear that? I say.

– What?

– That honking.

– Yeah.

The closer we get the clearer we hear it, honking, over and over, coming from the lump along the highway.

– Just some truck, a car alarm, Khalil says.

Flanking away from the road, approaching from the side, we start to make out what the melted squares is. We see where windows once were. And the wailing repeats from those smashed holes, ghostly and weird.

The SUV sags tire-less by the road's shoulder, burnt down to the frame. Its hood arches like the brim of a ball cap. We're too far to see how it was destroyed. There's no need to know anyway. Khalil shakes his head.

– Wasted an hour 'cause of *that*?

– Had to be sure, I say.

He gives a frustrated sigh, throws a rock in the direction of the SUV.

– Next time I'll just go up to it and see.

– OK, I say, and it means *sure, whatever, asshole*.

* * * * *

Khalil stubs his toe. Both my knees are bells dinging with pain. Khalil sneezes five times in a row. Then four times. Then five again. He never sneezes less than three.

Then he says,

– It looked American.

I wait a bit,

– What do you mean, it looked American?

– You know, how it looks. The SUV.

But I don't want to ask him what the hell that means.

＊＊＊＊

I think we're almost half way there.

More farmhouses appear – mere huts along the riverside. We pass them like hitchhikers too tired to solicit rides, chins and shoulders melting under the pitiless sun. My head's lit like a candle.

A shepherd stands with a long pole in his hand. It looks like it's planted far into the earth until he raises it to wave. We wave back.

He yells,

– Where are you headed?

– Ramadi! To find the Internet! Khalil is quick to answer.

– *Fim Allah*! The sheepherder shouts, dismissing us with his free hand.

Maybe he hates the Internet I think and laugh to myself.

– Don't tell anyone where we're going, I say.

– Yeah. Like some peasant farmer's gonna follow us, man. Kill us in the night. Yeah, right.

– It's not him. He might get questioned.

Khalil has no defense.

– OK.

But his OK is just like mine: *sure, whatever, asshole.*

Sheep trot around the herder's ankles and he pats their shorn coats. They follow the lead of the herder's gentle pole. He looks like a gondola driver paddling through a canal of pillows. A breeze shivers them before we feel it ourselves, and it's an unsavory relief from the heat – only teasing, only a sneeze.

To the north of the farm there's a pyramid of cauterized date palms that've been plowed and stacked on their sides and torched with gasoline. Empty jugs litter the smoldering mound. We can't take our eyes off it, smoking like a dead black comet. Seen from the river and the road, it's a totem warning all resistance fighters that the world will burn before they're given control.

I believe this now.

* * * * *

Later, Khalil offers to take the backpack and bedding. I give him the bedding. We drag our feet. It's past noon. My shins feel like they've been whipped. I have to shit.

We rest under a cluster of palms, and Khalil decides to swim again but I just watch. Welcoming banks invite him to the water. There are few rocks to scale. He lowers himself in, arms shaking.

Then he dives. He loves to challenge the currents, swimming deeper. Reemerging, his head hovers in the tiny crests of whitecaps like a buoy.

I take the paper towels under a cluster of trees and get it over with. I wonder if Khalil's been relieving himself at night or in the river – he hasn't asked for the paper towels once. I look around to make sure no one is approaching before I lean on a tree and squat in the sand. My mouth waters. Weakness shivers my legs. I'm suddenly nauseous. My head's a microwave. Snakes coil in my guts again, and, shaking hard enough to topple over, I feel some indescribable toxin exit my body.

– Shit, is all my mouth manages to say.

In a few minutes, the nausea passes. Little relief though. I try to relax.

Past the trees, there's a sea of wheat where a cow's rear sticks out. I watch its tail jump. Then the cow clomps somewhere into the high weeds, gone.

These are the paragraphs Rana won't read, the ones I'll later delete.

* * * * *

We were totally different people less than ten years ago.

Hanging out with Khalil wasn't like hanging out with anyone else. We ran through the streets like tyrants, orange peels flipping over our shoulders, cars swerving to get out of our way. The poorest princes of Fallujah.

People watched us, shaking their heads.

Khalil taught me to chase dogs before they had a chance to chase me. We stoned them when they nipped at our ankles – a good rock to the ribs – a chunk of concrete between the eyes. Getting bit was much worse.

We chased the screaming freight trains. At night. Beating the afternoon. Pretending the trains were speeding beasts. Threw stones at them, too. We even tried to run down the cars sputtering through town, the scrapped and dented Nissans and Toyotas, trucks with partly crumpled beds. No vehicle was allowed to enter Fallujah unscratched. I counted the mismatched colors. Green side panels on yellow sedans – spray painted bumpers – fiberglass patches slapped on by blind hands.

All of this was under Saddam. And before this war. Before my Mother left for Baghdad, and we never heard from her again.

Now no one watched us. Men and women were always looking to the sky, their ears diced by the thick chopping of helicopter. Black metal bugs. Machines mounted with hot death.

Dad finally asked,

– Why do you hang out with that stupid boy?

– I don't know, I said, head down.

I really didn't know.

– Savage, was all Dad said, a fly dive-bombing his shaking head.

When we did hang out, I never let Khalil tell me what to do. He'd try to boss me around.

– Breathe really hard and let me sit on your chest, he said.

We hunched and started breathing deep, over and over, windpipes stretched and bunched. We did it for a whole minute, foreheads throbbing. Then he laid me on the ground and put all his weight on my chest, suffocating. Impossible panic. The air sucked into blackness. My whole body sank into the earth. Cold beds of nothing. Brain drumming. I came to a second later. Daylight stars through bedrocks of near-death. Khalil grinned above me, said,

– Do it to *me* now. Pass me out.

I coughed back alive,

– You are an asshole!

Words like that meant nothing to him.

He said,

– But it's my turn now.

I figured this was why Khalil was stupid. And why he'd stolen that bell.

* * * * *

Khalil stands in front of me.

– Man, you really need to get in the water. It's cold, but it's great, really, he says, patting his face with a shirt.

He hands me a rusty bottle cap he pulled from the river, says,

– Got this for you. I know, I know, you told me not to splurge, but I saw it and was like, Sal's gonna love it. I just had to. *Don't be mad.*

I snort-laugh and ask,

– Man. Does your stomach hurt?

– Yeah. I'm starving. I didn't wanna say anything, but I've been hungry all day.

– No. I mean, *hurt, hurt.*

– Naw.

He pads his shoulders.

I roll the bottle cap between my palms. I wish it were an antacid.

* * * * *

Khalil dries in minutes and with the sun as intense as it is, we can't continue much longer. An hour or two. That's probably all. Sand flies like someone's kicking it in our faces. We dig at eye sockets with our fingers, scooping grit blown from the dusty womb of civilization. I wonder where these same sands have traveled and what other wanderers have tolerated this irritable scourge – Arab conquerors, Romans and The British, legions of mounted marauders, murdering agents pledging allegiance to greed, great tides of shields and helmets glowing through sand-storms. I wonder how Khalil's holding up. He asks about my stomach and I tell him it's the riverwater. He offers to take the pack, but I don't give. He must have a stomach like a clay jug. Maybe he always drinks from the Euphrates. Maybe that makes him a better Iraqi.

Ridiculous.

As thirsty as I am, I stare at the phlegmy strands of vegetation in the banks and fight the urge to drink. We stomp shirtless through overgrown weed as high as our elbows. I wonder what microscopic larvae have metastasized in my guts.

I say,

– We might have to boil some water at some point.

– You feel that bad?

I nod like speaking is too much effort. We have no kettle or pot and the plastic gallon is long gone, but Khalil doesn't point that out. He's being nice.

* * * * *

Standing guard, Khalil's a barebacked genie with his entire head wrapped. His tracksuit pants crack in the wind. I take another insane shit behind a boulder that even has a carved-out arm rest that I can lean on. When inspiration strikes, I complain to myself in compound swears.

Khalil never looks back or makes fun.

At least that's something.

* * * * *

By four o'clock I've had enough. When we spot a properly shaded grove, we relax, our minds stymied by the timeless repetition of the land, the sienna sameness of the sand. All the same aimless sienna. Khalil takes the paper towels and I remind him to conserve as much as he can. I feel like a jerk for reminding him, but maybe I have to be a jerk.

I don't feel like eating but we have to. There's a banana we'll split with some coconut milk that'll be better than the tainted water.

When I was younger, I'd go shopping with my mom to stock up on weekly things – cabbage and carrots from a vendor down the block, sugar and tea at a spot further down, close to the *Jolan*, the best in town – once in a while she'd let me get a *kahi* except she'd make me save some for later because it was too much to eat all at once. She'd point out signs and I'd read them out to her, but I was more concerned with the way they looked, not what they said. Arabic fonts jutted like hooks across storefronts. My favorites were the exaggerated letter forms and colors.

Back home, she'd set the groceries on the counter and we wouldn't say a word. It was my job to get the glasses, two tall pints from the cabinet. And, silently, with a sly smile curling, she'd pour milk into both. Right to the brim.

We'd stand in the kitchen and drink them at the same time, slow and silent. We'd move our wild eyes around and put the glasses down at the same time, and the crazy grins on our faces would probably terrify anyone witnessing our weird ritual. We did this once a week for years and years until she disappeared.

I never told my father about it.

Now I sip the coconut milk as slow as I can.

Khalil's gone for a while.

Taking off my sandals, I pop my big toes like I'm cocking the hammer of a gun and rub my feet, sinking them in the baked soil. I want to take out my laptop and write, but I'll wait until dark.

A wood plank surfs slowly downriver. It disappears. My

feet feel better.

Khalil appears out of nowhere.

– Where you been? I ask.

He plants the roll of towels in the sand like a tent stake, and I pull it out and put it in the bag.

Khalil asks,

– We stopping here for the night?

– Yeah.

– Can I get the scope from you?

– What for?

– I just want to look around. Might be a checkpoint up ahead or something.

He squints into the distance, shielding his eyes from the sun with a flattened hand. Says,

– Way off there.

– We'll eat, I say, already working the old rusty wheel of the can opener along the lip of another can.

– Here.

Khalil takes a can of kidney beans. He cranks it open, peeling back the lid, and savors each spoonful. He runs his tongue along his gum after every swallow, rooting up bits inside the slaloms of his mouth. I try to swap cans but he says I should have all the coconut milk – lay off the water – and I thank him and eat a few beans. I wish I'd packed some pepper or spice, anything to mask the blandness of plain old beans. The more I dream about sweet yellow curries and okra and blood-red tomatoes stewed in *masala*, the more homesick I get.

– I wish we had some chicken, just a few bites is all I need, I finally admit.

– Man. Some lamb kebab.

– Yeah.

– Marinated cabbage, cucumber.

– OK. That's enough.

– Pizza.

– Shut up, man, I say.

Lounging on the blankets, head to head, we pass an infectious yawn back and forth until Khalil starts laughing and I laugh too. He pushes out a fart that's so impressive I can't believe he did it on cue, and when I don't respond he asks what happened, and there's nothing I can do but howl laughing.

– You're supposed to fart too, man! he roars.

– I'll shit my pants, man. I'm sick!

And we both laugh and that's all I remember. My eyes burn a little. My eyes close.

* * * * *

Saturated blue ceiling. A cloudless, continuous haze. The sky is like tile imbued with cobalt, glazed and fire-fixed until its impossible blue avows a depth so impregnable you can't fathom its end. Blue that'd drive you crazy if you let it burn your pupils. Lifting my *keffiyeh*, I lose myself in the upside-down ocean above us – a gulf half-swallowing the Earth – deadly blue and a blue-from-the-birth-of-time. Little worms scurry in my vision – floaters. I blink back to focus.

It's six thirty. Been asleep for two hours. The shade's shifted and my legs have been sun-exposed for who knows how long. I bet they're burned. They feel alright.

Khalil's gone, of course. And the scope is gone, too. The bag's peeled open, but that's the only thing missing. He might have bitten an *Awat* and put it back. He can have it. Even with the land as flat as it is, he's nowhere in sight. Not a spec on the horizon and no reason to call his name. I finish the coconut milk – sweet and gritty – then consider drinking some water, but my stomach feels terrible. I'm going to have to relieve myself by the trees again. I'd rather have Khalil spotting, but I can't wait.

This camp isn't ideal, but it's still hidden from the road. Any river farer has plain sight. Whatever. I go around some palm trees, and it feels like there are tourniquets around my intestines.

I wish I brought a book.

* * * * *

When I was younger, my mother – who made me promise never to tell my father – would read me a chapter from a Steven King novel every night before bed. Sometimes they were real paperbacks, but most of the time they were photocopies of the originals. Contraband from *Al Mutanabbi* Street in Baghdad. She'd read *Carrie, Needful Things,* the one about the cemetery for pets, *It, The Stand* (the abridged version) – all of it was weirdly American. She'd skip the really scary parts. Hearing her describe the bizarre characters and details made me feel more adult than I was at the time, more responsible with this new knowledge.

Sometimes I still read with her cadence.

One time Rana asked me what my favorite book was and it took me an entire day to decide, worrying that she might think I'm a nerd. I don't think I ever answered her.

* * * * *

Slowly, the sun nuzzles its way into its daily extinction. Buttery yellows and oranges fade. Pastels melt inside the skillet of the sky like they were never there at all, and I think about all the things that were here once that left no trace.

In half an hour, we won't be able to see across the water or the road. I won't be able to see Khalil coming either. The river bends like a horseshoe, and on this slight grade, I'm sitting high enough to see both ends coil into the plains. I try to imagine how far Ramadi is, but it's still so far, and I know we haven't made enough progress.

Darkness overcomes the day. It erases me the same way it erases the details I slowly can't see. I sit here, alone.

Disturbances sound in the dusk that I have no explanations for – yelps from wild dogs, helicopter thumps that aren't there at all, toads, gulls, a crow. This loneliness is new. Brand new. Khalil better get back soon.

I power up the laptop. Its humming and welcome-tone is briefly pleasing. I start writing. Thinking of Rana. Why am I so worried about someone forgetting me, someone whom I've never even met? Might never meet.

I've written over twenty pages by the time a nearby splash makes me hunch and fold the laptop. Ripping off the white blanket so no one can spot me, I lie on my stomach and study the water, but nothing is there except unyielding black. It's silent for a minute. There's enough moonlight to illuminate echoing ripples in the water and then the sound reappears – more splashing and movement upriver.

I see a rowboat emerge from marsh grasses. It's Khalil. Head down, rowing. He looks confused.

I think I see him make some face of recognition. He hurries to paddle inland, dipping the oar. Not calling out, I let him pull ashore. He strolls to camp with his pants rolled to the knees, his sneakers laced around his neck. He drags the oar. His crazy smile proves he is out of his mind.

I don't let him speak.

– Where's my scope? I ask.

– We have a boat! he declares, waving his hand at it like he's proving a point, adding,

– a good boat.

– We don't *need* a boat. *Where's my scope?*

He jabs the oar in the sand, crosses both palms on its handle, and rests his chin on top of them before crossing a leg. Says, with more authority than required,

– It wasn't doing us any good, anyway.

Standing, I let my hood droop to my shoulders and, for the first time, I get in his face.

– That's not for you to decide, man.

I step back.

A fresh cut on his cheek looks like it might have come from a thorn. In the moonlight, his features seem magnified. His strained and narrow stare, his sharply arching eyebrows giving him an undue conniving expression. Unshaven, scraggly, a natural chinstrap of beard has grown over the past few days. It only exaggerates the shifty mask that's even hard for *me* to see past. I know kindness is there, somewhere in there. His smile is only a shallow reference to what he's thinking.

– I know, I know. But we *do* need a boat. We've gotta cross the river sometime and it's better to do it sooner. At night, he says, extending the oar to the river.

– Where'd you steal it from? I ask, arms crossed.

Khalil pauses,

– You won't believe me anyway.

– Doesn't mean I don't wanna hear it.

– I rented it with the rest of my money. There's a farmer, up there. About a kilometer up. Before the canal.

– Huh? What canal?

– Not far. We'll hit it tomorrow if we don't cross now.

I bite the inside of my cheek and look upriver, chewing the blubbery flesh. He's right. With all my planning and packing and worrying, I'd forgotten about the massive tributary cutting us off from the west, a canal dug above Al Habbaniyah before the Euphrates coils tighter into Ramadi. It flows south, emptying into the great lake – too deep to wade through.

He must have walked pretty far to get that boat.

There would be farms nestled in the fertile land surrounding the marshes, and, if he'd really walked all that way, if he were telling the truth, Khalil would have had his choice of houses to approach. A rancher or herder might have had a spare boat, might've been willing to part with it for a night. He probably wanted my scope as part of the deal.

Khalil says,

– I told the guy we'd leave the boat by the shore when we've crossed. I even told him about you, about what we're doing.

– Great.

– He's not going to tell anyone.

I can feel my nails through my cheek, between my teeth as I scratch my beard. I push the cheek-flesh in and keep chewing. Stop when it hurts.

– And you didn't even think of asking me, you just steal my shit and run off to get a boat. You could've been caught!

– But I wasn't, Sal. And I got us a way over the river.

– We're *safer* on this side.

– How? You don't know that, he says, digging with the oar like some beach comber, not even looking at me.

– There has to be a bridge.

– Might be. But if it's unoccupied, it'll definitely attract attention to us. Someone will spot us, we'll get arrested. This is safer. We can cross right here. We've seen the other side. We're safe.

Khalil's had ample time to compose these rebuttals in the hours he hiked and dealt with farmers or tradesmen. He's obvious about it, too.

He waits. Shrugs. He doesn't stare at me too long or pressure me to answer.

– Whatever. You're an *asshole*. Grab the blankets, I say, and shove the laptop in the pack.

He doesn't gloat, though he wants to. Letting the oar slap the sand, he folds the bedding and I don't help.

– I'm not an asshole. I'm trying to help, he says.

Packing the dirty spoon, I leave the empty can of beans in the dirt and feel guilty, but there's nothing to do about it.

– There's so many reasons why you *are* an asshole, it's probably easier naming the reasons why you *aren't* one.

He's quiet after that. Maybe because he's trying to figure out what I mean. We go to the shore.

No lights up or downriver. We're at an awkward bend where, if a patrol boat approached, we'd have little time to hide. At least we would hear its motor. It could be worse. The current could be stronger and the distance to the other side would be greater without the bend pushing us part way, but it's still a long crossing. It should take five minutes, no more. Khalil, trotting by, stuns me again.

Says,

– C'mon, man! *It'll be fun.*

* * * * *

The rowboat is hardly seaworthy. Weather-beaten and half-rotted, its white paint peels like birch bark. It will cross the river.

Clouds snuff the moon. The light is fickle. Khalil tosses the blankets in, and I rest my pack on them like a bundled infant, making sure it won't tip. A single bench stretches across the hull, and with our cargo there's barely room for two. He says,

– Get in first, I'll push us out.

If my computer gets wet, I'm going to hold his screaming head underwater until he's limp. I swear.

We heave the bow and submerge the rickety thing and I climb in. It's less of a boat than a crate that happens to be water-tight. My hands clamp both sides. Khalil holds it steady, but I'm still balancing on a needle. Looking down, I see that gouges scar the floor. Some are so deep that only paper-thin wood seals out the water.

– OK. Alright, Khalil nods.

The scope's on the floor of the boat.

– Khalil. The scope's right here.

– Yeah.

– You said you lost it.

– I thought you'd be happy to have it back once we got in. You surprised?

Grabbing it, I peer through, aiming the reticule over dunes and spiky clubs of palms, but I'm really just making sure he hasn't cracked the lens.

– Guess so, I say.

– I didn't break it.

Tapping my arm with the oar, Khalil hands it over and pushes the boat off shore. I spin for a second. I can't believe we're doing this – crossing the Euphrates – crossing the great Euphrates in a teacup, and I've never been on a boat in my life. Khalil wades, throws his leg over the side and hops in like he's jumping into bed. The boat rocks. He takes off his shirt.

– Don't worry, Sal. This thing's solid. Been floating for hours on it.

– Guess what? I ask.

– What?

He says, holding the oar like a javelin, composed to push off.

– You're still an asshole.

I shoot him a grin.

He sighs and digs into the sand, jabbing.

If I could make him feel worse about what he's done, I would.

* * * * *

Outward, the riverbed vanishes – devoid of definition or dimension. We float like a stalled plane ready to plummet. Slimy weeds reach up from the bottom, but in seconds they disappear and we're coasting deeper. Two holes punched in the boat's cheeks hover above the waterline, sipping water with each rocking dip. The boat's creaking complains, saying we're too heavy, the journey's too far, that it can't possibly do what we expect of it. I agree.

The river's changed.

It's no longer just an artery on a map or a predictable course for us to follow. We're not its eager pupils letting it lead us. The abstractness, the alluring attributes all fade and the river is just a crack in the earth filled with spillover from richer ground, richer nations.

I can't look at the water. Khalil's bottle cap pokes my thigh. I take it out and roll it between my palms. I pass it from hand to hand, trying to create some game to play, but there's nothing I can think of. Khalil's shoulder blades jab and retract as he digs into the water, maintaining a honed rhythm. The practice he got earlier is an asset. He's efficient, wasting no energy. He pants quietly. He takes breaks every thirty or forty strokes, then inhales for another set.

The boat wants to pop.

We're leaning into the current, but Khalil's strong and summons everything he's got to speed us – knowing he can't let me down, knowing he'd let himself drown before he'd let me drown. He sweats and the beads collect on his back like procreating amoebae, and they cascade and join into larger amoebae. The river doesn't care if he sweats. Nebulous torrents stir underneath, an archaic habitat bubbled up long before the maxims of theology and governance, a cold haven where the first children of the earth took root, taking in every nutrient of hydrogen and protein. I know they'll take *us* at our first mistake.

What's down there?

The black water says nothing.

Mute leviathans – stripped of pigment and devoid of conscience. They croon hungry, kindless as knives. And the river knows we're here too. Sons of the river and sons of Baghdad, we're here, and I know the drops leaking out of our armpits and eyelids were once molecules of the river. It smells us as we float, knowing our bodies belong to its ancient body. It won't hesitate to swallow us whole.

I scratch my beard like it's strapped on with glue.

Rowing, Khalil turns to me. Smiles. Rows.

* * * * *

There's a rat in my stomach. It jumps from wall to wall,

hooking with little talons. It scurries in berserk circles, pausing before causing more havoc. It hurts a little less when I lean over.

My tongue is gauze.

Skimming the river's surface with my tin cup, I scrutinize the water for floating grit, but in the pale night it's impossible to see. I sip with both hands. I keep my backpack safely clenched between my knees, a little above the boat's floorboards. A puddle sloshes dangerously close. It might be rising.

Jabbering, Khalil talks about how strong his arms are going to be after all this rowing, then he describes the farmer he rented the boat from – how he wanted to be a barber in Ramadi, but ended up taking over the family land, falling in love with it all over again even though he vowed never to be like his father in any way. I don't say a word. He asks if I'm OK and I say,

– Don't talk to me.

– Fine.

Ripples pulse like sound waves on the water. Khalil rows harder. He rests a second, the oar napping on his lap, and stares straight ahead at the expanding shore. We coast straight and graceful.

– You know, I'm not gifted like you. I didn't have all you had, he says.

It's evident I've dislodged the dry rotted stopper plugging up his pride. He continues,

– You've got your art and computer stuff. You're good with computers. I'm not. Everybody knows you for the stuff you make.

Letting him vent, I sigh, sip, and sigh.

– People know me, they're like, oh, *there's Khalil*. He's the guy that *waves*, he's the guy on the news that *waved* when the *Mujahideen* lynched those guys. Big deal. Big fucking deal. Now look at me. We're homeless, man. Homeless cowards.

I expect him to start paddling, but he's not. Our idle floating loses momentum and we're nabbed by the river's pull. He dabs at his back with his balled-up shirt.

– I don't even have a webpage or anything.

Chuckling, I empty my cup overboard, say,

– I can make you a profile once we get to Ramadi. It's easy.

– Yeah?

– Sure, man.

– Really? You will?

– Why not? Yeah.

– You're a *khosh* guy, Sal.

He goes back to rowing. If we continue straight we'll slide into shore perfectly, and part of me thinks Khalil paused his rowing, planned that conversation so we'd align there. I wouldn't put it past him.

– You can't use that photo from the bridge though, I say.

– OK. I know. OK.

* * * * *

The boat coasts with the current. We let it catch a patch of sand and Khalil leaps out, knee-deep and doing all the work. He drags us over snotty brine to the river's edge and yanks as far as the boat will go. I toss him the blankets and strap my pack on, and he tells me to throw it to him and I say it's OK, I've got it.

– We're just leaving it here?

– Yeah, the farmer said he'd take his other boat and find it in the morning, he knows about where we are.

– OK.

I jump to shore, relieved to be on stable ground. Flakes of

cracked mud cover the beach. Agreeing the boat might attract attention, we move from the waterway and hike the plain between the river and highway where Al Habbaniyah sits. I know we both consider stopping in town but don't bring it up.

South. Headlights pounce the road like fireflies. They're too far to spot us and it doesn't look like there's military stationed there – can't be sure. We shuffle carefully with the bedding over our heads. The terrain is hard, then crumbles into ground chalk. Khalil holds out his arms to cool off. He's still hot from rowing. We're like two tattered clergymen cast out from the house of whatever we believed. There's no home for us like there's no home for anyone.

The river looks the same on this side.

– You didn't see any food or anything while you were out, did you?

– Uh-uh, Khalil says.

I figure we'll walk until he starts talking again, but he's silent, shuffling behind instead of taking the lead. When I look back he's always spacing out like there's something captivating in the sky, in the treetops, over and through the diminished landscape. Maybe he's just exhausted. The shore tugs us onward.

An owl hoots like an echoing ghost.

I scan the trees in the hopes of seeing it. Humps by the water must be buffalo hunched among choppy wheatgrass. They're motionless. They're the old sages of Anbar Province decreeing *leave us be, we've been here so long, leave us be.* My mouth is like someone dumped a pocketful of sand in it and made me swallow – never been this thirsty. Khalil's at the riverbank drinking with his hands, and I join and know it's a terrible idea.

I gulp. Kinked guts tell me it's going to come straight out the other end. My reflection grimaces in the river, a weary portrait waving in the ether and my eyes are evaporated olives. I look down at my palms blurring in the water.

I watch myself say to Khalil,

– We should sleep here, over by that grove there.

Khalil nods, quietly compliant.

He drinks another handful and wets his black hair.

7

Here's a list of the *stupidest* things I've ever done:

- My Uncle's wife passed away and he spent all his savings on her funeral. The next month he came to my birthday party but couldn't afford a gift. He must've felt terrible. In front of all my relatives, I mistakenly thanked him for a new dictionary my other uncle gave me. Later that evening I saw him crying through the cracked bathroom door.

- When I was seven, I pulled a seat out from a kid as he was sitting down. Now he plays on the Iraqi Olympic football team. Dad says, *you went to school with that guy*, every time he's on TV.

- I stopped going to piano lessons. I can only play *chopsticks*. Now I want to play guitar.

I'm always the first to wake.

For some insane reason, I didn't turn off my laptop. It was probably when Khalil showed up with the boat, or right when I started yelling at him. That's when I stuffed the laptop in my bag. It's morning when I figure that out. So it's been on all night in my bag, on sleep mode though. I'm trying to decide if that ranks in my top *stupidest* things I've ever done. Right now it does.

Khalil's passed out, face down on the blanket, and this is the first time I've ever seen him sleeping with his eyes open. I knew he did it, but I'd never seen it. He looks like a zombie – mouth agape, a thread of drool waiting to hit the ground. It's my fault, the laptop, but I still want to kick him awake.

I sit on the hard earth and feel useless.

The morning is cool. If Khalil were really undead it would take a breakfast buffet of brains to reanimate him. Folding the end of the blanket over me, I eat some flat bread and stare at him. I accidentally chew some sand and spit it out.

* * * * *

Khalil's cell phone is flipped open, but the screen is automatically dimmed blank. The phone rests on a ripped-up piece of newspaper, parts of which have blown away. Careful not to wake him, I snag the paper.

It's Khalil's photograph.

Half of Khalil's face is in the photograph, the green bridge on Highway 10, the lively men and the deadened remains of men, just halves of them. Khalil is different in the photo – neither an expression of joy nor dread. It's impossible to know what he was feeling at the time – overwhelming frustration or excitement – but either way, whatever fortune the photo might have brought turned quickly to a curse. Other torn pieces flutter like spent fireworks, but most of them were taken by the breeze hours ago. I let this one go, too.

I hold some bread under his nose.

– Hey, Khalil. Breakfast.

Eyes flutter, he moves his mouth like a horse. I tap a nostril with the rough bread.

– What? He moans, pushes up on his palms.

– Here, man. Breakfast.

– What time is it?

– Eight.

He takes the bread, sits with his head between his knees and grinds his eyes with the heels of his hands.

– You still mad at me?

Khalil doesn't look up, so I nod yes, but say,

– We're still alive, right?

– Guess so, he says.

– So.

And he seems fine with that.

＊ ＊ ＊ ＊ ＊

I shit again while Khalil finishes breakfast. It's the same sickness coming out as before. I feel like I've been eating nothing but chilies for months straight. Dizzy, I'm squatting against the trunk of an acacia tree. The paper towel roll is getting thinner and thinner – disappearing faster than planned. I've never been good at improvising. I wonder what I would do if I had no paper towel left.

The ground is crusty crag.

There are no leaves around.

Back at our camp, Khalil asks if I'm OK. It's the only thing he says all morning as we skirt Habbaniyah's probably hospitable cafés and storefronts and burgeoning fruit stands for more desert nothingness. The heat arrives quickly. Our sweat evaporates before it surfaces. Skin tightens and cracks. Khalil keeps running his hands through his hair, feeling for something that's not there.

The landscape's refrain repeats unchanged.

The river drags us along. Any trees that don't strangle the Euphrates are starved naked. We watch them wilt as we walk.

I glance back and Khalil's lagging behind.

– Ah! he yells.

He's trying to dig a rock out of the hole in his sneaker. He pries the sneaker off by the heel, rattles it out, and rubs his sore foot.

– Stop for a second? I ask.

He shakes his head no.

Khalil points at a greenish smudge in front of us – wrecked machinery. I don't bother with the scope.

Defeated tanks languish along the outskirts of the highway. Their sad barrels bend downward, fixed in the position in which they were left after the first war – crippled vestiges of tyranny. Scabbed with rust, most are peeled open like storm-damaged houses – instrument panels, levers, seats, and dials open to the sun. Anxious sand creeps into the chassis, burring axels and their great iron gearboxes. Parapets and pillaged gun mounts are all that are left jutting out of the little dunes. A woman's purse hangs from one of the massive barrels.

I stick my hand into one of the treads, imagining what it ground between belt and iron wheel.

I'm surprised Khalil doesn't want to check them out. He barely looks. One of them points its massive gun at us as we pass. I want to put my whole arm in the barrel.

– They might be booby trapped, Khalil warns.

He might be right.

And people have been known to get sick from touching blown up vehicles –inhaled particles, causing tumors, birth defects, babies with no mouths.

Mortar tubes lay like pieces of fallen satellite. We avoid an outpost fortified by sandbags – long abandoned – and traverse the sienna nothing between roadway and river.

I know I should drink some water, but I don't. Can't.

My *keffiyeh's* soaked with sweat. I hang its salty skin over my own salty skin like a veil, and I'm a Pac-Man ghost again. I wonder what the pellets that Pac-Man eats taste like. The insides of my thighs are raw. My bowels feel power-washed. Wilting and tacky, I take off my watch. The leather band is gamey and gross against my wrist. It goes in my pocket where it clicks against the bottle cap Khalil gave me. It makes a nice rhythm when I step, clacking like a metronome. It's a nice distraction.

Flattened short grasses grow close to the shore.

Coasting downriver, a man in a *mashoof* trolls with a small motor rigged to the stern. Somehow I know it's the farmer retrieving his borrowed boat. Khalil watches him until he disappears around the bend. He smiles at me.

While Khalil drinks with the tin cup, I take out the scope, buffing the lens with the slack of my shirt. Rolling it over, I notice, for the first time, initials etched into the cylinder – RBK – Russian? No way to tell. The letters are so thin, smoothed over from use. Khalil leans over my shoulder, looking at the letters. He offers me a sip of water.

– No thanks, man.

Stowing the cup, I hand him the scope.

– Take it for a while. Someone should be looking out.

He shrugs, stares off again, wrinkles his nose, says,

– It's OK. You should have it.

– Really, I'll take the blanket, you keep an eye out.

So he takes the scope.

– You sure? he asks.

– Yeah.

Then I let him spy the man in the *mashoof* until the river erases him from us.

* * * * *

Khalil always had something interesting. Used TVs, huge umbrellas, binoculars, bifocals, camping equipment, cases of soda and cartons of fruit, speakers for car stereos with wire dangling like jellyfish – all of it, I assumed, came from his dad who owned a second-hand shop in the *Jolan*. I never asked. One afternoon I helped him sell boxes of batteries. He even gave me some of the money but then made me buy us dinner.

We never held hands like childhood friends because we both knew we weren't childhood friends.

I finished middle school. Then high school. Dad said if the Americans do invade Iraq, I should wait until after the war is over to apply to Baghdad University.

Bad luck followed Khalil like a stray dog. He would be fine for a few months, nothing out of the ordinary, and then, without warning, something weird would happen, and then another thing. Right in a row. Other people might say it was a curse. *That Khalil is cursed! Better luck to that young man, inshallah!* I wouldn't say that.

There was a week when the electricity was out most of the time. No one really knew why.

Mom would whisper,

– It's Saddam.

Dad would hush her,

– You think everything is Saddam. Be quiet.

The ceiling saw more of her rolling eyes than the top of her head. I emptied our refrigerator so we could eat the last perishables for dinner. Beef was valuable and spoiled too quickly; cheese was pure gold.

Khalil had his own theories,

– No. It's not Saddam. He loves us.

It was cool that morning. We sat in the sun.

I watched Khalil scoop runny eggs into his mouth, cumin framing each sloppy chew. He dabbed flatbread into the yoke. Sopped the runny yellow clean. He must have ordered six eggs at the café where he eventually got fired from, but now that Khalil had an unlimited supply of secondhand goods to sell, he could afford six eggs whenever he wanted. Six chickens if he really felt like it.

I waited for him to offer me some bread. He said matter-of-factly,

– It's aliens. They suck our power. They need it. To return home.

Khalil's pepper-freckled finger pointed up.

I shook my head,

– Right.

– *Right* from their mother ship.

– Yeah.

But what Khalil didn't know was all that power that got sucked to the mother ship hadn't been powering the café's refrigerators or keeping their milk or their butter or their eggs cold. Just one of the six he'd shoveled into his mouth that morning had spoiled enough to poison his entire system. Venom-shocked.

Pissed with sickness. Both of his ends bubbled so violently that he didn't leave his parent's bathroom for two days. Sisters cracked the door to see him doubled over in shivers, yelling,

– Close the door! *Ugh.*

A week later, still slightly green, Khalil managed to fall off a ladder and break his wrist. My mom helped reset the bone. No one even knew what he was doing on a ladder, anyway.

There was the time he lost 500 dinar on the bus. There was the time he was running and accidently stepped on a dead sheep and lost his sneaker in its rotted guts. He skipped home in the hot dirt. Overburdened, carrying three things at once, he'd always drop at least two. He'd fill tea to the brim and scorch his fingers every time. That was Khalil. But I never called him cursed.

Televisions appeared on our doorstep from time to time, the black and white sets Khalil had a harder time selling. Anything in his inventory he was tired of carrying around crawled into our living room, crept into our bedrooms. Cracked lamps with dribbled rivers of glue, old shoes, fish tanks, a pair of roller skates that could have fit a giant.

Mom would hold her head.

– Not another lamp.

Our tenants and neighbors ended up with most of it. I kept the best for myself.

Peering into my bedroom, Dad asked,

– Where'd you get *that* thing?

It was the first computer I ever owned. It took up my entire desk. Sounded like a dentist's drill when it was on too long. Words appeared hazy on the dim screen – pecking at the keys. I shrugged,

– Uh.

– Khalil?

– Yes, sir.

Dad scowled. Turned his back into the hall, yelled,

– Give it back!

I kept typing. Swampy green letters glowed like magic.

Mom convinced him that I should have a computer, no matter where it might have come from. Dad didn't understand what it meant for someone like me.

Maybe Dad knew the debt I would be in. Not financially, but in some way to Khalil. I'd have to see him more often, which was way too often in his opinion. But Khalil kept bringing over newer or better quality parts – keyboards with almost all their keys, color monitors, more disc drives and discs than I ever needed, and even a mouse that was somehow resistant to sand. Khalil loved giving.

– Look at this, man!

He pulled piles of ink cartridges from a wooden box. Smiling, he said,

– No one buys this stuff.

I knew he was lying. Someone would buy them.

Maybe what I liked most about the laptop were the English keys. They force me to read better, to write better. In both languages, really. Mom knew this, too.

Software was harder to find, but Khalil somehow dug up pirated versions of recently outdated applications. Every third or fourth disc actually worked, but when it did, I would spend nights, eyes burning, trying to teach myself layout design or a spreadsheet's arithmetic. As my English got better and better, my curiosity increased. Even though he had no clue or wish to know about operating systems or graphic design, Khalil knew how important it was to me.

Ducks wiggle downriver, followed by a yellow sandal, a wax wrapper like a little parachute, foam packaging, chips of plastic, a shoelace – I wonder where it all comes from.

Occasionally, Khalil peers through the scope and hunts for threats along the shoreline, targeting with the crosshairs. I even hear him making mock explosive sounds. It's something I have done myself. I used to ride in the car with my uncle, my mother in the passenger seat – a speck of dirt on the window would become the sights of a gun. We'd pass apartments and stores. Closing one eye, that speck would take aim and spray quick bullet bursts. Every bump in the road made it harder to keep on target.

I was just a game. Harmless fun.

– Where'd you get this thing? he asks.

– Found it on a neighbor's roof.

It was attached to a rifle. He doesn't need to know that. The rifle is still on the roof.

Palm fronds hiss in the breeze and the breeze carries mist off the river, cooling us, but we know it can't last. Khalil pauses. I pause too.

A truck speeds away from Habbaniyah. The transmission strains to shift like the driver's never driven stick or the engine is blown. We follow it like a fly buzzing by a television. There's nothing to worry about. We're glad to have the town behind us. Whatever was there to hurt us is too far away to care.

* * * * *

Goldenrods hug waterfront fields where swaths of cinnamon-colored sands dot the lowland. We descend a rocky hill, stepping sideways, sending rocks bouncing down. Khalil drops the blankets twice. Then the scope. It's fine. Reaching the bottom, I have to stop to relieve myself.

Leaving the gear with Khalil, I duck into some thick shrubs planted near the surf where it's private and safe. I notice the paper towels are almost gone now. There are no rocks or stumps to sit on, and, looking around, no leaves or brush of any kind that would serve as paper. My *keffiyeh* is tempting to use, but there's no way I'd disrespect my mother's headscarf even if she would understand. And she *would* understand, I know. For a second I consider going in the river, but it's too late.

My bent knees shake.

I didn't think it was possible to shiver in this heat.

If it wasn't hard enough to crap with nothing to brace myself with, whatever is coming out of me is like boiled mouthwash. Everything burns. When it's finally bubbled through me, the last two paper towels aren't enough. Sweating, I flip the coarse paper towel roll in my hands and twist a grimace at it. Following the scored spiral along the cylinder, I see a long code printed on the inside, letters and a date and more numbers.

My fingers shake, legs cramp. The longer I wait the worse everything gets. I crush the middle of the roll with my fingers. It dents easily.

The tube unrolls into a long, narrow strip, and I bend it back and forth thinking that it might make it pliable. I drop it once and have to blow the sand off. Seven ragged pieces tear from the roll. I clamp all but one under my sandal in case the wind kicks. I wipe as gently as I can. It feels like a bicycle tire breaking in my ass cheeks. Thinking I still have to conserve the pieces, I fold one in half after using it and use it again.

Khalil yells,

– You alright?

Knees cracking, I stand and the needles in my legs disperse. There are four pieces of paper tube left. They go in my pocket. I kick sand over the evidence and leave.

* * * * *

Raw desert opens. It spills endlessly, left and right. River and road separate briefly, leaving arid stretches of land. Dwarf shrubs group along the most fertile soil, but lose courage once drier ground overtakes the moisture. Palms trees triumph, green and stately. They're timid to leave the Euphrates. Like we are. The river is our chaperone. If it weren't for this heat and my screwed-up stomach, we'd be in Ramadi by now. We're going too slow.

Khalil asks for an empty plastic bag and I say,

– For your sneaker?

– No.

At the river he washes the breadcrumbs out and fills the bag as full as he can, twists it shut, and pokes a small hole in the bottom. I shake my head and smile.

– You said you weren't creative.

– It's no painting, he says, holding the bag over my mouth like a canteen. I open my mouth and chuckle with water dribbling over my beard, gargling. I say,

– It's a lot better than a painting.

Harsh terrain spills ahead and where healthy marshland was, there's just sand and the malignant sun. I can't tell if we're drowsy or fatigued. The bag of water contracts, and we drink it before it turns to vapor.

The river and road finally bottleneck into a narrow pipe where small farm houses appear. They're like tissue boxes painted dark plum with sable roofs, some of them as sapphire as the river itself. One even has an Iraqi flag hung vertically from a front porch. A mother and daughter sit under their awning, both reading, a cat on the table between them. Only the cat sees us.

Little slopes tuft the dust. The sand is ruffled linen.

Houses disappear as rocks commandeer the riverbanks, cordoning off the waterway. Walking paths lead us through elongated corridors tedious in their lack of character or color. Spatterings of bramble repeated over and over. I almost step on a dead bird. There used to be a fence. Wooden posts mark our pace where the trees grow and where fence wire would hang taught. Stopping, Khalil squints, leans forward like it might help him see farther. I stop too. He levels the scope and immediately crouches, drops the bedding, and grabs my calf.

– What?

– Dunno.

I get down.

Kilometers ahead, a cluster of rocks might be stacked into a makeshift den, but otherwise there's nothing but crumbles of shore and weed along the river. Too far to tell. I ask,

– What's it look like?

– An outpost maybe. There's a boat sticking out of it, I think.

Khalil makes short sweeps up and down the river, studying the rock cluster. He rolls his tongue in a circle behind both lips. It looks like there's a grub or something fighting to get out of his mouth. I guess he's thinking.

He hands me the scope. I can't make anything out.

– I don't see it.

– Where the water meets the rock, there, he says and

points, but that doesn't help much.

– It's just some rocks. I don't see a boat.

– There's a round part sticking out. See?

– Not really.

He takes the scope back and stares like a captain crazed by illusions of shore. I sit on the backpack while he's transfixed. Low, he crabwalks closer to the water, using wheatgrass as cover, but can't get a better view and comes back. He raps the scope against his open palm.

– Definitely something.

I ask,

– So we're going to wait?

– I think we should.

* * * * *

We trade off the scope. We hold our breath and listen, but there's nothing. Every five minutes Khalil perks up like he's seen something, but there's obviously nothing.

With the sun glowing head-high, we languish like rotting pumpkins, and I *know* it's all for nothing. The pile of rocks is just a pile. It's so far away it could be in another country and if the road weren't such a menace we'd just go around whatever the hell it is.

Khalil squats and sits, shifting curiously, on constant watch. He looks like he's about to say something, then doesn't. Using his pinky finger, he scoops grit out of the spiral of his ear.

– Anything? I ask.

He says no.

Stalking prey, a hawk circles between us and then makes a loop around the rock pile, thirty, forty, now fifty-seven patient circles before it dives and misses whatever snake or varmint it eyed. Riding a gust, it banks upward, jerking left and up until it regains its vantage and repeats. The hawk's wings barely flap except to maintain altitude – circling wider – thirty, forty, fifty times. Then it dives. Khalil doesn't see because he's fixed on the pile of nothing. Counting. Every second is counted. Is time an accumulation or the slow expulsion of remembrances? Loosening my watch, it slips over my hand. I tighten it again. Is time different for everyone or does it govern our bodies the same?

I scratch my beard. He's snatched his dinner. Looks like a small fox or something. It thrashes briefly before the hawk carries it off like an empty purse. Khalil takes a break from staring, rolls up his pants above the knees.

I'm so hot I think I've stopped sweating.

– I dunno. I dunno, Khalil mumbles.

– Think we should go?

– No. Uh-uh.

– Not yet?

– No.

Khalil takes the water bag down to the river every so often and brings it back as full as he can carry it, and we drink. The water's deceptively clear. There might be a bar of soap melting in my guts, the way it feels, but I keep drinking.

– We might'a missed this outpost entirely, if we were on the other side of the river, he says.

I snicker,

– *If* it's an outpost.

Khalil pauses and scopes and says,

– It's something.

I lay back. Eyes shut.

Hearing the dial tone and the weird whining twang of the Internet connecting for the first time in my bedroom made my arms electric – made the ceiling ripple and vanish – images burst like confetti between my ears – stayed up until dawn – searched everything, everything, everything – good things – gross things – *Day of the Dead* – dancing babies – garage bands from New York City – peanut butter cups – sweater vests – people thrown into volcanoes – the Lakers – weapons from World War One – Hawaii – Honda – chat room acronyms – and Rana, her profile, her covered head and bashful shoulders, her messages sent late at night and my swollen heart bursting like pollen-soaked sunflowers.

War waged. Everything changed. Dad was reluctant, but agreed that Mom would be safer with relatives right outside Baghdad. She left. She never liked Fallujah. I knew this as much as Dad did. She always longed for the city's culture, the beauty of Baghdad – poetry and music and everything. We kissed her. Over and over. She wanted me to go. Then to stay. I don't know. I don't know. We kissed her cheeks and mouth, the first mouth I knew before my own. Dad paid her driver extra. Keep safe. We waited. Dad checked the dial tone. Over and over. She never called. Weeks then months. Our relatives cried with us. Everything changed even though it felt like nothing changed.

A Kalashnikov on every shoulder.

Fire-breathing clouds.

– This is a great opportunity, man. You have to.

Khalil was good at a few things, but not at convincing me what was a good idea. We sat at the table in my parents' backyard patio, shadowed by a constellation of sunflowers. He tried flipping a coin into his empty glass. I groaned,

– No. I don't want to be involved. I can't.

Khalil flipped the coin into my water glass.

I didn't know he was working for Mr. Hassnawi until Khalil started bragging about the money, how he didn't really need to sell junk anymore. I asked,

– What are you doing for him?

– Errands. Delivery stuff. Not much.

I had no idea. I stayed out of those circles. Men cleaned their rifles. Woman baked their bread. But at the beginning of the occupation, there was no other work.

Always needling, Khalil badgered me to design propaganda flyers for the uprising, mentioned my name to Mr. Hassnawi's subordinates, said how great of a designer I was even though I wasn't that good at all. I could hear him now:

– He's good, man. He'll make it look slick.

And I was called to Mr. Hassnawi's office one day, asked to go by two men in the street, escorted, heel on heel, through the *Jolan* and its confined alleys. We entered a little storefront with only a sheet for a door. We passed the clerk and the shelves to a back room. Pillows lined the walls. A prayer rug. Pop music played softly on a giant square stereo. I was told to sit in a chair at a table. The two men left.

I waited a minute, trying not to fidget or look nervous.

I never met Mr. Hassnawi, but I did speak to a man that

answered directly to him. He slumped in front of me. Spoke softly. The man's polo shirt barely covered his enormous belly. He touched his face a lot – scratching cheeks, fingers tugging on earlobes, pulling on his lip like he might be trying to take off his face right in front of me – and he asked me about my design experience, just like a job interview. He seemed nice, repeating,

– Good, good.

and, smiling modestly,

– I see.

He never asked me if I wanted to help the uprising or join the *Fedayeen*. The words never came out of his mouth. But, after asking about my computer and software, when and how and why I like design, after offering me tea and kahi just like the kahi Khalil brought to my house a year later, he slid a pad of paper across the table. Said,

– Write down anything you might need.

I paused. I looked over at the stereo. The man said,

– Software. Laptop. Anything.

I didn't know what to do. The man pulled his earlobe and waited. His other hand slid the pad of paper closer. Temptation overcame me. The pencil found my fingers. I wrote down everything I'd ever wanted – the most modern laptop, most recent software – I even listed brands and names of applications I'd only read about online, almost thinking that if my request was ridiculously unreasonable, they'd dismiss me completely.

When I was done, the man read over the list and nodded. I could tell he understood very little. He left the room. Minutes later one of the two men who'd bought me in took me out, and he didn't say a word, and I didn't say a word either.

A week later, Khalil showed up at my house with half of what I asked for. A few days later, the rest. He said,

– Here's what Mr. Hassnawi needs.

And I got to work.

Taking every precaution to hide my involvement with the uprising was vital. My dad would have thrown me out. I never would have thought of taking that computer equipment if Mom was around. But we needed the money and this was the only real paying work.

I was detached enough from the people and the violence to feel uninvolved. Propaganda would have been printed anyway, with or without me. After delivering each leaflet design, I'd promise myself that that would be the last one. No more. I told myself I'd pack up the laptop and everything that came with it and drop the box off to Mr. Hassnawi myself, but that never happened.

* * * * *

Clouds coat the sun for a minute and melt away.

I take the scope, make broad sweeps over the sand and across the water.

No hawks or birds of prey or cattle grazing sparse pastures. No farms except one humble dwelling, hugged by barbed wire, way off beyond the delta. Palms make a perfect passageway. Verdant and thriving crops form emerald grids around an unfinished oxbow that nearly completes its circle, but stops short of the Euphrates. Little black dots gallop inside the barbed fence. They might be goats, or children.

Maybe eighty meters away, a safe patch of palms sways invitingly. I'm sick of waiting.

– Let's go for it, I say.

– Yeah?

– What else is there to do?

He does that grub thing with his mouth, circling and circling, tongue in the trench of his lip.

– OK. Yeah, he says.

Khalil grabs my backpack and shoves the rolled bedding between the straps, keeps the scope ready. Says,

– Hopefully we'll just go around it. Maybe there's no opening on the other side, like it just faces the water.

– Yeah.

– Lemme go first, he offers.

– Yeah.

Rushing a few meters at a time, he pauses to peer through the scope.

– OK, he whispers, gesturing to advance. I follow. All I see is the backpack bouncing, the blanket and sheet flapping like wings, thin shoulders and thin arms. Unchanged, the pile of rocks looks more and more like a pile of fucking rocks, but Khalil sees something entirely different. It's a hidden coalition stronghold meant to snare watercraft traveling to and from Fallujah – resistance ferries shuttling fighters or re-supply ships carrying food or weapons. Almost to the trees, Khalil stops and says,

– They'll have a turret facing out, facing the road, right here.

He points at the pile.

– Maybe we should run.

– We'll be OK, I say.

– I'll go first, you come when it's safe.

– OK, I say, playing along.

And he dashes as fast as he can, skipping a little on his sore foot, holding the pack straps like loose suspenders, and reaches the palms without taking more than a few breaths. We wait. I can see him raising the scope to the pile, to me, to the pile. He waits. Then he waves, *come on*, and I run.

* * * * *

Khalil has his right sneaker off when I get to the trees. His face crinkles when he prods the sore on his foot where the tear in his sole keeps swallowing stones. We keep low. There's no way to tell what the pile is or isn't, and we discuss how long we're going to walk and how close to the road we're willing to go. Neither is safe. Khalil says,

– You OK?

– Yeah. Fine.

* * * * *

Reaching the northwestern side of the pile, it's still an abstract chunk. We continue, keeping the road and the river equal distances between us. Khalil wears the pack and I root through the remaining food, settling on a can of peas, but I can't find the spoon.

– Did we lose the spoon?

We put down the pack and rummage until we find it. The whole process takes all the energy I have left.

– We must stop, I say.

– OK.

Khalil surveys with the scope. I can tell he loves using it. But he doesn't spot much other than some growth closer to the river. Says,

– We could settle over there, or keep going a little. See

what's up ahead.

– OK.

– OK, what?

– The last one.

– OK.

For an hour, the sky is queasy and gray. It looks like it might rain, but the sun appears.

I follow Khalil, and he eventually finds a field of tall wheat far enough from the river and the road, and though we're exposed a little to both, it's OK. A few mangy acacia trees offer little shade. We settle down under their torched and bony limbs. We groan with relief. We rub our feet and calves and thighs, taking off as many clothes as civility allows – Khalil in his underwear, me in my rolled up khakis – and suffer in the meek shade like stray dogs.

Finished with the peas, Khalil pours water from the plastic bag into the cup and passes it to me and I drink as much as I can. Not much. Not nearly enough. Khalil says,

– I just want to go swimming.

– I'd probably join you, I say.

It's too dangerous.

Scraping the inside of the can, Khalil makes it sound like a washboard, running the spoon over tin ridges, and scrapes out a strange tune. He makes a slow zip pushing in, a quick one zipping out, and the elementary rhythm is calming. He taps the can's bottom like a little drum.

He stops.

We look to the road. We lay flat on our stomachs. We count three, then four white Suburban SUVs tail one another in a coiling advance. They float on the horizon, swerving both lanes of the highway, speeding away from Ramadi in a slithering serpentine pattern. Khalil asks,

 – Is that how they avoid being attacked?

There is no way they can see us, but we stay low.

 – Private security, I say.

 – Yeah.

 – Escorts.

In a minute, they've shrunk silently into nothing.

* * * * *

Khalil kills time bringing back water from the river and the empty can becomes his personal cup. We split another *Awat* cake – somehow it tastes better this time and it settles my stomach a little. He talks about his cousin Anmar in Ramadi and how he's some big shot in the resistance – *no one would ever betray him* – and how they hadn't spoken since the photo of Khalil and the bridge was published.

 – He's going to be happy to see me, Khalil boasts.

 – You sure he has the Internet at his house?

 – If he doesn't, he can help us find it.

 – Cool.

I take out the pocketknife from the pack and flip it open. It's duller than I remember, and the cedar handle is dark with oil from years of use. It was my father's and maybe his father's, too. After digging some grit from the nail of my big toe, I clean the blade on my pants and hand it to Khalil.

 – You should have this. Just in case, I say.

 – You sure?

 – Yeah.

The sun makes the landscape quiver.

* * * * *

The full cup of water is nearly evaporated when I wake. Khalil's asleep on his stomach with both his hands under his crotch like he's pissing into the center of the earth. If I had a camera I'd take a picture and send it to Reuters. *Man in Blackwater Photo Pisses into Center of Earth.* I drink the rest of that water and lay back down.

* * * * *

Khalil wades waist deep the next time he fetches water. His whole body is red. The violet sunset alchemizes overhead. Eerie bronze embers stir inside the cloudy cauldrons. Khalil looks like an obscure and forgotten pharaoh, walking back, bulging water sac in hand. *God of the plastic water sac.* He hooks a finger in his mouth.

– My tooth hurts, he says.

He can have the knife, but I'm not going to let him use my toothbrush.

After taking inventory of our supplies, we decide to ration more conservatively, knowing our progress has been slower than planned. Half a can for breakfast, half for lunch. Bread might be dinner by itself.

– We might run into some food, Khalil says hopefully, still messing with his sore molar.

– Can't count on it.

He pauses.

– I know. There were ducks by the river. Maybe we can hunt them.

– You can try.

I yawn, and he yawns and we both keep yawning. I take off my wrist watch, not wanting to know the time. *Could be walking*, I think, yet it's unimaginable now. We gulp the water he brought back, and Khalil stands to get more, but we hear a growl in the distance – combustion-driven and steady – a humming at the rim of the river.

– Shit, Khalil whispers.

– A boat?

– Yeah.

– Get down.

Flattening on our stomachs, I ball up my *keffiyeh* and hide it under my chest. We pass the rifle scope back and forth. Our trembling fingers make it impossible to focus.

– Yeah. Shit, Khalil says.

A Banana-shaped, black coalition patrol boat chugs up-river. Men squat packed in its hull. One soldier leans forward with his hand on a front mounted turret. Another holds a large pair of binoculars. The driver, partly concealed by amour plates, speaks into a radio. A few others are sitting, attentive. Helmets and goggles and breastplates all matte green. Some smoke ciga-rettes and some don't. Portside, *Ride the Lightning* is painted in scratchy white. I think that's from a movie. Khalil and I look for the same thing: prisoners, *Mujahideen*, or unlucky civilians, anyone – a shepherd or farmhand or the man we borrowed the boat from.

There are only young troops.

My lungs contract. Khalil tries to hand me the scope, but I'm frozen. He keeps it. The soldiers must wear some technologi-cally advanced headgear that can see through sand and can spot humans in daylight, or have heat-seeking laser-guided mortars that make no sound before impact. We wait for them to turn their main gun and empty it at us.

Bobbing, they surge against the glittery current, but there is little life along the shore to be disturbed by their wake – few gulls or ducks, and the ones that are there to see them pass pay no mind. Everything is the same.

– Same shape as I saw by that outpost. Must be the same boat. Has to be, Khalil says.

I play along.

– OK. You think they saw us?

Aiming the scope at the boat, Khalil makes the same explosion sounds as before, says,

– No way.

The Euphrates drinks up the boat as it glides away. We keep our eyes locked on its exhaust smoke until it is completely gone.

– Definitely the same boat, Khalil says again.

* * * * *

We're silent while the ochre plains blacken, and the sun is finished with its daily chore. Our darkened shoulders mark another day closer. Closer to what, I'm not sure.

It doesn't matter that Khalil sees me taking out the laptop. I clear sand from the keyboard. It blinks on. I run the corner of my *keffiyeh* through each key and over speakers, scrubbing ports and the CD drive and it's impossible to get all the grains out of the square where the tab key was. The battery is low. I'll spend it typing as the warning messages flash and the screen finally flickers dead.

– Be nice to make a fire, Khalil says.

– Yeah.

– I can stare at a fire all night. Wonder why.

– Dunno.

I try to write while he talks about primordial instincts, how he can just stare at a fire, how it's the only thing that relaxes him. Just staring. He's silent for longer than he's ever been. Then he asks, out of nowhere.

– Do you pray, Sal?

– Huh?

– *As-salat.*

– Not anymore, really. Sometimes, I guess, I say.

Khalil loses all expression in the fake fire he stares into.

– Yeah. Me too. Sometimes.

We're quiet then. He doesn't ask why I stopped, and I get a sense he already knows, so I don't ask him why he's stopped either. We both know what *sometimes* means, and sometimes no reason is the best reason.

* * * * *

Khalil and I sit under the white sheet and I show him a few photos of Rana. He doesn't even make fun of me. I explain how to set up an online profile, username and password and everything – but we can't do it now. I say,

– We'll get you hooked up, man.

– Anybody can see it?

– Yeah, anybody.

– You think I'll meet a girl on there?

– Sure. Yeah. There're tons of girls on there.

He smiles so wide his eyes disappear.

Then he lies down. I lie down, too.

Head-to-feet so one of us can watch the river and the other

the road, there is just enough sheet to cover both of us.

Things scratch the desert's back, picking in the reeds, bowling little rocks along the riverbanks. The sky is paper. The moon is just a watermark.

Warning messages say the laptop is losing power, so I pull up Rana's folder and the one pic I love, and even though it is etched into my mind, I have to see it one last time. Messy dark hair like a bird's nest, her nose tangled up in mid-laugh. This is the one she took for me and posted right after we emailed for the first time.

I unroll my pants and dig my feet into the sheets. Earlier, when I said I wanted a pair of hiking boots, I might've been wrong there. Socks would've been perfect. A thick pair of thermal socks to keep out this nighttime cold. My elbows rest into the blanket like two eggs in a carton. It's uncomfortable to type, but I bang the keys as fast as I can.

Everything is sweat-stained.

Salt in our sweat hardens shirt fabric and pants. While this night's cold is welcome, it fossilizes and starches our clothes and it calcifies the river running through our veins. The river that is part of our bodies just as it is part of the country. We will carry this river with us. We were born from it and we will return to it. And like the soldiers in the boat riding its cordial passageways, the river treats each visitor equally – with the same complacent undertows and swells, currents gravitating seaward. Khalil and I struggle against its flow, against the natural order of war and whatever follows the war.

If we're escaping one thing, we're following something else. Are we brave enough to admit this?

Another warning message pops up. I click it closed and keep typing.

For some reason, all I want to do is draw.

If I had some paper and a few good pens, I'd draw *Sasoki*, a cartoon character from my childhood. *Sasoki's* face is as round as a ball. He's really the only thing I can draw from memory, probably from hours and hours of sitting in the living room with a pad of paper, pausing the VCR and sketching from the off-color screen. I could see my mother restraining herself, leaning in the doorway. Her long fingers crumpling her dress. She would be trying not to tell me to stop staring at the screen because she wanted me to keep drawing whatever I wanted, as long as I was drawing something. Anything. She would move the coffee table so I could prop my drawing board against it like an easel. Maybe it was her creative way of keeping me a reasonable distance from the TV. That videotape of *Sasoki* cartoons got played so much it wore out.

He's a simple character to draw. And even though my mother hated when I drew blood on his sword, I did it anyway. Red and dripping – that was the best part. I wonder if she still has

Two in one Grave

8

With sunburned nipples and lips as cracked as bark – wheezing in the heat, and hair wild with snotty grease – Khalil imagined them appearing half-crazed at the Ramadi border like escaped slaves. He and Sal would emerge out of the wiggly mirages fuming off blacktop. Legs gimped. One side of their bodies flash fried as red as rhubarb. It wouldn't matter. It wouldn't matter at all.

But they would have to get a little cleaned up.

Days in the desert whitewashed all traces of their city roots. Even though Khalil still had his black Adedas and black pants and black windbreaker, he knew they would be reduced to a vagabond's attempt at assimilation. His sneakers were dry-rotting off his feet. Pant hems wrinkled from rolling them under his knees. Once they had finally stepped into Ramadi, Khalil would dial Anmar's number and Anmar would have his friends along when they arrived. No doubt, each of them were experienced fighters appointed to honorable positions within the loose structure of the resistance.

Mud stained the side of Khalil's pants. Fifteen minutes of

scrubbing couldn't get it out. It didn't matter. He repeated to himself it didn't matter, but it really did.

Of course they looked insane. They'd escaped Fallujah. They'd traversed kilometers of soldier-filled desert. But Anmar would be honored to have his cousin, *famous* Khalil, seen on every television from Fallujah to Houston, as a guest.

It was dawn.

Dew glossed Khalil's arms and eyebrows. The morning was a cold fish across his face and neck and belly, and he knew he smelled worse than fishy in his reeking track pants.

Thinking he felt his cell phone vibrate, Khalil flipped the phone open just to check. He laid his cheek on the coarse wool blanket and couldn't close his eyes. He held the phone close to his face. Its glow illuminated his nostrils, his nostril hairs. He tried to see himself in the screen's shining plastic, but couldn't. Turning it off to save power, he rolled over and sat up, his back to the road, and read the long sentence of the river – right to left – no patrols or troops in sight.

Comatose, Sal curled into a tranquil ball. Khalil wanted to touch his hair, wake him, except sunrise was a dying bulb above the berm and Sal needed the sleep. He should sleep as long as he could. He wasn't looking good. All that stomach cramping and constant shitting.

Morning was already warm.

* * * * *

Khalil stood, safe in the dark. Tucking the folding knife and scope in his waistband, he went to the river, accessing the shore over a shelf of rock bypassing thickets and wiry shrubs. He scaled the rock, stripped naked, and slid into the water. Though the air was warm, his body shivered in the coolness. His teeth clicked like a stopwatch. He fought to sink past his crotch, stopping twice, and danced in place, arms flailing.

"Man!"

Shocked awake, his body began to acclimate.

He wrung his clothes. Standing waste-deep, he scrubbed and twisted them in the coolness. When his salt-stiffened pants, socks, shirt and underwear were properly soaked, he draped them over a bush. They would dry quickly. He knew they would still stink, but not nearly as bad now, and, once they reached Ramadi, they would have to be clean enough. From what he remembered, Anmar and his friends stunk anyway.

Khalil submerged and scratched his scalp underwater, freeing sand. He did the same to armpits and crotch and between his toes and he wished Sal had brought a bar of soap – surprised he hadn't – a bar of soap in its own bar-shaped case. The water felt great on his sore foot. He plunged it into the river's silt – felt like an unbaked cake.

Khalil swam out further.

He dove. His cupped hands scooped until he reached the bottom, scouring for a stone, something for Sal. He found only slicked algae and vegetation, and then he darted back toward the tinsel above.

His eyes adjusted. Chevrons of sun blasted the day. Billowing tarps lit red-orange overhead.

Relaxed, floating on his back, he watched dawn develop into morning. Bands of light broadcasted off the river. Minnows squirmed. Catfish kissed the surface for breakfast. A rusty *Seven Up* can bobbled in the willows, and Khalil doggie paddled to it, inspecting its aluminum reds and greens. He worked the pull-tab until it popped off. He threw the can to shore. He held the tab between his lips and swam.

* * * * *

When his clothes were nearly dry, he collected them, dressed, and returned to their simple camp with his plastic bag bloated with riverwater. Sal was awake. He lay calmly with his hands folded on his chest.

"Went for a swim?" Sal asked.

"Yeah. Washed my clothes. You should, too."

"Too dangerous," Sal said, sitting up, folding his sweatshirt that he used as a pillow, packing it away. "Trying to say I smell?"

"We both reek, man – "

"Yeah."

Khalil filled the cup from the bag and handed it to Sal. He drank a few sips and put it down.

"Still feel sick?"

"Sorta."

"You should drink as much as you can."

* * * * *

Through the barren valley between the river and the road, they marched a deviated line into the gravel. Their shuffling feet steered around jagged formations and mounds of unidentifiable steel – mangled chassis of Jeeps and a charred wing of something manmade and outdated. A rectangle grew on the horizon.

"A bus," Khalil said.

They stopped to stare and then moved closer. Long panels of chrome flashed. A marquee above the windshield gaped desti-nationless – no city or town spelled out. Abandoned and leaning crooked on the shoulder of the road, the bus sat empty, raided for anything that might be inside. There was no baggage or passenger to be seen. The storage lockers between the wheels hung open, but the vehicle was otherwise parked as normally as someone might park a bus. Metal strips shined against its baby blue paint and all but two windows were down. It was as if it were waiting for people to step on. Khalil took inventory with the scope, peering into each streaked window frame, then the wagging emergency door.

There was nothing to say about it so they said nothing.

The distance between the river and road grew. They kept closer to the road as rocks clustered, cutting off access to the water.

Undeterred, they continued their path northwest, the bitter terrain offering little shelter from the sun. Whatever shade they found was made from leaf-stripped branches, not the canopies which accompanied the riverside. Sal walked slower than usual. Khalil slowed too, hauling the bedding, keeping the corner of his eye on Sal. He wanted to offer him more water except he knew he wouldn't take it.

Finishing the last of the bread, they scraped their gums and sucked their teeth for every last morsel of grain, restraining from asking each other if they should open a can of beans. The folded pocket knife poked Khalil's stomach with each step. The scope chewed his hip.

They came upon another bus in the same condition – spotless and left to the elements. Closer, they saw two holes crowned by spider web cracks in the windshield. There was nothing to say about that either.

* * * * *

The second time Sal asked to stop in the shade, Khalil insisted, "Lemme take the backpack for a little bit."

Sal handed it over. They drank some water. Khalil took off his sneakers to air out his socks and noticed a blister on his smallest toe – this one on the foot that wasn't sore yet.

Just down the highway, a bullet-punched sign on the road read *Ramadi 8 Kilometers.*

* * * * *

Khalil felt he needed to know what time it was.

He wanted to know if his cell phone had a signal yet, but wasting his battery out of curiosity was stupid. He kept it turned off in his pocket. *Too far from town for a signal anyway,* he thought. If they reached the city limits and couldn't call Anmar, Sal wouldn't be happy. Khalil would have asked the time, but Sal hadn't spoken since the last break.

"Only eight kilos to go, man. We're good, we're good."

Sal only nodded.

"When we get to Ramadi, Anmar will have dinner for us – lamb and cauliflower and potatoes – we'll be treated like heroes," Khalil said, his arm over Sal's shoulder. He walked awkwardly so the rolled bedding wouldn't bump his friend. "We've survived and lived to tell the tale," he chuckled.

"Survived what?"

"The siege – the battle. Now we seek refuge," Khalil boasted, squeezing and shaking Sal with one arm. "Anmar's probably got a great house and if there isn't enough room for both of us, he'll know someone with a bed."

"We didn't even fight."

"Huh?"

Clearing his throat, Sal said, "We didn't fight in the battle. We ran."

"No one has to know that," Khalil said and punted a rock with his sneaker. "Whatever."

Passing several houses, they saw two residents fixing their roof. Asking for handouts would be a waste of time. They traveled onward, without stopping, heads wilting. Khalil dislodged another stone out of his sneaker. The plastic bag he used as a makeshift sole had worn too. He ditched it.

"Not far now," Khalil said, keeping his eyes on the dirt for a flat stone. He picked up three before he found the right one.

They rationed their water when the gnarly crags and plant life blocked easy access to the river. When Sal went silent for too long, Khalil sang an American song they had downloaded late that winter – but he could only remember a verse or two and gave up.

He said, "Tonight, we'll take baths and drink tea with lemon and sugar and we'll watch a movie. Anmar's got movies. He's probably got pirated DVDs and satellite TV, you know – the last time I called him he just bought a motorcycle and he said he was going to build a sidecar for it. He's a handy guy. Good mechanic."

Khalil's side was sore.

Taking out the pocket knife, he unfolded it, and holding the handle in his right hand, the flat stone in his left, he spit on the speckled surface. He ran the stainless blade over its back. Ten swipes on one side – he flipped – ten on the other, careful not to slice his hand when returning to the stone. The sound reminded him of skidding to a stop on his bike, pivoting with a heel to spin out in the gravel road. He took comfort in the rhythm.

Every fifty or so passes, Khalil'd consult the edge of the metal, checking for sharpness, finding it forever dull.

Within the hour, they stopped once and drank and Khalil refused to give up his duties of carrying their load. When the shoreline was accessible, they refilled every canister they had with water, paying little attention to the algae and moss along the shore. The bottoms of Khalil's feet soaked through. There was nothing he could do. He ran the blade as if he was buttering a petrified piece of toast and when he felt inclined, he grazed his arm hair with its razor edge – sharp to the tip – but continued sharpening to pass the time.

Sal was a quiet as a mosque.

He'd stopped wiping his forehead and scratching his beard. He just tucked his chin to his chest and fought the day.

"Should be there soon," Khalil said, eyes fixed ahead at the road. The asphalt spilled ahead of them like oil. The heat fuming off made it look ignitable. Khalil wanted to drop a match on it, strike a dancing fence of flames connecting two burning cities. Sharpening the knife, he kept to the tempo of their steps. If he kept it up, there would be no blade left – scrape, flip, scrape, flip – *just a handle in my hand* – scrape, flip.

"A few more kilometers, man, that's all. Maybe there's a football game on. Anmar might even have a Playstation, man. We haven't played that in a while. We can play that snowboarding game if he has it still. You always kick my ass, though."

Satisfied with the blade, he let the stone flap to the ground and flicked his thumb along the knife's sharp edge. He turned to look at Sal, but Sal was meters behind him. Leaning over, one hand cupping his knee, the other waving in the air, he was calling something.

Then he dropped.

"Oh," Khalil yelled. "Shit!" And ran to him. "Sal!"

Mouth slack, Sal wheezed, "I'm okay."

"No you're not, man."

"Yeah," he said and sat in the sand, forehead on his arm. "Headache. I have a crazy headache."

Khalil dropped the pack and knife, feeling Sal's dry fore-head, "You aren't even sweaty. You're dehydrated."

"Yeah," Sal kept repeating.

Holding the jar of water to Sal's lips, Khalil forced him to empty it and untied a plastic bag of water. "I'm going to dump this on your head, man."

He poured more water over his shoulders and down his shirt and told him not to move. He spread the sheet over Sal's body and Sal slumped woozy, sandaled feet sticking out. All Khalil could see of his face was a dripping beard. "Why haven't you been drinking enough?"

"I've been shitting it all out."

"Oh."

Sal groaned.

"Did you bring aspirin?"

"Why would I bring aspirin?" Sal asked, groaned again, and held his head with shaking hands. His ears were as hot as light bulbs.

Biting his thumbnail, Khalil looked at the river and looked at Sal then back at the river. It was too far to carry or drag him, too far to make him walk. Khalil would have to run.

"I'm going to get you more water, okay?"

"Yeah."

"It'd be better if you just came with me, take a swim."

"Can't," Salim shuddered.

"Can't move?"

"Yeah."

"Okay. Alright. Just stay right here."

Grabbing both plastic bags and the knife, Khalil sprinted. He didn't care if his blistered feet would mash into blood-pink hummus or if the stinging would last for the rest of the trip. The

185

sand was mostly soft. The shoreline bounced and grew and he sucked in the hot air, skirting mournful Joshua trees with twisted antlers clawing out of the earth, and when he skidded to the water, the gravel shattering, he clenched the knife in his teeth, panting, nose gargling snot. He filled one bag until it swelled. He looked back at Sal. He was still there, still melting. But when Khalil twisted the fat bag closed, it tore loose and all the water he had scooped splashed back into the river.

"Idiot!"

He filled and spun the other bag tight and started back, holding the squishy thing close to his chest. Sal seemed so far away – just a white lump in the sand.

Khalil tried to run as fast as before. He cradled the bag and trotted, nursing his injured foot. He wondered, once they reached the city, if Anmar had an old pair of shoes he could borrow. He wondered if they were name brand – real Adidas with no crusty rips in the rubber.

Watching Sal, watching the road, the water sloshed and bulged his fingers and he felt like both hands were pitchforks juggling a balloon.

His feet clomped the sand and the more he listened the more he heard weird grinding, a low clacking engine.

He slid to a stop, looking for something coming from Ramadi. Nothing. He scanned southeast to where the road bent backward. There, barely visible – a stout machine crept toward them. Enormous tires churned along its backside. Worms of dark smoke grew out of its tall exhaust pipe.

Squinting, blocking the sun with a flat palm, Khalil saw a cloaked rider sitting high behind its wheel. He rushed – nearly leaping – to Sal who turned his head to the machine instead of standing, as if willing to let the thing roll over him.

"Hold on, man!" Khalil yelled.

The bag was ready to rip, Khalil knew. His sneaker gulped sand through the worn sole, collecting a lopsided lump and his other foot throbbed every time he stomped.

Almost there, he thought, *almost there*.

Sal pointed at the machine, showing his friend. He had the scope leveled at it, not taking it off the thing as it ground closer.

"What is it? What – " Khalil panted, finally standing over him. Sal looked even weaker. Khalil knelt.

"A tractor, I think," Sal said, voice hoarse.

"Here. Don't talk," Khalil passed the water and took the scope. Sal poured a cup. Sipped. "You might want to pour some over your head, man. You look terrible."

"What're we gonna do?"

"Dunno," Khalil said, studying the thing. "It's a tractor alright. A farm tractor. There's one driver," he said, holding the scope steady with two hands, "a woman, maybe. No others."

"How do you know?"

"She's shrouded."

"It could be a shrouded man."

"Yeah," Khalil said. "Stay here. Don't talk."

"Huh?"

Khalil marched head-on.

Sal only protested with a meager wave, sitting there wheezing.

Jogging, Khalil drew an invisible barrier between the tractor and his friend. He unfolded his knife, holding it backwards and behind his thigh and took his time engaging, side stepping to get a better look. He tried the scope though he couldn't focus while he jogged.

It was still a minute away.

A billowing cape of orange dust followed the thing and the cape projected a tricky silhouette of the machine, blurring steel appendages and then obscuring the rider. When a thick cloud kicked up around the rear, the contraption became solid again. The rider, black and lanky, sharpened into view. Khalil almost anticipated an army to emerge from behind it – materializing out of the dust – though he knew the machine and its rider were alone. Its two rear wheels spun like windmills. Its long nose clanged with dull twin headlights over a grill composing a face that grimaced and choked.

An old machine, Khalil thought.

Wobbling, a front wheel leaned too far inward, but rolled confidently along as the rider pumped the gas, shooting oily exhaust upward. Smells of diesel brewed and burned. The vintage tractor sputtered closer. Khalil could see that no plow or scoop detracted from its speed, but it crept with its rider stooped attentively in her black *abaya*, only eyes and silence. She bounced in the bucket seat, gripping the wide wheel with one hand. She had no face or stated features. She held a pole, something Khalil mistook for another exhaust pipe at first – a long spear jutting up with a thin white flag flapping at its tip and a string of dangling bells.

Khalil backed down to a defensive stance.

She was on him.

The grill of the tractor was within reach. He should wave, he thought, offer a truce – if she pulled a rifle, he would dive, try to run around and under the tractor – somehow attack from behind. He knew it was ridiculous. Khalil wiggled his fingers around the knife's cedar handle, keeping it hidden, the blade's tip needling his forearm. The engine's clatter pinged louder, hissing. Break pads squealed. Khalil kept his chin high.

The rider halted and idled, unmoving.

She revved the engine, her other foot hard on the brake,

and the rattling machine bucked like a tied horse, pissing smoke with every pump of the accelerator. Parked a meter in front of Khalil, she patiently lowered the spear, drawing it down, and fixed its sharpened point chest-level, square between his nipples. She said nothing. The end of the spear tucked under her armpit, she kept her elbow out and hand steady. She revved the engine and the engine shuttered and rumbled the tractor's loose frame.

The spear leaped forward and stopped.

Brakes ached and moaned.

The tip of the spear hovered a finger-length from Khalil's chest. The rider revved the engine louder.

Khalil stood his ground, looking the rider in the eye, and he knew he was a break release away from impalement. The heavy spear dipped and lifted and scribbled its threats on the paper of his chest. She couldn't hold it straight for long.

Khalil held his arms out and dangled the knife, pinched in his fingers, before dropping it to the ground. She revved the accelerator lighter, making the machine grumble. She tilted her head. On the tip of the spear, the brass bells jingled and the narrow white flag snapped in the wind. She sat straight and stoic like a mounted knight and waited.

"*Alsalamu Alaykom*! We're walking to Ramadi!" Khalil shouted over the rumbling.

The rider moved her head a little.

"From Fallujah!" he added.

She didn't move at all except her foot on the gas, lightly pulsing the engine. Khalil inspected the spear for blood, but it and the attached flag were both clean. Khalil swallowed hard.

"To find the Internet! My friend is in love with a girl on the Internet!"

Somehow he though that might help the situation.

She seemed to be taking it all in.

The rider took her hand off the wheel. The engine sputtered and choked and stopped dead. The grateful machine hissed in thanks. She raised the spear as slowly as she had lowered it, then planted it in a makeshift holster fashioned to the tractor – bells twinkling in the sunlight – and that was the only sound but the pinging from the engine. The rider leaned on the steering wheel. She rested both arms and pulled out a bottle of water, lifting her *abaya* enough to drink, and then set the bottle down on the tractor's long hood. Condensation rolled along its ridged plastic and sizzled on the rusted metal. Cascading lines evaporated.

She tapped the cap of the bottle with her finger.

Khalil went to cross his arms, but cocked his elbows instead and turned back and forth to stretch his spine. Look casual, he thought. Pointing back at Sal, he said, "My friend's sick. I think he has sunstroke. He needs water."

She tapped the water bottle cap like it was a button for something.

"Tell me why I shouldn't shoot you right here?" Her voice was worn, thick as suede.

"You have a gun?"

The rider lifted a silver pistol from her lap and waved it in the air, then set it next to the bottle.

"We're not *Fedayeen*. We're escaping," Khalil explained, his hands in the air.

Nodding, the rider leaned close, her lashes curled long and thick. She lifted her chin and said coldly, "You're the man from the photo in the news."

Khalil sighed. He laced his fingers behind his head and kicked at the sand. He couldn't deny it. "You're right. I was there."

She lingered, staring.

"So *you're* responsible for all this."

Khalil couldn't tell if she was joking.

"*Khala*, please," he defended, "I was only there, I promise you, that's all."

The rider glanced over her shoulder at something above the horizon. Khalil followed her eyes, but he saw nothing. There was nothing. She took her time returning to him.

She restarted the tractor and put it in gear, retrieving the pistol and water. She sipped from the bottle before rolling forward. Khalil stepped out of the way. "Lemme tell you, just listen for a minute!" he called up to her, jogging alongside. "I was out buying sodas for my sisters that day! I'm always buying them soda! Their teeth are going to rot out of their heads if they keep drinking it! It was hot and I opened a can of soda and gunfire started and I dropped the can. There was shouting and everyone was running to the bridge! I didn't know why!"

The rider didn't look down or acknowledge him. Her bells rang quietly and her flag was a long white fingernail above her black covered skull. A tear in her *abaya* ran down her back, exposing deep red cloth underneath. It looked as if she'd once had wings and the wings had been removed by some clumsy surgeon.

"So I ran over! At first I couldn't tell what was going on and people were going crazy! It was crazy! Yelling and shooting and pulling! Taking photos! Hundreds of photos and they happened to use the one of me! *Khala*! You have to believe me."

An ice chest rattled, tethered to the tractor's rear, clinking bottles and cans inside. An oil lamp swung, its handle looped inside the securing ropes. Khalil wondered what wonderful meats and cheeses and fruit might be under the dented metal lid – freshly cooked chicken or even goat might be wrapped in cloth and packed in ice. Steady drips tearing from the lowest corner of the case painted his imagination with wildly delicious visions.

"*Khala*, please, my friend might be dying!"

He wondered if she was crazy. He considered jumping on the tractor and stabbing her throat. *That'd be insane*, he thought. And Sal would be pissed. He knew he shouldn't think like that.

The rider rolled onward. She came upon Sal standing in the white sheet like a ragged Sheik. He put his hands up in a strange and pathetic surrender. She steered around him – stopped the engine.

She leaned down.

"And you're the cameraman? Huh?"

Sal looked blankly at her and spoke in the clearest Arabic he could muster. "Sorry?"

"Your friend, the media star. You the photographer?"

"Oh."

She shook her head and tossed Sal her bottle of water, just short of his reach.

"No," he struggled to say, reaching for the bottle. "We're headed to Ramadi."

"Joining the resistance in Ramadi?" she pressed.

Khalil didn't interrupt.

"*Escaping*," Sal said sternly, "I have to contact someone in Syria – we have no way to do it in Fallujah. Not now."

"So what is it then?" the rider pried.

"Sorry?"

"Are you escaping or are you communicating?"

Sal looked at Khalil and Khalil at Sal and neither answered her until she dismounted the tractor with the pistol tucked in her *abaya*. She swooped around to the ice chest and unhooked the bungee cords hugging it.

"We just need to send a message to someone," Khalil said.

The rider waved him off.

"Other fighters, I'm sure," she said.

Sal gulped the fresh water and joined them behind the tractor. "We're not fighters – we've been walking for days."

"And now I'm willing to wager," she said, handing Khalil a gallon of cold water, "you'd like a ride."

Sal spoke before Khalil ruined the proposition. "You've already been too generous, we wouldn't want to add to whatever burden you already bear."

The rider slammed the chest shut and stepped to him.

"And what burdens could *you* possibly compound onto *my* sorrow?" she hissed, gripping the tractor's great tire with one hand, the finger of her other aimed at his face. Sal back-stepped. "I've tolerated cruelties beyond the creativity of *Allah* and I've been *un-mothered* – and I will *un-mother* anyone who speaks of it. Understand?" She shoved his shoulder, knocking the bottle down. "*Do you understand that?*"

"Sorry," Sal cowered. "I'm sorry. I meant no offense."

Her pointed finger was an arrow ready to pierce his eye. She stepped again.

"We can just go, we're okay. We're okay," Khalil said, stepping back, too, giving the gallon to Sal. "No offense."

The rider grunted and secured the ice chest after taking out a hunk of cheese for herself. She mounted the tractor. Khalil and Sal returned to their belongings like scolded children – Sal sipping from the water, sloshing some on his neck and beard. Khalil did the same and they waited for the tractor's ignition, the jerky sputter and gear engaging.

Sal whispered, "That cheese looked good, man."

Khalil nodded, gave a vigorous grin. The rider sat in her tall seat – a black stencil cut out of the horizon. She called to them,

"Give me your blankets and that knife, then you can ride."

Sal grinned. Khalil shook Sal's shoulders with both hands, nearly hugging him.

In minutes, they were sitting backwards on the tractor's warped bumper, asses tenderized with each rigid bounce.

For the wool blanket, the sheet and folding knife, the rider agreed to take them as far as the city limits, but for caution's sake, as Khalil might be recognized by troops or unsympathetic rebels, the two would have to hop off and walk into town before they reached the border. This was fine. It was a *khosh* deal. They wouldn't need the bedding once they reached Ramadi anyway.

Acknowledging Sal's condition, the rider let him wear the sheet, but the blanket and knife were stowed in a suitcase also strapped to the tractor. Two gas canisters sandwiched it, keeping the broken lid from spilling open, and a paisley scarf tied around the handle piqued Khalil's curiosity. He saw a passport and family photos and folded clothes before the rider snapped the case shut. He knew not to ask.

They rode the jittering lummox. Cautious, the rider swerved around obstacles and suspicious mounds that could have been landmines, except they were just dark scabs of rock. The engine cleared its throat and choked, but kept firing steadfast. High on the spear, the truce flag snapped on the wind.

They passed little houses and then a big house with two satellite dishes. They saw kites circling like frenzied moths. Three children flying them.

Khalil put his arm around Sal, and Sal leaned into his friend.

When they least expected it, the rider pulled back her *aba-ya* and let her thick black hair flutter. She shook her head and scratched her scalp, made sure the backings of each earring were clasped, and she blew her nose in a cloth stashed below the tractor's console. Then she hid herself again, tucking and folding fabric while her knees steered the tractor's vibrating wheel.

The tractor slowed over the loose sand. The rider turned straight west, away from the road, taking her time and a safer route.

Khalil yanked off his Adedas and hung his socks to air out, dangling both feet above the scrolling earth. He felt bad for any animal or man unfortunate enough to inhale their putrid funk. He imagined river snakes and bison, gazelles and geese, asphyxiating wherever tractor treads hoed the sand – hordes of choking lizards scurrying to escape the smoke wafting off his toes. Sal took off his sandals and their four heels swayed unsynchronized. They both passed a hunk of goat cheese, torn off from the rider's share, back and forth. Khalil and Sal nibbled like grateful mice, using the sheet to keep sand off their food. Their eyes spiraled at the tangy galaxies found in even the thinnest residue smeared on their fingers, and they licked each digit in triplicate, stripping them clean, and even nipped at knuckles and nails.

Not walking made the cheese taste better. Cheese made the water taste better. And the ample chugs of cool water seeped into their skin, creating a shield between them and the unbearable sun. Everything was much better.

"How you feeling?" Khalil asked.

"Better, man. Better."

Under one of the back fenders where oxidized psoriasis crusted orange-red, a cobweb stretched just millimeters from the tire. It flexed, ready to snap. Wispy silk stretched in the arc of road bumps – expanding, contracting – before settling back. No flies or snared insects struggled in its tangle, and no fanged attendant waited for them to snag. The web went unnoticed until, detached by a ricocheting rock, it collapsed.

All three heard the ping of the rock, but only Khalil saw the silky strands waving from the fender.

Sal leaned back and drank.

* * * * *

Dusk descended. Suggestions of copper and burned polymer pricked their noses. Twilight filters slipped sepia over their tired eyes. Sal took off the sheet and held its corners, letting it whip the air, and he handed Khalil one corner. They both wanted to let it go.

From her high vantage, the rider stood, saw Ramadi's sparse flickering, and turned straight west, crossing over the road with a thump.

"What's she doing?" Khalil asked.

"Probably knows a safer route."

"My ass hurts."

"Mine too."

Khalil opened his cell phone and turned it on, waiting for the neon screen to brighten. Sand crusted in its hinge. He cleared the dust off with the hem of his shirt, tapping the cheap plastic against his palm. He scrolled backwards through his contacts to Anmar because Anmar was listed alphabetically and he had nothing else to do.

"No reception yet."

"You think he's —" Sal paused, scratching his beard, "he's okay?"

"Yeah, man," Khalil assured. "If anyone's okay, it's Anmar." He turned off his phone. He rubbed his hand over his forehead and cheeks. "Do I have any zits?"

"Huh?

"On my face. Do I have any zits?"

Sal squinted, surveying his friend's oily face, his hairline, where floppy black bangs hid his brow and hovered above his sharp and sunburned nose. "You're scraggly, but no pimples."

"Good, good," Khalil mumbled, rubbing a finger over his teeth, scrubbing plaque, chiseling with his thumbnail.

Small-arms fire of different calibers cracked in the distance – American rifles, then others, then American again – two groups reciprocating shots. The rider ducked and slowly rose, trying to see. She held a hand out to them to keep seated, but they didn't notice.

Khalil asked, "Can we trade shirts when we get to the city?"

"Why? You have to be in all black?" Sal asked.

"I wanna look good, man."

"Yeah. Okay."

* * * * *

Under the cover of a grain field, they approached another farmhouse where empty fences secured parked tractors and a few date trees and a dog, chained, rolling on its back – happy to see its owner. It flipped and kicked. It made no fuss except submissive whines. It crouched with its belly flat on the ground, its front paws paired at the perimeter of a circle worn in the dirt. Parking behind the house, the rider dismounted and pointed at the city, not looking at Sal or Khalil. She untied her suitcase. She popped the lid of the cooler, but left it there, open. She took the bedding and suitcase before walking up a footpath to the farmhouse.

Someone clanged pots together from inside.

The rider never looked back. She disappeared into the candlelit dwelling. Greeting her and taking her luggage, an elderly man shuffled through the fickle glow, eyeing Sal and Khalil briefly before shutting the door. The dog whined with its nose between its paws.

"You think she'll mind if we take some more water?" Khalil asked, nodding at the ice chest.

"I'm not going to stop you."

"She left it open for us right?"

"Sure."

Thick clouds snuffed any starlight there might have been.

They gathered what they hadn't bartered for the ride: another jug, and, along with a hunk of cheese, they collected a few stray grapes hiding at the bottom of the box. Khalil pulled off his shirt first, swapping it with Sal's, and slipped on his windbreaker. In the bashful moonlight he was a walking shadow with a gait more confident than before. He straightened his hair with his fingers and went back to cleaning his teeth.

"Let's go," he said.

A scythe sat orphaned at the edge of the property. Khalil wanted to steal it, but let it be.

Through partitions of hearty grass, Khalil led Sal as if he had used this path hundreds of times, brushing away weeds as high as corn stalks until they came upon open range. An unguarded field stretched between the desert and Ramadi – urban buildings lined that boundary where no towers or checkpoints could be seen – only random streetlamps and a tiny string of decorative lights dotting a veranda. The road faded off to the north. Headlights appeared like low-lying comets as vehicles turned toward and away. The night was peaceful except the random snap of riflefire.

Sal shook with fatigue, hiding his hands in his sweatshirt.

"We're lucky," Khalil whispered.

"Why?"

"Anmar lives around here – if he hasn't moved."

"You think he has? You think he's moved?"

"Naw. He likes his house."

"How old is he?"

"Older than us."

"How old?"

"Twenty five," Khalil said. "Not much."

* * * * *

Street lights never looked so welcoming.

They dashed low through the field toward the city. Khalil shooed horseflies swarming in the brush. Stopping every few meters, they scrutinized roof ledges for snipers and moved on. Bypassing a flattened building – a corner of which still stood – they scrimmaged over pummeled walls spilling into streets like clumped porridge. Office chairs and a photocopier mixed into the powered wreckage. Toppled reams of copy paper sprayed with every wind gust. What was once a carpeted lobby was now an open lawn.

Khalil led Sal past the rubble.

Fire-damaged cars lined the block.

Across the street sat apartment houses and the cars parked there were intact – a newly washed van and three sedans, a truck, a motorcycle – as if this block wasn't part of the same neighborhood. They could see where someone swept the street free of debris. Dunes of concrete crowded the sidewalk.

Khalil skipped ahead to peer around corners.

"Do you see any patrols?" Sal asked.

"Only people."

Chatter echoed above them.

Three men on a veranda gawked at a television too large for the card table supporting it. A girl brought them each a saucer with hot tea. They thanked her. Below them, a boy did pull-ups on a pole fashioned between two rafters. He dropped and another boy took his place. A younger voice counted off – *1,2,3,4.*

Dinner smells permeated the air – spiced vegetables and buttered loaves, stewed meats slow-cooked and stripped of their bones.

"Man," Khalil said, sniffing loudly.

Their stomachs tightened like prunes.

Simple ochre hovels lined the streets tethered by power lines and cables crisscrossing. Hundreds and hundreds of strung cable. Electric wire held canvas canopies like pillowcases. Iraqi flags hung from doorsteps, windows, ledges, rooftop decks, any pole available – red and green and white swishing.

They stopped. Hundreds of flags circled them.

"We're here man! We did it!" Khalil cheered, grabbing Sal's backpack with both hands and shaking him. "This is amazing, man!"

"I can't believe we actually made it," Sal said.

"Yeah! Wait till you meet Anmar. He's a *khosh* guy, man. You might not want to leave Ramadi." Khalil did a little jig in the sand, shimmying his shoulders, gyrating his hips.

"Stop that," Sal said.

"Whatever. C'mon."

Down the block, a playground flanked an empty school-yard. Khalil led them past monkey bars and spiraling slides to a carousel where he sat and dialed Anmar. Sal got on the carousel and pushed off, sending them in a circle, pedaling his foot.

A fire in the distance produced a thick cone of smoke. A gas station sabotaged by rebels or coalition misfire. The incandescent point of the cone flashed sulfur-white, and with every rotation of the carousel, they saw it obscuring and refocusing – the oily plumes smoothing out detail then dispersing. Khalil lay on the cold painted metal and pressed one ear to it, listening to the squeaking axel and the grumbling steel. The phone rang and rang. Sitting up so Sal could hear, he left a message,

"Anmar. It's your cousin Khalil. Uh, I'm in town, man. Me and Sal – give me a call. On my cell. Yeah. Okay. Okay, later."

He looked up at Sal.

"That's it?" Sal asked.

"I guess. He'll call back. He never answers."

"You have enough battery power?"

Khalil flipped open his phone. "Yeah."

"I'm going to have to charge my laptop."

"Okay."

* * * * *

Spinning, they watched the fire burn silently. They swung their legs and waited for the phone to buzz and blink. A few kids came and sat on the monkey bars. but only climbed and lounged, smoking cigarettes and laughing. Two sat on bikes, afraid to leave them unattended. One of them kept burping. Another mooned Khalil and Sal, and they all ran toward the apartments except for the kids with bikes who wanted to ride the playground. Everyone laughed.

"How do you feel?" Khalil asked.

"I haven't been mooned in years. I feel great."

Pedaling madly, the two bikers took turns breaking, skidding out, trying to top one another. The older of the two sped to a stop and sprayed a fan of gravel over a seesaw. Pinging stones chimed like a hundred dinging bells. They both looked to Sal and Khalil for approval.

"Remember that time you wiped out on your bike when you were staring at that girl?" Sal snickered.

Khalil's phone vibrated on the carousel's metal floor.

He fumbled opening it, "Hello?"

Anmar yelled at someone on his end and then yelled hello.

"Hello? Anmar? Yes!" Khalil yelled back.

Sal leaned in to listen but could only hear shouting over the line. Then chuckling.

"Okay," Khalil said, "Yeah, we're here. Where are you? Okay. Okay. Now?"

"What?" Sal asked, eager to know what was going on. Music and shouting and hooting. The kids on the bikes raced away.

Khalil laughed, "No, my sisters aren't with me man, you're a dick face. I said a *dick face! A face made out of dicks!* Okay. You too. Yeah. *I know.*" He made mouth flapping gestures at Sal with his hand. "Okay, okay. I know where."

"Ask about the *Internet*," Sal said.

"Yeah? No!" Khalil jested, laughing harder. "*Iché!* You're lying. Shut up, man. Okay."

"What is it?" Sal pressed.

Khalil waved him off, "Alright, see you in a few minutes."

He hung up the phone and turned it off.

"What's so funny?"

"Those guys are seriously damaged, man. Retarded."

"Oh."

* * * * *

They hurried through the hushed commercial district on the south end where shops had just closed – an audio store specializing in microphones and megaphones, corner markets with colorful awnings, an instrument seller with empty display windows, its sign covered by a tarp, a photo mart in the same condition, barbers, variety stores, butcher shops, auto part depots – all locked except one late night café crammed with men.

Khalil felt comfortable here. He'd visited often as a child. He had family everywhere. Cousins across Iraq. In every Sunni tribe, it seemed. And he knew that Sal would trust him as they walked through the small town.

A salesman slept in an armchair on the curbside. A book lay, pages-down, in his lap. His shop was lit by a single bulb dangling from the ceiling. They walked between rows of bed frames and mismatched living room sets, stray ottomans, amber-stained end tables paired with corduroy lounge chairs, dining room tables accompanied by three and five chairs. One piece always seemed missing.

Sprawling tenements, no more than three stories high, overran the market. Khalil ushered Sal down a well-lit main street with bland apartment buildings stamped out as if from muddy molds, each with a simple balcony enclosed by ironwork. More flags waved from railings, everywhere.

Pop shots echoed off brick walls and building tops – just someone disturbing the night – but it was otherwise peaceful.

"It's around here," Khalil said.

"You sure?" Sal's voice seeped.

Armed squads made their presence known.

Mujahideen strapped with bullet belts and shoulder bags, cradling Kalashnikovs with banana clips doubled together with tape, roamed the roads and cruised in white pickups. They left Sal and Khalil alone. They drove slowly through alleys, backing out for men to peek from the safety of sandbag-lined truck beds with barrels leaning steadily.

"Don't worry."

"I'm not," Sal said.

Someone prayed. A woman. Her window was cracked and from it they heard her repeating verses familiar and comforting. They didn't linger.

A young man hurried past, heaving, out of breath, holding a plastic tarp in his arms. Something sloshed inside. Another man tripped at his heels.

"It's dripping. It's dripping!" he yelled, running a body length behind with a gas canister in each hand. "Hurry!"

"What the hell?" Sal asked.

"Weird," Khalil said, "Maybe someone is hurt."

Their racing steps diminished down the street until Salim and Khalil heard a door whip open and slam. Cheering erupted from inside. Then arguing and more cheering and one of the men laughed louder and longer than the rest.

"What was that all about?" Sal said.

"*Or* not," Khalil said.

Following the drips, they came upon a smaller tenement with a single purple door facing the street. Two men on the rooftop peered down, head scarves tangled around their skulls. One coughed. Their cigarettes made them into two cyclopes, each with a single glowing eye. One of them leveled a rifle.

Khalil looked for an address.

The building was a tired box. Water stains spread from the roof like liver spots. Beginnings of graffiti blotted the brick as if their writers ran out of paint or forgot what they meant to say. Like stretched accordions, sliding metal shutters covered a storefront on the bottom floor. Both were padlocked and dented from forced entry. Several dusty motorcycles, most of them outfitted for off-roading, leaned in a neat row with mirrors cracked and fenders missing, padding picked and pulled out of ripped seats. Khalil recognized one as his cousin's. It was the most well-maintained of the group.

The cyclopes on the rooftop glared.

More cheers shot out of a second story window.

"I think this is where those two guys went," Sal said.

"This is it. Anmar's place."

"You sure?"

"Stop asking that."

Khalil rang the buzzer.

No response.

The cyclopes tapped their triggers.

Khalil rang again, leaning longer, the buzzer zapping their ears like the school bells. Sal closed his eyes, and when he opened them the men on the roof were gone. Their smoke plumes proved they were sitting close by, listening. In each slot on the intercom's box, names were crossed out or removed and streaks of bubble gum were pulled across the slots like gooey pink tendons. Khalil wanted to touch them. A head appeared from the same window where the laughing had cackled, and it quickly ducked back in.

"Was that Anmar? You sure this is it?" Sal asked, tugging a beard hair with pinched fingers.

"Of course. I've been here before. I think."

They heard stomping on the staircase behind the door, reverberating loose hinges and screws. The door cracked open with exaggerated caution. The man pulling it appeared. Smiled wildly. Another face stacked its chin on the first man's scalp, wearing old aviator sunglasses and a wooden match in its mouth.

He smiled even wider. His teeth were yellow kernels.

"*Khalil*," the bottom face said.

"*Anmar*," Khalil grinned.

The top face cackled, letting his match flip out of his mouth, "Yeah!" And he blasted open the door.

Anmar stepped out and gripped his cousin's shoulders with fingerless gloves before drawing him close, hugging tough, slapping his back. They kissed each other on each cheek and then pulled away, palms on shoulders again and hugged and slapped backs and cheered. "Cousin! Cousin!"

"No sisters?" Anmar asked. "I thought you were just kidding on the phone."

"Man, my oldest sister is fifteen, man. C'mon."

"And she is my *cousin!*" Anmar roared.

For some reason everyone laughed, Sal the hardest, laughing and looking to see when to stop. Anmar pinched and twisted the skin at the tip of Khalil's elbow like he'd done to Sal days before and Khalil swatted him away, laughing, too.

"I'm sorry, I'm sorry. I'm being rude." Anmar sighed and said, "This is Hassan," who was leaning against the wall with a pint glass of iced tea. Hassan grinned, his smile so wide his cheeks might have been slashed. He postured behind his streaked sunglasses. He hooked his thumb in the strap of a rifle behind his back, pointed downward. It was an American rifle, Sal and Khalil both knew. Taking a lemon slice out of his drink, he sucked it down to the rind and said nothing.

"We were just saying. Hassan's a *compassionate conservative*," Anmar clarified.

"This is true," Hassan confirmed, exhaling through his nose and pinching the toothpick in his front teeth. "Very." He spit the lemon skin onto the sidewalk.

"*Compassionate*," Anmar doubled.

"I have," Khalil paused, "no idea what that means."

"Neither do *I*," Anmar said, jiggling his shoulders and laughing again, getting everyone else to laugh. "Salim Abid?"

"Ah, yeah," Sal said. "Hey."

"You guys," he said plainly, shaking Sal's hand, glancing left and then right, "look like *shit*."

"Yeah, could use a shower," was all Sal could say.

Hassan roared. The ice in his glass bucked and clinked. Anmar roared too.

"We've got a Jacuzzi in the back, man. A sauna too. Very nice," Hassan joked as he tapped his fingers on the rifle's long magazine, jingling its staggered bullets.

"And a lap pool if you guys really need a good workout. It's the best exercise in the world. I do about fifty, maybe sixty laps a day," Anmar lied, flexing his arms and looking down at invisible muscles.

"Yeah, yeah," Khalil drank from the water jug and gave it to Sal. "Maybe we'll take a *swim*."

Hassan rolled the match to the corner of his mouth and managed to drink. When he lowered the glass it clinked again and everyone stared at it, like his cup was filled with uncut diamonds. He kept one of the diamonds in his mouth, chewed it to slush.

"Anyway," Anmar said, reopening the door, "we've got something important to do. Need your help. C'mon up."

"He stays here," Hassan said, staring at Sal.

Everyone froze.

"Yeah. You're right," Anmar agreed. "Salim's gotta stay outside. Won't be too long."

They exchanged expressions – Sal of concern, Khalil of reassurance, and Khalil said, "It's cool. Sal, just wait here."

"Okay."

"Yeah?"

"I'll be fine."

And they left Sal in the street.

The men on the rooftop never looked back down again.

* * * * *

Cavernous stairs led to a landing where a man sat on the top stair, a white ski mask pulled up over his nose. He drank iced tea too, from a pitcher with a long straw, and stared at Khalil with eyes as wet and black as leeches. His flackjacket squished his thick frame. One side was duct taped shut. Karabiners clipped to his chest held prayer beads and a braided lock of brown hair. A Kalashnikov lay next to him on the landing. He moved it out of their way.

Anmar pretended to ruffle the man's hair that wasn't there, his fingers wading over the white ski mask.

Children's toys scattered about the concrete landing – a few foot-pedaled cars, one the shape of a red crayon, kickballs, a ninja turtle with no arms, a plastic sword, dolls and more dolls contorted into headstands, and dolls sitting serenely on the upper steps with their hair combed and their dresses straightened. On the second landing, Khalil knocked over a broom and stood it back up. Its handle pointed at a spray-painted saber dripping pink down the concrete wall. He assumed it was by the same writers who did the outside graffiti.

"Sorry we can't let Salim up here. It's not that we don't trust you, y'know," Anmar assured.

"Yeah, man," Khalil said. "I know."

"We trust *you* – means we trust him. Just not yet."

Hassan stopped to listen, shaking his head as laughter flushed the stairwell from above. Every time he stepped up, his rifle swiveled, aiming at Khalil's eye socket, his stomach, his shins, dead square at the top of his head, and though it was unintentional, Khalil felt it might fire at any minute.

There must be a whole group upstairs, he thought.

Khalil recognized the voices upstairs from the people cheering out the window – someone beatboxing badly, the others cackling between his spits. Hassan followed closely, clicking the *select fire* switch on his rifle back and forth like a ticking clock.

Anmar opened the only door at the top of the stairs to an open room where young men stood with glasses and big plastic cups of iced tea. The two guys from the street who had run past him sat on a folding table, the gas canisters one had been carrying tucked under the table. Still beatboxing, the guy in the center of the room balled his fist up to his mouth like a microphone and vibrated his lips, his other hand paddling the air.

"Awe *shit*," one of them belted.

"Ladies! Ladies!" Anmar announced, "*Iche*! This is my cousin, Khalil Hammadi!"

"Hey," most of them said.

Anmar chuckled, "He walked – *walked* – all the way from Fallujah."

Everyone nodded. Khalil waited for them to say something – about the photo, about the bridge.

"Yeah shit," the one sitting over the gas canisters said.

"*Yeah* shit," Anmar seconded, "someone give this man an *iced tea*."

The beatboxer two-stepped over to the table, shoveled ice into a large glass, and poured tea the color of cedar, adding two slices of lemon along the rim. "Sugar?" he asked.

"No, no, that's perfect." Khalil took the glass, drank half. Icy coldness streamed down his throat. He had never felt anything so good. Everyone in the room, even if they had never walked three days straight, knew his relief. They smiled and sipped. "Amazing. Where did you guys get ice?"

"Addel and Abbas traded two gallons of gas for it," Anmar said, pointing at the two men sitting on the table. "And this time, *this time,* they brought back the *canisters.*" He shot the two a wide-eyed bucktoothed face. "Get off the damn table! I've told you, you're gonna break it!" Everyone but Addel and Abbas cackled as they put their heads down, shuffling onto the floor.

Refilling his glass, Anmar asked, "You hungry man? We've got all this stuff from the soldiers."

Anmar went to a table and opened a fresh snack bag of Cool Ranch Doritos and handed them to Khalil. "Have you had these before, man? They're *amazing.*"

"No," he said, lifting one to the light, the flaky tortilla glistened greasy with flecked seasoning. "Never."

"We've got Fruit Loops, too, but they kinda suck," Addel said, giving him a single-serving box which was already open. Khalil emptied a few in his hand, studying the little pastel rings of coral. "Try 'em," Addel urged, on the edge of smiling.

He did – deciding if they sucked or not.

Anmar pulled Hassan and two others to the side by a column of rice bags and whispered, explaining something Khalil couldn't hear. One of the men argued quietly as Anmar held out his calm hands. The man shook his head and eyed Khalil before Anmar pulled them out to the hallway.

They must be talking about me, the photo, Khalil thought, and licked his fingers. He finished the bag of chips and grabbed some Doritos for Sal. He tried another Fruit Loop and liked it, but only ate one more and put the box down next to the jug of tea, asking, "Do you guys have the Internet here?"

"Naw," answered the third guy, "I haven't checked my email

for weeks."

"Oh."

"Or my profile."

Abbas chuckled.

"Am I the only guy on this planet without a profile?" Khalil asked.

"Probably," the guy said. "We're a free country now, man. You gotta take advantage of that."

"Yeah."

Where there weren't stacks of provisions, bare walls stared back at Khalil. Looking for a clipping of his picture from the papers, he wondered why no posters or portraits were hung. *Just a storage room*, he thought, looking for a recent newspaper, *and maybe my hair's too long, they can't recognize me. Or it's the fatigue. I probably look like an entirely different person, and Anmar didn't want to brag about his cousin. He's just being modest.*

He considered making the same expression as in the photo, mouth open, teeth showing, but that was too much – too obvious.

He waited.

Cast iron skillets hung next to a microwave and tabletop range where UNICEF boxes made a little tower. A butter knife stuck out of the side of the highest box. Dueling gunfire cracked outside and the snaps rattled the single window. A whistle followed, then a muted concussion. The window shook harder.

They tried to show no sign of notice.

Abbas got up and paced the room. He swept a row of rifles lined barrel-up along the outside wall, sticking his fingertip in each muzzle. He wore Adedas, black Sambas, laces whipping untied. They were the same off-brand and style Khalil was loyal to except his pair were spotless, straight out of the box. Their white saw-toothed stripes could not have been whiter; their leather sides shined like new plastic, and felt details wrapped the toes without a blemish. Khalil could tell he had never worn them outdoors. Not once.

After his walk around the room, Abbas leaned against the wall, stared out into the street. He placed his palm on the window, expecting it to vibrate again, but it never did.

Khalil sat himself on the shorter of the two stacked bags of rice, but they weren't rice bags now. They'd almost become fluffy cushions that could build the most comfortable bed. Next to them, a sack of beans could easily become a squishy pillow, one that he wanted to sink his face into. He nodded, nearly dozing. He gulped down the last of his tea so he could abandon the glass in case he nodded again, but the Internet profile guy refilled it.

Sal would have loved some tea, Khalil thought.

Murmurs from the hallway made him wonder what private things Anmar had to say. Addel drummed on the table loud enough to drown out their conversation.

And then Anmar came back. He whispered, "Khalil. Come here."

In the hallway, the two other men stood with crooked posture on the landing, talking, and Hassan – his lenses reflecting the staircase, concealing his eyes – sat on the metal banister, rocking back and forth, both knobby knees racking his rifle.

"You think Sal's okay out there?" Khalil yawned, thinking it would make him seem unconcerned.

"He's fine, man, fine," Anmar assured. "Check it out. We've got a really important thing to do. A mission."

"Okay."

"Which, like, we can't really let you in on," he explained, pinching his square chin in thought, "It's –"

"Sensitive," Hassan finished, hopping up and strolling

around his friends. "Sen-*si*-tive."

"Yeah," Anmar agreed, "it is. But we need you to do something for us."

"Okay, cousin. Anything," Khalil said.

"We can count on you, right?"

"Of course. Yeah."

Anmar nodded. "I know. I know."

Hassan walked and cracked his neck. He slung his rifle over his shoulders with both arms hooked like a scarecrow hanging on a pole and flicked the match in his mouth up and down like a light switch. He could clear the landing in two wide steps with his giant legs.

Slinging the rifle once more, Hassan slid a thin plastic comb from his back pocket and raked the teeth of the comb across the banister as if he were sawing it in half. Prongs twanged an eerie song. Flakes of paint snowed.

The heavy man on the landing whistled a tune, too.

Then he stopped.

* * * * *

Khalil carried the small bag of Doritos. He wondered if Sal would like them.

Anmar and Hassan led him downstairs, passing the man on the landing and front door, to the back of the building where a dim hallway joined the adjacent tenement. The hallway felt more like a tunnel as it cooled. Gradually absent of light, it ended with a sharp left to an open room. Like the space upstairs, it was decorated with rugs and a single reading lamp in the center of the floor. Whoever had last left put an orange *keffiyeh* over its shade, an attempt to let the lamp's glow somehow warm the walls and low ceiling. The smell of mildew ruined any cozy illusions. A table was pushed against the wall with a radio and a few empty cups. Tires formed a black pillar in the corner.

Anmar asked Hassan to get a rifle from upstairs. He said they would be leaving in a minute. "Bring everyone down, too."

Then Anmar sat at a table with two folding chairs, and Khalil sat next to him. Khalil put the bag of Doritos on the table and ran the tip of his finger over the rippled seal at the top of the package. Its edge had the same saw tooth as the stripes on his Adedas.

Anmar waited until Hassan was far from earshot. He tightened his lips into a smile.

"It's good to see you, Khalil."

"Yeah. It's been like, forever, man."

"*I* trust you Khalil," he assured, looking down at the rug, "It's just them, you know."

"It's okay," Khalil smiled. "I understand."

"I've always trusted you."

"We're family."

"Exactly." Anmar checked his watch. Its gold face threw soft reflections around the ceiling. "Family can rely on one another, in crazy fucking times – like these."

"Yes," Khalil agreed. "Definitely."

Anmar leaned back in his chair, its metal creaking on two legs, and he rolled his sleeves, folding both cuffs tight above the elbow. Chewing on the inside of his cheek, he leaned forward, exhaled, and said, "Yes. Yes." He turned the tuner of a radio even though it was unplugged, cranking it to the lowest band and then to the highest and back, the red indicator manually rising. He chewed and chewed his inner cheek. His forearm was marbled with pink burns – some of them puffy and raised; some of them devoid of pigment like cooked cabbage fused to his skin.

Khalil knew Anmar wanted him to see these scars. Anmar repeated, "Yes. Yes. Yes."

The radio's dial returned to its original setting.

Multiple footsteps clobbered the stairs above. Sandals and sneakers crashed like cymbals and splashed through leaked puddles where pipes drizzled unfiltered seepage. Cackling, high-pitched screeching preceded the steps as men entered the hall and then the room, and there all seven men gathered, Hassan in the center. He placed a long rifle on the table.

He told everyone to quiet. "Let Anmar speak."

"Yes, okay." Anmar said, slapping the table.

He rose, and, with Hassan following, walked over to a battered wooden door across the room with several round holes shot through it. No light came from the holes. Khalil thought it might be a closet or a bathroom.

Anmar flattened his palm to the wall beside it and tried to look through one of the black bullet holes except it was too dark to see. "C'mon," he said, still peering. "Khalil, come here."

Hassan slid closer, too. Anmar and Hassan cupped their ears on the door, their noses almost touched. The men at the other end of the room hushed and shifted their weight. Hassan grinned wide and whimpered a little under his breath like a wounded dog. Anmar hushed them. "You hear it? Shh –"

"What?" Khalil asked.

"Put your ear up to the door."

"*Why?*"

"So you can *hear* them," Anmar said and moved out of the way, his scarred forearm grazing Khalil's wrist, electrifying goosebumps from fingernails to forehead.

Khalil took Anmar's place, facing Hassan. Hassan hunched lower, putting his face in Khalil's, his red and white head scarf slackly bundled above his eyes. The cool wood of the door was smooth against Khalil's cheek; a sliver from one of the bullet holes tickled his skin. He stared at himself in Hassan's metallic lenses, feeling Hassan's nostrils exhale, forceful, a smell like sour milk and tobacco and fear. Patches of burn scar blotched the side of his nose, creeping like a web up and under one opaque lens. Khalil wondered if those burns were from the same fire that scarred Anmar.

Hushed, Hassan asked, "Hear them, man?"

Everyone was silent.

"No," Khalil answered, swallowing hard.

Water pipes groaned. Abbas whispered something, and Anmar flicked his ear.

"The youngest one," Hassan said, leaning closer, "he cries all night. All night like a little falcon."

"Huh?"

The crew behind Anmar snickered.

Hassan clicked and clicked his rifle's *select fire* switch with his thumb and locked his shielded eyes with Khalil's.

"No," Anmar disagreed. "Do you even know what a falcon sounds like? He's more like… more like a *puppy*."

Khalil realized they were talking about the people on the other side of the door.

Anmar frowned, his brow furled down, and spun toward the men – the third guy from upstairs, Addel and Abbas, and the two other men, and the big guy from the landing. Anmar let out a loud squeal, repeating it over and over, so the men couldn't help but mimic, their pursed mouths usurping all the other sound in the room. Like six sustaining fiddles, they aimed their little squeaks at the door – each man maintaining a slightly different pitch until Anmar fluttered his hands in the air and hushed them. The man from the landing continued longer than the rest.

Hassan tilted his head. Khalil could tell he was rolling his eyes under his sunglasses.

"No, no, no," Hassan said, with a *Strike Anywhere* match tweezed between his front teeth, its red tip dipping. He whispered through the side of his mouth, "He's like a *falcon*."

The others laughed.

"A puppy!" Anmar yelled, squealing his rendition over Hassan's. "C'mon, like this. *Reeerrwwhhh Reeerrwwwhhh –*"

Hassan shook his head and his head scarf loosened and fell from his scalp. Long dark hair unwound – curling brown locks that matched his handlebar mustache growing from neglect. Stubble caught little marbles of peculating spit.

"You'll hear him," Hassan assured Khalil, plucking the match from his mouth, flicking it across the room. Hassan made a weird *whooshing* noise as if the match had sparked and combusted.

The men wouldn't stop laughing.

"Shh!" Anmar commanded, stomping his foot. "C'mon now. *Iché!*" He wandered over to the table to pick up the long rifle that Hassan had retrieved earlier and dragged its wooden stock against the cement and rug, then lifted it to Khalil. "Here. Take it."

He did.

"We've an important mission tonight," Anmar said again, leaning an elbow on Hassan's shoulder, "a mission I wish we could bring you on, but –" he paused, "we're not all comfortable with that." Clearing the barrel of his nostril with his thumb, inspecting it, he said, "You're my cousin. I trust you. We can trust you, right?"

"Yeah, Anmar. Yes." Khalil tried not to nod so aggressively.

"You *hear* that, guys?" Anmar shouted, "We can trust him!" The man from the landing started squealing again like a puppy, and one of the men smacked his back – choking him to a stop. Everyone straightened up. "See? We're already comfortable making jokes. Good."

Hassan kept the convex mirrors of his sunglasses facing Khalil, creating an elongated diptych too alluring to ignore. Twin images of Khalil with the long rifle stared back at himself. He nearly expected one of his two reflections to dash for the exit.

Khalil wiped his brow and held the rifle one-handed with the old oak stock inches from the concrete, smelling the sappy cosmoline that once coated its internal levers and springs. The heavy thing slipped in his sweaty hand as if someone was pulling it away. A draft from under the door brushed his ankles. The same wind channeled through the three little holes punched in the door, grazing his neck. Cold air. Nothing air.

"Yeah," Khalil said. "Okay."

Anmar leaned forward and rubbed his thighs, asked Hassan, "You had to give him *this one*?"

"It works. It's Russian," he said.

Anmar snorted hard, spit at the foot of the door, and rubbed his thighs again like he was ready to sprint. "Russian," he said and that was all.

Anmar stood straight and tilted back, stretching with his hands on his hips, and asked for the time.

"Almost seven," Abbas said.

Groaning, Anmar nodded at the exit. That was the crew's cue. They filed down the hall with benign chins square and tight like boxers, heads low and shoulders high, though they sloshed through stagnant pools and soot, jingled brass shells and gun oil, and the straps of slung weapons slapped ribcages and backs with irresolute congratulations for unfinished tasks.

Sal, Khalil thought, *Sal will have to deal with them now.*

"Ya know," Khalil said, "I could help with the mission, whatever you guys are doing. I've got experience and y'know," he trailed off, fumbling with the rifle.

Pipes moaned behind the wall again. Upstairs, the front door slammed.

Grumbling, Anmar shuffled halfway to the exit and turned. "We need you to guard for a few hours."

"Guard who?" Khalil asked.

"Whoever's in *there*," Hassan pointed at the door.

Anmar, without elaborating, disappeared into the hall. His footsteps faded, ending with another door slam that ricocheted off the shadows sticking to the dim.

Hassan rolled the match between his lips.

Vague scratching came from where the doorframe loosely sat and where semidetached nails, bent and rusted, struggled to keep the trim secure. It quickly ceased. *A person or a mouse*, Khalil thought, uneasy.

Tightening his head scarf with fold after fold, Hassan carefully tucked his hair into its nest, clamping the lip of the fabric with his finger tips and combing strands with his palm. He rounded the crown, inserting a finger, making certain no stray hairs dangled over his brow. He did the same over each ear with the attention Khalil wished he could give himself, now that they were out of the desert.

Hassan patted the head scarf, squishing it flat, "This a *khosh* look?"

"Uh, yeah," Khalil said.

"Really? Do I look good?"

"Yeah, man. Fine," Khalil said, his voice wavering.

Hassan smiled the smile Khalil feared more than any razor or bullet – like two hooks hiking his cheeks – a wound of tongue and tea stained teeth. Hassan pointed at the flimsy latch securing the door: a bolt without a padlock, copper wire holding it snug.

"It's really not locked," Hassan whispered, "the door."

"Huh?"

Khalil felt Hassan's nostrils streaming hot air against his chin. "Shh. They don't know. *It's not really locked.*" Breathing deep, he whispered, "They could just yank it open if they wanted." He sniffed and smirked with a bottom tooth as brown and rotted as a turd.

"Who are they?"

"Doesn't matter, does it?"

"I don't know," Khalil said.

"Right," Hassan said. "Right, right, right, *right,*" and he pinched the muzzle of Khalil's rifle, rocking it slowly back and forth. "All you need to know is, if they make noise, if they make *one little squawk,* just shoot through the door." He fingered one of the holes. Splintered paneling warbled. Hassan withdrew his fingertip and sucked it though no splinter had stuck. "*Pow.* Not too low though. Don't hit any of them."

"Seriously?" Khalil asked, pulling back with Hassan's grip still wrapped around the muzzle.

"Oh, it's hysterical, really. You might wanna cover your ears." Hassan covered his own ears, face mockingly sullen. "Loud in here. *Loud.*"

Wanting to protest, wishing he could talk his way out, Khalil watched himself cower in the reflective lenses of his own captor. It was a far different picture from the one he thought people knew. There was no shouting crowd or panicked energy surging through the exposure, no cameramen or news outlets or journalists – only him, alone.

Had they recognized me at all? Khalil thought. *Anmar hadn't mentioned a thing. Nothing.*

"Well. Okay," Hassan said, recomposed, his expression suddenly yanked into serenity. "You can sit over there. Not sure if the radio works. At least you have some Doritos, man."

"Can you give those to Sal?" Khalil asked.

"Who?"

"Sal. Outside."

"Oh yeah. Yeah. Backpack guy. *Cool Ranch.*" Snatching the bag and turning away, his shoes snapped on the cement when they cleared the rug. Hassan added, "Thanks again, man, we appreciate this."

"Yeah."

And Hassan lifted the Doritos in the air with one hand and opened his mouth in a silent scream, mimicking the pose from Khalil's photograph – holding the stance in mock salute, frozen like a mannequin. He captured the expression, the gesture, the impulsive salute perfectly. He held it for a few seconds, then loosened.

Hassan grinned his grin and dropped his hand.

He couldn't decide if Hassan was mocking him or if he was just out of his mind.

Khalil sidestepped back from the door.

He wanted to get as far away from the door as possible.

Hassan turned to leave. As nonchalant as a butler bowing away from a banquet, he Hassan screeched a sustained *Eeeeee!* and became a shadow amid the hallway, the catacomb hollowed out from misery and grief.

* * * * *

Wood smoke and tinder curled under the eaves of buildings. The city.

The carbon-soaked wind whistled through alleyways like air through tired oboes, and in the chimneys, the same eerie notes did little to soothe the families bundled there.

Doors shut. Windows locked. Carrying the song of the night through drainpipes and keyholes, the draft reminded herdsmen and seamstresses that the oncoming fire was as unpredictable as the descending spears that delivered the flame.

Oil smoke and burned furniture smoke and smoke from wilting plastic side mirrors. Sal sniffed and waited.

Some kids wrestled in the dirt.

* * * * *

The sidewalk was cold. Sal's ass was cold on the sidewalk. And the wind kicked, spitting sand up his ankles and up his beard.

Sal was certain Khalil would appear minutes after he entered the tenement. Soon enough, he would open the door, popping his head out with a smile to call Sal in, but as Sal's wristwatch's minute hand moved half-circle, he started tallying all the things he could have done while waiting.

A cup of coffee and a pastry or some warm soup. He imagined a comfortable chair to prop up his sore feet. There would be a cat to lick the milk spilled on his saucer. There would be the comforting chatter of bakers, welders, and handymen, but most of the patrons would be unemployed mechanics, obviously, still fixing whatever they could get their hands on. This was all Sal needed. With the dinar he hadn't spent, he might have found a café with an electrical outlet. Even if there were no Internet, he would still be able to write and look at Rana's photos again.

She thinks I'm dead, he thought. *I know.*

And he felt dead. Sticky and dead.

He scratched his beard, pulled his cheeks toward his bent knees. There was nothing to blow his nose on, so he sniffled and snorted hard and spit.

A good café would have a restroom where a sink would serve as a washbasin, but for now he sat on the sidewalk in his stinking khakis and calcified sweatshirt, convincing himself he didn't care. Between gunshots, he nodded off. But his ass was too cold.

Sal snuggled his backpack like a pillow. The vinyl crackled like starched silk.

Settled in, his stomach gargled, making it impossible to relax. He thanked *Allah* the python puking in his guts had quit. He slid his hand over the paper in his sweatshirt pocket. He couldn't believe he had wiped his ass with cardboard.

A car cruised slowly by, its headlights out, the driver's hair barely visible over the steering wheel.

Footsteps drummed from behind the door.

Sal stood and waited – hands crawling for somewhere to hide, retreating inside pockets – but no one came. Then he slid down again, almost grateful for the chilled asphalt. He shut his eyes.

The stomping restarted and his knees cracked as he straightened and the men finally emerged.

"Hassan *better* fucking hurry," Anmar said, leading them outside.

"We're gonna miss it," another man complained, tripping on a wood plank teetering on the walkway. He caught himself and placed it back at its original angle. "Stupid thing."

"No we won't, no we won't – he can catch up." Anmar whipped around and saw Sal, his back to the wall. Clearing his throat, he said, "Oh, hey!" motioning for the men to be quiet.

"Hey," Sal mumbled, trying not to address them all.

Each man surveyed rooftops and side streets, some pulled open their rifle's breach to hear the sliding mechanical *click* – a warning to whoever might be out there.

"Khalil's just in there, man. He's going to housesit while we do this *thing*," Anmar explained, gesturing his men to flank the block – two up one side, two up the other – with the remaining man, the man with the white ski mask, standing guard at Anmar's heels.

"Okay," Sal nodded.

"Okay," Anmar said, his eyes darting along the street.

Sal did the same. He studied the edges of the flat roofs for proof of life, hallucinating helmets and goggles and radio antennas that weren't there. The two other men on the roof of the tenement building, the guards, gave a nod and Anmar nodded back. "We'll be back soon."

"Okay," Sal repeated.

"You alright, man?" Anmar asked, cocking his head, "You look like shit."

"Just tired," Sal said, trying not to sound pathetic.

"Sit over there. We'll be back in a little while."

"Sure. Yeah."

Anmar put his index fingers to his lips. With a whistle, the four scouts advanced up the block. Anmar trailed his escort down the street, dark panels of abating light cloaking their approach as the men commingled shadow and self. Silent as the dark. At a yellow blinking stoplight, they veered right and disappeared.

Sal lingered, not thinking.

He didn't think about lying down. He found the sidewalk and waited.

Unoiled hinges squeaked. Hassan opened the door. Peeking out, he asked, "They *left* me?" with something in his mouth.

Sal couldn't speak.

"*They* left *me*?" he repeated, stepping outside with an open bag of Doritos in his hand, munching openmouthed with exaggerated disappointment. A key slid from his pocket. He locked the door. "Those dick faces."

They must have used the term after hearing Khalil use it on the phone, Sal thought, and he wanted to say, as a joke, *a face made out of dicks!* but instead, "They're down the street."

"I know where they are. The fucking football game." He handed the empty bag to Sal then licked his fingers. Seasoning peppered his lips. "Big mission." Sucking index and middle fingers, then his thumb, he alternated each hand and hummed with pleasure. "You gotta try these man. They totally have *Down's Syndrome*."

"Huh?"

"Americans say something's *retarded*," he explained, faintly self-righteous, "So these chips, they have *Down's Syndrome*."

Hesitant, Sal chose his words as carefully as possible, "I thought *retarded* meant *bad*."

Hassan paused, an index finger stuck above his puckered grimace. Sal thought he might be smelling it.

"Yeah. Yeah, yeah, *yeah*. That *would* make more sense. Yeah. Retards aren't any good, are they?" Hassan said.

Sal didn't know how to respond.

Hassan turned away. "I've gotta go."

Is he high? Sal thought.

Hassan wiped his palms on his thighs and slapped them on Sal's shoulders, scooting him to the right with rigid arms. Sal shifted, foot over foot, tripping on himself.

"Over... over... over here," Hassan instructed, pushing Sal backwards to the sidewalk. "There," he said, peering northeast and pointing. "You see that tower way down there? Way, way over there?"

"Yeah," Sal said.

A narrow spire jutted from the skyline, tall enough to pencil the clouds.

"I know it's far away, but snipers – they've got nothing but time to practice around here."

"Oh."

"You see that plank lying on the sidewalk?"

Sal looked down, nodded *yeah*. It was the same that got kicked minutes before.

"Whoever's in that tower can't see you if you're to the right of this wood plank. Understand?"

"Yeah."

"Keep to the right. Right here," Hassan repeated. "Someone should have told you that an hour ago."

Hassan looked down at Sal like a father bestowing precious knowledge to his son. He pulled the reins of his face into a wicked smile and held out his hands, pinky fingers tucked in and wiggled them. "You know why Mickey Mouse only has four fingers?"

"Not really," Sal said, smiling a little, too.

"Take a guess."

"Uh."

"Because," Hassan said, face stern with authority, "he is a *demon*."

He flexed his fingers in and out. Grin deflating, he paced backwards a few steps and swiveled on a heel, leaving Sal dumbfounded.

Hassan took a different route than his friends. He shrieked a shrill and inhuman call to the night and to the town, to the neighbors harboring ill wishes of opposition.

It sounded like a bird call.

Sal slid even further right of the wood plank, taking note

of the fist-sized chips hacked out of the building where – a meter from where he was sitting – mixed with dust and crumbled cement, rusty swirls baked like glaze on ceramic tile. Someone had stood there once. Someone had fallen like a dropped sack. And the person who had cleaned the splatters and puddle hadn't scrubbed hard enough to erase the evidence, so that maybe that was left as a warning as well.

Hassan's call faded into the night.

"*Eeeeeee ...*"

Craning his head, Sal couldn't see anyone in the tower, but he dragged his bag away from the stain and away from the plank, and when he was clear across the street – away from the tower's view – he shouldered his bag, his laptop, his everything, and followed Hassan.

* * * * *

Khalil knew just enough not to want to know any more.

He stood in the middle of the room, away from the door.

A discolored path was worn in the rug from foot traffic. Well-tread patches were ground as fine and pale as cheese cloth by boot heel. Ashy concrete bled through. Dirt stained wherever the wool was white, so that the dyed oxblood and burgundies of the fabric were now muddy browns. An extension chord wound out from an outlet, under the rug like a long, thin root, to the radio on the table.

Could've charged Sal's laptop, Khalil thought. And he thought about getting up to check on his friend, but then the hostages, the people behind the door, would be unguarded.

He was closer to the door than to the table.

The exit was closer to the table than to the door.

He didn't want to turn his head to the table or the door – so he didn't, for as long as he could, allowing his eyelids to slide closed like bashful clams, and he pretended not to be there at all.

Minutes passed without sound.

He drew papery breaths, minimizing any noise in his skull, concentrating, and though distracting thumps tumbled from the adjacent building, he couldn't hear the people behind the door. He tried his hardest to hear. Khalil rocked on his heels. The rifle shook. Anything not to look at the door.

Nothing worked.

Around the door frame, heel marks streaked the wall. In some places, yellowed chunks of plaster had been kicked to resemble piles of crackers below. Surrounding those urgent streaks of rubber were footprints of differing sizes, and Khalil had a difficult time discerning what age their owners might be – thirteen or thirty. Some were just toe scuffs; others caved great dents in the wall.

An ant ventured from the jagged pieces of chipped wall. It climbed and circled the rim of a spent roll of duct tape by the door.

"C'mon, Anmar. What is this?" he whispered to himself, not wanting anyone to hear.

There was nothing to do. His heels led him with noiseless poise away from the door, his rifle like a cast iron cane.

When it was the only option left, he sat at the table. The seat was still warm from Anmar. He tried to make no sound.

Khalil unlaced his sneakers, peeled them off and sat them on the table. He folded two pieces of notebook paper from a pad next to the radio into thick squares and reinforced both rotten sneaker soles. He wanted to toss the ratty pair away, burn them in effigy, pour gasoline down their throats and dance around the foul smoke. As of now, they smelled like rotting fruit covered in old Band-Aids. Socks smelled nearly the same.

Maybe there would be work in Ramadi. *Maybe sneakers were cheaper here*, Khalil thought.

Stooping, he found the radio's plug and connected it to the nearby power cord. The metal box hissed with static. No station could be found, but he kept the volume low so only he could hear – not them, not them behind the door – this was the only sound he wanted.

He rested the rifle by the radio and picked at its stock. Flecks of varnish splintered under his fingernail. The stock and handgrip were chipped and oily, but the surface had aged well.

Old, he thought. He hadn't seen a rifle like this in years – not since his father returned from the southern borders of Kurdistan with a carload of bric-a-brac to sell in his secondhand store. That first Russian rifle, the one his father ended up keeping, had been thrown into the estate sale – just another heirloom among the womanly-shaped lamps, ornate nightstands, tarnished silver, tea sets, and endless rolls of rugs his father hauled home.

Khalil flipped the rifle belly up. He unclipped the internal magazine to see how many rounds were left. It opened with a *ping*. It was filled to capacity; ten bullets stacked inside. Then, with his smallest finger, he wiped as much gritty molasses from the housing as he could, swabbing around the mouth of the magazine, and knew whoever assembled the weapon hadn't scrubbed it clean first. It probably wouldn't fire – *might blow up in my hands*, he thought. Slapping the magazine shut, he stood the gun muzzle-up on the floor, aiming away, and pulled down on the spring-loaded bayonet. A metal tooth that held the blade in place disengaged and Khalil spun the blade upward, aligning it with the muzzle and secured it into another tooth facing upward until it locked into place.

The bayonet nearly doubled the length of the barrel.

It wasn't razor-sharp, but scuffs along the blade's sides proved someone had spent time working the edges. Uneven lengths of cutting edge threatened Khalil's thumb as he plucked the blade. With the equator of his palm, he patted the blade's tip and inspected the center of his hand for blood. None appeared.

Khalil scratched the back of his head. He tried his hardest not to look at the door.

It would be so easy to leave – grab Sal, keep walking. But there would be nowhere in Ramadi to hide. Anmar was everywhere. Anmar and his crazy friends.

"C'mon," Khalil whispered impatiently. "C'mon."

The floor was freezing.

Khalil wanted to let his feet air out longer, but he slipped his sneakers back on in case Anmar returned. *Any minute*, he thought. Every street sound echoing down the passageway convinced him they were coming home. Any minute.

Khalil scratched the back of his head. There was no itch. Then he counted the cracks in the ceiling, cracks that grew in crooked circles like unfinished countries drawn on a map, and he followed water stains down walls where plaster separated from hidden slats.

Images of Hassan with his mouth open, his hand raised, flashed on every wall, the ceiling, and sand sprinkled rug. *Was he making fun of me*, Khalil dreaded. *Was he even mimicking the photo at all? Could have been my pose, my pose from the photo, but he could have been just waving goodbye.*

Creep. That total creep.

Khalil's nails pried at the back of his neck.

It was Hassan, definitely Hassan who didn't want me going along on the mission, it was him. Anmar wouldn't have cared. And this was his way of isolating me, showing me who's who and who's in control. This is how it's gonna be.

Fuck him.

A cigarette butt sat on the table. Khalil pinched it. He took a matchbook off the radio. He lit and smoked the last of the tobacco until the stub was just cotton, and he followed the uninspired spirals of gray upward. The smoke drew rivers inside the map of the ceiling then quickly disappeared.

Smoke covered everything Khalil didn't want to see or smell or taste, and the static covered his ears, too. This was good.

The radio fizzed without reception.

Fuck him.

Wet iron and wet feet, bodyrot and burnt hair — all the smells of the room overtook him. The cigarette smoke covered the grossness for a few minutes and then the smells came back even worse.

He kept an ear for the door, but focused more on the radio — its hiss like someone blowing their nose forever. But then the static would hiccup or gasp lightly, perking his ear, and he lifted his head off the desk to hear. Lifting his hot cheek off his arm, he picked out muted consonants from the buzz but would find no words or voice, and Khalil rested his head again.

Whatever, he thought.

He jimmied the radio's knob. The red needle tracked past each station, unsuccessful, attracting only static. He let the dial rest on a random frequency.

A draft fluttered up Khalil's ankle and over his shoulders. Goose bumps prickled his arms. Then another vowel would allow itself in — just a slice of a word sneaking through, ghosts in the wattage seeking attention.

But maybe it wasn't the radio at all, he thought.

Khalil deadened the airwave's static and listened harder.

Voices groped this new air – smothered voices from under blankets – voices, soft and confused by barriers, thick and compacted, murmured. He flipped his head, resting his other cheek on his folded arms.

The door was closed, the same as before.

Is it them, he thought. *Are they children?*

A neighbor flushed his toilet. Sewage smells overtook the room.

It can't be them, Khalil reasoned, crossing his arms, gnawing his cheeks, looking at the ramshackle lock and the bullet holes and the heel marks. They would have spoken up earlier. They would have called out depending on who or how old they were – if they weren't gagged or tied.

Who the hell were they?

Shia businessmen captured off buses speeding to Syria? Bankers and salesmen embarking from Baghdad, ambushed and ransacked and shackled with tape? Had they been beaten, their feet turned eggplant by steel rods? Bound on the floor, their herringbone jackets pulled off by their buttons and inside-out pockets. They could be women. They could be young sisters sleeping forehead-to-forehead.

Khalil counted the bullet holes in the door.

Five.

Or are they Iraqi police? Military trainees? New recruits, survivors lucky enough to be shielded from a car bomb, but too fazed to fight back – scooped up by *Mujahideen* – some of them still wounded? And those were the same wounds Anmar and his crew leaned into, pressing overgrown thumbnails deep inside sinew and meat until the new police bucked hysterically, fainting from the pain. Men like that would have tried to escape. Men like that would have for sure.

One of the bullet holes was low enough to have struck a shoulder or a chin of a person standing on the other side of the door. The other two were shot upward, too high to kill, but Khalil knew that wasn't the shooter's intention.

Khalil chomped the loose pocket of his inner cheek so hard the taste of pennies stained his mouth, and he swallowed the beginnings of blood. With his rifle standing between his knees, he swiveled in his seat to confront the door. His hands shook.

He listened for more voices that never came.

In his mind, the men and women were arranged in rows, facedown, bellies naked, bellies fat like peppermints melted to the concrete, their beards and unwound hair collecting dirt. In the pitch black, they wiggled close for warmth. Girls and boys. Socks strewn in corners. The more Khalil imagined them roiling there helpless, the more he was convinced the foul odors seeped from behind the door and not the running toilet.

He gripped his rifle harder, trying not to shake.

"Hello?" he called softly.

Khalil pressed his nose to the bayonet's cold steel, then his lips, savoring the coolness before pressing it to his forehead – cooler still – leaning hard, embossing the peak of the blade into his skin. The blade's tip ironed a steeple between his eyes. With the tip of the blade flat, he pressed harder, holding the rifle straight, and searched the air for whispering pleas. He thought somehow, somehow through the door, they might feel his pain, too, and that would summon them to speak, though he knew that was stupid and the voices were gone because they were never there.

A pile of rags, he thought.

They could be artists or pirate radio operators or writers, pressmen using defunct facilities to print radical newspapers, daughters of elected officials, councilwomen, clergymen, anyone.

They could be Christians – Christians seeking asylum in Jordan. They were pulled over in the night by bandits and herded into vans, driven and sold to the highest bidder, and now they waited in the starved light with the trestles of their ribs showing – with less and less hope for rescue. A father, a mother. Their sons and an aunt. They could be. Huddled close on the floor. A family, probably – some of them curled into impossible shapes like brass instruments, limbs bound by electrical cord and tape. The youngest son's wrists suffocating and strapped and yanked behind his ankles. He'd lay cranked toward the door. His shriek would be a foot on Khalil's heart, bursting it like a water balloon.

Would he screech? The falcon? The little boy?

Khalil listened.

He listened and was dowsed with guilt for wanting to mimic the falcon's cry like Anmar and Hassan and the crew, but he didn't. He couldn't.

He bent down.

There was nothing more to see.

He gripped the rifle and he bent lower – eyes almost level with the bar of blackness under the door – trying to see the likeness of shoe or blouse or the dome of a knee, but he could only see darkness.

They could be sleeping. They could be tucked into corners, crawled as far from abuse as possible.

Khalil closed his eyes again and saw their faces on the ashen floor, cracked lips squirming for leaking water, and they'd whisper to one another – hushed reassurances and coos – but sparingly, every few hours, cautious not to provoke their captor's eager fist and the furious weight behind it.

Could've been us, Khalil thought. *It could be me and Sal in that room.*

"Hello?" he called, a little louder this time.

Any minute, he thought. *Anmar will be back to relieve me, any minute.*

Khalil scooted backwards against the wall, distancing himself further from the door. The chair legs scraped a miserable howl throughout the space. He aimed the rifle at the door from his hip, feeling ridiculous, cowardly.

Had they starved to death?

Were they there at all?

Could be nothing – nothing but empty chairs in an empty room.

The silence resonated harsher than any prayer or sob or shriek. Khalil shifted his weight onto either foot and chewed his cheek until he thought his teeth might bust through. He sat and stood and sat and tapped the rifle's steel butt plate on his shoe laces, believing the falcons on the floor were never going to pray again.

The war

We sat and watched from the rooftop. The insurgents came running. My brother's key and my dog tags hung from my neck. Hanging. The key that my brother gave me so many years ago – the key that opened doors he never imagined it would.

I watched.

Beautiful. Weirdly green. The insurgents ran, ducked next to buildings, ran.

They were phantasmal beacons dashing from block to block, using umbrellas of dark – two lookouts waving *forward,* the rest weaving in tow. Pulsing. Ghostly green. Their exposed skin glowed molten, but the rest of them, their bodies, were dull olive like the landscape. Their rushing arms and legs blended into the pixelated background. I tried to follow them all the way, 'cept they either turned down an alley or entered a café, 'cause they were gone. Quick fuckers. Illuminated by the night vision, it was the backpack-wearing-kid that came jogging behind.

He was the only one unarmed.

He paused and slithered sideways. Looked to be in his early twenties.

"Who's tailin' them?" Gunnery Sgt. SnackWell asked.

"Dunno," I said.

"*Muj*," SnackWell slurred under his goggles, monitoring the kid as he crept behind the group. "Muj's got a backpack," he said in the weirdo Muppet voice he used when he was trying to be funny. We watched the kid trot across the road where he hid behind a pickup and waited until one last insurgent joined from a side street. "*One* more."

"Roger that," I said and radioed in.

* * * * *

We took position after clearing the building, SnackWell covering the exit while I waited for the target.

We could see all of Ramadi from that roof.

I remember the dump mostly.

Cooked by the evening sun, moldering dunes of garbage fumed putrid and persistent. Westward gales flapped great aprons of rot over the rooftop. A recent avalanche had breached a hole in the garbage mountain, releasing pus and milky seepage into the breeze. No one dared roam too close to its perimeters spread deep – and neither did we – as concoctions of boiled piss wafted off the range. It only added to the misery of the inflicted city.

It was perfect. Who would spot us here, three stories above the sizzling junk?

"Anything?"

"Target's in route," I said.

We knew where they were going.

"Target has entered site Calico."

Site Calico was what we called the café. They'd been there night after night.

We coughed and gagged, trying to stay silent, and even though SnackWell had eaten half a box of SnackWell chocolate mints cookies, he seemed unaffected by the rankness. Every time he finished a cookie, he'd wipe his hand underneath his knee. His pants were his napkin. As if under his knee was the equivalent of wiping his hand under a chair or dinner table. No one cared – no one cared 'cause we were filthier than our mothers and wives ever thought imaginable, and our armpits itched red, and our monkey-butt asses were chapped raw, and there were never enough baby wipes around to spot-clean our junk. We dreamed about showers like we used to dream about women.

My eyes never left the café.

SnackWell offered me a cookie. He kept his night vision on the insurgents, too. I said no. Then he repeated the same stupid line he always did after I passed up a cookie – something about *low fat and guilt-free*, but we both knew it was a joke.

I hate mint anyway.

And I'm probably diabetic or will be, one day, and don't need that shit in my body. There were two jalapeño cheese crackers in my MRE. I'll eat those later.

"Stinks like hell."

"Yeah," I said.

When SnackWell had his eyes on our target, I cleared my eyes of sand.

With a clear view of the open landfill, we saw dogs yank on naked things and fight over twisted knots of marrow, softened and fermented in the crock pots of sedans. Occasionally satiated, they'd howl and leap, spinning in the air like they'd been hooked by fishing line. A few were injured, limping. One of them might've been a border collie, but looked a little too mangy and fierce.

"There's so many of them," I said.

"Dogs?"

"Yeah."

"Yup."

Two mutts chased each other around what looked like an overturned Jeep, flirting and nipping at heels. Rolling in the dirt, scratching his back, the border collie kicked his legs then followed the others, running like a spooked rabbit.

"You think they used to have owners?" I asked.

"Don't care, man," SnackWell said, sucking on a cookie like a communion wafer. He straightened his knee pads that always seem to be sagging, said, "Hate these turtle shells."

Other dogs howled and chased one another, but the collie was suddenly quiet and alert. He tried to keep up with the rest but seemed disinterested. He rocketed around a tipped truck and sat with his paws draped over a tire, hiding.

I said, "That collie – his name's Clyde."

SnackWell looked up and cracked his neck.

"No it ain't."

"Sure is. I just named him," I said, watching the collie lose interest in his pursuit, distracted by sheets of raw garbage. He found a sash of fabric to rip with his teeth, and his head whipped left and right like a crocodile. SnackWell sipped from his canteen when he really wanted to chug.

"Careful there," he said.

"Why?"

"If you think they might'a had owners."

"Yeah?"

"Can't rename a dead man's dog." SnackWell paused and sipped a little more, sniffling, "Very bad karma."

He recapped his canteen. Offered some to me. It's like giving someone a bit of wisdom and then something to wash it down with. He was right. Seemed like all sorts of bad karma.

I fought the urge to yawn. I rubbed the back of my neck and pulled out a wild hair.

"We got a while, right?" he asked, already knowing the answer.

"Yeah," I said.

I knew SnackWell wanted to pry open the Velcro of his cargo pocket. He wanted to pull out his PSP with the cracked screen and the broken speaker, both disabled when he slid down a staircase after clearing a house, the time he discharged his weapon clean through the ceiling as he hit ground.

He raised his rifle at the exit door instead.

No one could see us, not from up here. No one could see our swampy asses sitting in our swampy fatigues or the long burn scar branding SnackWell's forearm like an earthworm, branded there from an overheated barrel of a mounted SAW. And no one could see the weeks of grime manicuring our nails, oily slivers of dirt that grew back minutes after digging them clean.

"Alright then," SnackWell whispered in his Louisiana drawl.

It was more thug than cowboy by virtue of color, not geography, and he peeled off his wristwatch where his LiveStrong bracelet used to be. Lieutenant Jasper, who everyone called *The Law* – who probably loved being called *The Law* – had told SnackWell that John Kerry wore a LiveStrong bracelet – "For the votes," he'd said – and SnackWell sliced it off with his K-Bar the second the LT left the barracks.

Everyone would'a called him *LiveStrong* after that if *Snack-Well* weren't such a snappy handle. His wrist wasn't nearly as tan where that yellow band used to be. I knew it was probably a constant reminder of what used to be there. He didn't need me saying nothin'.

I adjusted my helmet's strap, loosening it some. It itched like burlap and rode my chin, and every time I straightened my helmet the microphone for my radio rode up. So I fixed that, too. Quietly, in my earpiece, the unit gave the insurgents' position and arrival time, and reported that we'd all meet down there and take the café once positioned outside.

We could hear them laughing once in a while. We could hear the soccer announcer on the television inside the café.

"Who's playing tonight?" SnackWell asked, rifle sight still on the exit door.

"You don't really care, do you?"

"Rather be watching football – even if it's *fake* football."

"I guess," I said, and spit, and the spit bubbled between my boots. I kept my head low over the roof. No one was around. No dogs were in the dump. The street was a cutting board. Vehicle scraps were pushed against sidewalks like gnarled hunks of fat cut off the city; overturned garbage barrels rolled; little rugs, milk crates, pushcarts, stacks of bricks, wooden boxes were all shoveled to the side so late-night traffic could flow, 'cept there was no traffic.

The backpack kid stayed put. He didn't enter the café.

"We have one Tango outside the Calico," I radioed in.

I flicked on my rifle's night scope, and hanging the barrel over the ledge, I lowered its reticule just above his head – combing the red bead through the kid's hair and around his scalp, my finger outside the trigger guard. The safety was on. He looked too scared to move. And even though he was tin in my scope at half a block from our position, I could sense the hesitation in his posture, almost able to feel his shaking hands.

"Tango's just watchin' the targets, *over*."

The kid rummaged through his backpack. He took out something and ate it. My eye itched. I thought there might be some sand in it, but I blinked until the scratching stopped and my eye blurred teary.

"Shitty sand," I said.

"Yeah."

The soccer announcer screamed a few sentences in Arabic.

"Status, bro? How much time we got?" SnackWell wanted to know.

"Fifteen *mikes*," I said.

He shifted his weight.

We sat shadowed in the tired light.

The building was still empty.

We took the stairwell slow the same way we cleared it the first time, taking each step as if it were ready to snap. No mistakes.

We made sure the ground floor was secure and snuck out to the street, making as little noise as possible. A helicopter approached – one of ours. The AC-130 passed overhead as if it were milling the clouds to powder. Massive and almighty. The chopper rounded back overhead. Though it wasn't supporting us with fire, it offered comfort. Its chopping covered the sound of our footsteps. We hustled, scraping our shoulders against bricks, avoiding windows and the oil slicked across the sidewalks. A rusted drainpipe snagged my fatigues and ripped them.

Across the street from the café, we took cover by a car with an open hood, kneeling, but pushed forward when SnackWell gave a nod. We circled the block and crossed the street on the same side as the kid and stacked up at the corner of a building.

He was still chewing on what he'd pulled from his backpack. He had his pack back on like he was ready to move.

I looked back every few seconds.

It was quiet – the way we liked it.

I picked a pebble out of my sleeve.

Like a totem pole, I positioned myself above SnackWell, both of us taking aim. He took a knee, using a corner as cover. The handle of my rifle tapped his helmet. Through my optical scope, I scanned terraces and walled rooftops, all the invisible nooks and open windows, returning my sites lower, northeast to the street where Ramirez and the rest of our patrol would appear.

Ten minutes. My watch read sixteen hundred. Only ten more minutes.

In the café, the insurgents spoke but we couldn't make out what really. One of them had his back to the only window.

"I'll stack up with the others if you get Backpack Dude," I offered.

"Roger," SnackWell said.

"If he moves, just let him go."

"Right."

"You got extra flash bangs? Only got one here."

"Should'a done this on the roof."

SnackWell handed me two, and I swear they smelled like mint chocolate. I lifted one to my nose, sniffing loudly. "Your dick smell like cookies too, bro?"

"You're my favorite homo," he whispered.

"*I'm* the one standing over *you*, remember."

"*Ho. Mo.*"

The insurgent in the window moved away – looked like he had an M4 on his shoulder.

The kid slid off his backpack and placed it behind the car's front tire. He scratched his beard.

"You think Backpack Dude's got explosives?"

"Naw," I said.

"How can you tell?"

"Dunno. He looks kinda brainy, though."

"I'm going to crack that motherfuck open," SnackWell snarled.

"Walk softly. No fuss."

"Right-o."

"Serious, bro."

"Yup," SnackWell said.

I blinked, but the itching still itched like an ant had pinched itself to my pupil.

Yells from the café jolted us. Someone hopped around in the window, arms berserk, celebrating. We laughed it off through our noses, keeping composed, keeping hidden. I looked out for Ramirez who by now should'a taken post on the highest building on our side of the street – his Springfield locked and loaded, his deadeye relaxing on soon-to-be-dead things.

Through the radio, Lt. Jasper said they were in position. They waited for my word. I did another pass for ambushes or mortar teams, but that's what we'd been doing all day, over and over.

I scanned above us for Ramirez's barrel, but he was invisible. Clouds clogged the starlight, the moonlight.

The moon was a sugar cookie.

* * * * *

I patted SnackWell on his Kevlar, giving him the signal. He swapped his M4 for his pistol. He knew there was a bullet in the barrel 'cause he checked it twice on the roof. I could tell he was excited. His knee jittered. We both knew if the insurgents in the café were alerted, if we somehow botched it, we'd charge straight in from right here.

"Good?" he asked, taking off his helmet. He palmed it with

his hand, placing the thing on the sidewalk.

"Live strong, brother," I whispered.

"*Fuck you*." And he went.

He was stealthy as a mosquito, sharpened by fatigue and burning reserve tanks of adrenaline. For a recovered thug straight outta the suburbs, he was good, creeping quick, not a boot squeak. We'd both had a lot of practice.

I kept my scope on the kid just in case. Petted his hair with the reticule again.

SnackWell was nearly there.

The patrol held, listening for my signal. Lt. Jasper couldn't wait long.

Nearly there.

SnackWell scooped around the kid's head and cradled him, a gloved palm over his mouth and the pistol in view, embossing a cold circle into the kid's temple. SnackWell eased him down on the ground. Neither of them made a sound. He kept the pistol to his face with a boot prying his shoulder blades. Flex cuffs zipped on the kid's wrists, he looked at me and slammed his eyes shut. SnackWell dragged him back by the ass of his pants, behind the car, out of view.

Thumbs up.

I throw a thumbs up back to SnackWell and radio in.

No one entered or left the café. Between shouts, glasses clinked and the crazed announcers on the TV spouted rapid-fire Arabic, and then the insurgents inside did the same. It was impossible to see them. There couldn't have been more than eight or nine. Out back, generators purred. We considered cutting the power, but we already had the element of surprise.

Our men jogged single file down the block, quiet and clunky

with their gear. As long as they were silent, it was fine.

Stacking up on the right side of the door, Lance Cpl. Swann positioned behind me with three men on the other side, Lt. Jasper holding one end of the battering ram, waiting for my go. Snack-Well covered the street for resistance flanking from either side. His elbows were propped on the car hood. I could see his boot heel still between the kid's shoulder blades – the toe of his boot working the nape of his neck. The kid's fingers wiggled.

I nodded.

Jasper reared back, and with one man behind him, throttled the door with the ram, blowing it off the deadbolt. The ram gonged on the concrete. Two flash bangs lobbed in through the door. They strobed like two split suns. Screams flung from every corner. Blinded, one of the insurgents started popping shots at the doorframe, shredding its wood as we ducked, rolling. Ricocheting metal whistled across the street.

Through the one front window, Lance Cpl. Swann punctured and smashed the glass with his barrel and burst fire at the insurgent, but returning fire pulverized the glass panes above his head and he ducked back. Chiming brass bounced out around boots.

"Might'a hit'em!" Swann yelled.

More rounds thwacked overhead and a piece of wood the size of a pant leg spun into Swann's helmet then bounced away. He swung his head to me and grinned.

With all this time, every man in the place should have been firing back.

"Something's not right!" Jasper yelled.

Ramirez radioed *six men exiting a side door, headed east* and he shot one before they dove out of view. SnackWell came running, pulling the kid by the shirt with Sal's nose bloodied, eye swollen.

SnackWell said he saw about five men escaping through an alleyway. He laid Sal facedown in the street.

Frantic cries called from inside.

Jasper cycled through a magazine, swiveled back, and reloaded. All I could see was his absurd mustache. He tightened his whole face up in concentration. Bullets thumped past our ears like acorns raining from trees, whizzing blindly. I hinged around to fire once Jasper was through, punching holes into an upturned couch, a table, another couch – and one of the insurgents chucked a brick out the window. It spun straight into my face.

My forehead opened. I blinked like I just opened my eyes in the shower. Stunned, warm wetness glazed my vision. Someone yanked me by my waistline. SnackWell. He pulled me down below the window ledge before rattles of Kalashnikov fire cut the air above.

On my ass, I tried to sit up 'cept SnackWell held me down, said, "Shit, bro. That's a grenade that didn't explode?"

"Tasted like a brick to me," I said through the blood, syrupy and everywhere.

"Definitely a *Muji* sand-grenade, bro. You *saved* us," he joked, slapping his PSP on my chest and tearing open a pack of bandages from the same cargo pocket. "Can you see?" He handed me the bandages.

"*Yes.* Christ."

Another brick arced over our heads, landing in the street.

"Run outta ammo," SnackWell huffed, taking back his PSP and clacking a few more rounds into the café.

"Back door, back door!" Swann yelled, and with SnackWell leading two men, they circled the neighboring building attached to the café. Jasper fired through a metal table both insurgents used as cover, and it sounded like pounding nails through a baking sheet. Both men silenced. Jasper had maybe ten rounds left in that magazine. He kept his rifle leveled and waited.

I mopped my face, pressed hard on the gash chiseled into my brow. I thought *Muji* probably played some softball in his early days, 'cause even with my helmet protecting most of my head, that was one hell of a shot. Popping up, I shot the table one handed – more ceremony than necessity – and from my angle I saw a crude passageway chiseled between both buildings. They'd escaped through it.

"Frag?" I asked.

Jasper shook *no.*

We should'a sent in grenades from the get go, I thought.

Reloading, we entered, covering the simple square room. Our boots crunched glass. It smelled like hot rust and cordite, like a car accident, the atmosphere spray-painted with salt. Generators hummed. Everything was cut up. The back counter had taken most of our fire. Chalkboards that once held handwritten menu items hung crooked, their wispy contrails interrupted by bullet holes. Some fragments of writing were legible on another chalk board 'cept most had flaked to the floor. A cash register, glass pitcher, kettle, and jar sat on the counter – somehow unbroken.

Rows of shoes lined the wall, dirty sneakers and a nice pair of dress shoes, and every poster on the wall had fresh eyelets punched from flying lead.

"Yup," Jasper said, his bottom lip stuffed with tobacco.

He lobbed a snotty wad, splattering thin strands of spit in every direction. The television survived. The announcers squabbled, spouting frantic syllables and the crowd chanted static while we tiptoed through the wreckage. It was like they were yelling at us.

Jasper kicked the outlet until the plug splintered out of the wall.

I stepped over CD cases. Some were still square. A silver boom box took a bullet straight in the tape deck.

Jasper kept aimed at the table we'd shot to shit. Approaching the dead insurgents, I kicked over a chair and addressed them like any other dead thing, wondering which one had the good arm, the keen timing, the balls to throw a brick during a firefight. I didn't want to get too close.

A hand stuck out from the end of the table, curled up like a claw, bloody and bright in the light coming from the uncovered bulbs overhead. I stepped around. One insurgent was on his back. His arm was bent weirdly around him. His elbow was red and rheumatic, probably broken. The other was turned a little, toward the wall. His face appeared dipped like candied apple, and he had no weapon – so he was the one who done my head in.

"We good?" Jasper asked, more in a *you good?* way.

"Yes, sir."

Across the street, well-timed shots whip-cracked the air – sounded like Ramirez.

"Buildings must be connected," Jasper explained, pointing at the hole carved in the wall, "We'll follow, you secure this mess here and the prisoner. Ramirez is coming with us. We'll send you wounded if we need to."

"Sir?" I asked.

I could see Sal frozen on the pavement.

Jasper peered into the hole.

Commanding over his shoulder, he said, "Keep that head from spilling out – looks like y'r hair's taking a piss all over y'r face."

Jasper ran out the door. Radioing for the squad's position, he clumsily vaulted over a bench and jogged down the block like some overburdened animal that just learned to walk upright. *Bastard.* I saw Ramirez run after him. Gunships growled in the distance.

Wetness dribbled over my nose and lips, and flipping the bandage over, the fresh side of the folded gauze was completely soaked. I swapped it out for one of my own. I swallowed and my head went fuzzy for a second.

I turned my radio louder to keep updated on their progress, took out the blaring earpiece. I heard Swann describing a tenement house, terraces with high railings, fire raining from makeshift pillboxes, from a front door. Shots crackled in my earpiece – sounds of rice pouring on a drum. Jasper calmly delegated and I waited for him to call me but he didn't. He wouldn't call unless he had to.

I took off my gloves and yanked a tourniquet from my cargo pocket.

Somehow, my head didn't hurt, but it gushed and I pressed on it hard, eyes blurring. It was tough to distinguish sweat from blood. Straps dangled below my ears. I set my helmet on the floor, fingers combing a sticky scalp. I tied the tourniquet across my forehead, sticking the bandage down as it started to throb. The room focused.

Colors on the wall sharpened into individual tiles. Molding grew out of the corners of the ceiling.

I approached the escape route joining both buildings, leveling my rifle. It was just a jagged hole hammered through the brick.

I shined my rifle's flashlight, spotlighting the crooked opening for tripwires. The hole was small – just large enough for a person to scurry through. A toppled bureau sat on the other side, drawers arranged on the floor.

I recognized our bullet holes in the rippled wood from the angle they'd sailed through – a miracle most of the insurgents managed to flee.

I wished I'd gotten some dip from Jasper.

Crunching back through the café, I got outside where the

kid was trying not to look at me or say anything that might spark conflict. He had his backpack sitting on top of his ass like Snack-Well meant to make some weird sculpture. *Insurgent with JanSport in Suppressive Position, Jeremiah "SnackWell" Christianson, c. 2004.* I almost took a picture. Knew better not to.

"You got some boom booms in that rucksack, Muji?" I asked, stepping forward, toe close to his chin. A bead of blood bubbled in the pipe of his nostril.

"No, sir," he whispered, looking up, eyes spiraled like red and white dinner mints.

"You speak English?"

He paused. Swallowed.

"Yes."

"Well, miracles never cease," I said, bending down to twist the shoulder of his shirt into a handle. "Hope you're a Chatty fuckin' Cathy cause we got some *quality time* ahead."

He didn't respond.

I didn't blame him.

I yanked his limp body up with the backpack in my other hand and we went back inside.

* * * * *

I cleared a rectangle along the wall with my boot, sweeping glass and dust fallen from the ceiling so the kid could sit with his flex-cuffed wrists. Even though neither of us could see the two dead insurgents behind the table, I found a rug and made them more comfortable, too. I threw it over them. No one should have to look at that. The kid watched me with his focus on the floor the entire time. He shook like a motorcycle ready to stall.

I dropped his bag between us.

"What's your name?"

"Salim," he said, perking up a little. It looked like someone swabbed his nostrils with a red lollypop. White specs of plaster clustered in his beard.

"Sally," I said. "Sally's a cute name. Knew a Sally in high school. Redhead. *Weird gal.*" I went through his pockets. There was only a rusty bottle cap and few torn pieces of what looked like a toilet paper role. "You write down notes to your insurgent buddies on this, Sally? Big plans?" The scraps fluttered down. A stone clicked on the floor, bouncing.

"No," he said quietly, "I'm not a fighter."

"Yeah?"

"No. I walked here from Fallujah."

Unzipping his pack, I took out some clothes and tins of unlabeled food, empty jars, a sock. "And that makes you *not* a fighter?" All that crap got piled on a table. He didn't say anything. "Sally, Sally, Sally. Fallujah Sally. What're we gonna do?"

In another pouch, I found a charger wrapped in two cables and beside them, an old laptop. My faced lit up. "Fucking score, bro! You got the whole *Mujahideen* blogroll on here? Emails? Chat room archives?"

"No," he pointed a cheek to the wall, eyes down.

"Cool Muji videos?"

Sal barley chuckled, "Only our profile pages."

"Cute, Sally. I like that." I laughed a little, too. The bag flopped empty on the floor. "You know, when we were following you here, I had you pegged for a Mac guy. You look like a Mac user, you know?"

"I don't know," he sighed.

"Skinny. Beard. Bandana around your neck and shit." I wagged an accusatory finger at him. "You guys are always flying international, can spot you a click away." The charger slipped off the face of the laptop and its wire snagged, saving it from the cement. I gathered it back up.

"Please be carefully with it, sir," he said loudly, sorta surprising us both, adding, "Please?"

"You dudes have profiles, huh? Online?"

Sal waited.

"I do."

"Yeah, right," I unwound the cables from the charger, opening the laptop and balancing it on my palm. The old thing was heavy. The battery must've been original.

"Know why?" Sal asks.

"Why?"

"Because I'm *not* a fighter."

"Right, right," I said, holding down the power button. "This ain't rigged to *blow*, is it?"

Outside, a mortar whistled and exploded, fizzling on the radio, too. Everything around us jumped. Sal flopped on his side, teeth nearly biting his knees, shaking. He couldn't cover his head. Ducking, I shoved my earpiece, listened. No one was shouting – only firing. Jasper's maniac orders came through clearly: they'd entered the tenement, rooms were cleared, two insurgents down. Apaches drumbeat like a dozen spooked horses.

Sal looked like I was going to hit him.

"Scary shit," I said.

His nostrils blew the dust on the floor. Grabbing his shoulder, I straightened him up.

"How you know English so well?"

For the first time he engaged my eyes.

"My mother."

* * * * *

With the back of the screen pointed at Sal, I kept pressing the power, but nothing happened. Every time I shot him a glance he looked away, finally saying, "Battery's dead."

"Well, you could'a told me that before, Sally. C'mon."

"Sorry," he croaked.

"Thirsty?" I asked, plugging in the charger, sitting next to him against the wall. He nodded. "Well, I'll give you some water after you tell me everything you know – and what's on this laptop."

He sniffed quietly. The corner of his mouth curled. "Boring stuff."

"Shit, Sally. I bet you've got some cool bomb-making memos on this bitch."

The laptop powered up and we sat there like fishing buddies waiting for oncoming rain, Sal leaning forward, trying to take the pressure off his bound wrists, face red and welling. He looked around the room, but mostly kept his face down, eyes avoiding mine. That was fine with me. My head started to pulse. It felt like someone connected an air compressor to my temple, turning it on and off and on. I loosened the tourniquet.

We listened to my radio. Another mortar shook the ceiling, hitting closer. Jasper's tinny voice called for an evac. Suppressive fire hammered through the radio and they seemed to be taking the building bit by bit. "You hear that?" I asked Sal. "I'm missing *everything*, bro. You better make this worth it –"

"My friend's in the tenement house," he whispered.

"Huh? Sally, you gotta speak up."

"My friend Khalil's in that tenement. He's not a fighter either."

"Sure sounds like he is."

"He's not," Sal sighed, sucking back tears.

I repeated something I'd heard days before:

"And I ain't no soldier, bro – I'm a *surgeon*." I opened folders on the C: drive, finding a photo file, some word docs. "Your country's kidneys are failing, dude. *We're* the *dialysis*."

"Huh?"

"*Dialy-sisss*," I hissed.

"Whatever," Sal mumbled.

The last mortar shook the cash register off the counter. The drawer popped open with a ding.

Two white trucks sped by the café and I warned Lt. Jasper over the radio. He confirmed. Apaches engaged. Tires screeched down the block and there was a second of silence before the helicopters lit them up. Rockets streamed out of their honeycomb tubes – walloping fire – sent one truck flipping. The other opened into blazing orange cauliflowers – black plumes of dirty red plum. The street flashed white hot. Debris pelted roofs, clanged on concrete.

Sal closed his eyes tight.

"Holy shit!" from the radio.

The rumbling faded.

With two in custody, the squad confirmed three dead. I can't believe I'm fucking with some Muji computer while they're taking out the rest of them.

Sal breathed heavily.

"What's dialy-sis?" he finally asked.

I didn't answer. Search words for files named explosives, bomb, and detonator came up empty. I started to open everything.

There was a file called *design work* and one named *Rana*. I opened that one and clicked through a few pics of a girl, all portraits, some with her family and friends.

"This your girl, bro?" I asked, turning the laptop toward him.

He nodded without looking. "She have a profile, too?"

"Yeah." Sal rasped.

"What a world, huh bro?"

"Yeah." 'Cept he didn't know what I meant, I think. Maybe I didn't know what I meant either.

"You gonna tell me what to open or do I have to sift through all this personal crap?"

"Khalil's a good person, I swear, I know he is," Sal said in one exhale, huffing frustrated. He used his shoulder to scratch the side of his face.

"We can make this really easy. You tell me where the bomb and suicide shit are and I'll make sure you friend doesn't end up in a dungeon. Cool?"

Sal just clicked his sandals together.

"Yeah?" I asked again.

Nothing.

Each design folder was empty when I opened them. I checked the trash bin. There were just some Word files and another pic of Rana. In this one she's with some other guy at a mall or something. When I clicked back to the desktop there was a folder with dozens of Word files, some dated, some labeled strange names.

"You aren't going to make me read these, are you Sally?"

I opened the most recent and read.

* * * * *

Sal breathed like a dog.

He breathed like a dog 'cause that's the best way he wrote it and that's the way I read it on his laptop. He breathed like a dog when all he could think about was Khalil and probably Rana, surely Rana too. He was anything but a dog.

We listened to the radio while I read.

Sal said nothing. He sobbed quietly, and when my eyes stung from the screen, I looked away and studied the ornate baby blue and maroon flowers painted on the tiles lining the bottom half of the café wall. They were beautiful and ancient like drawings by the first men, before words and before everything.

Tears spattered the concrete between Sal's heels.

I read as much as I could. Then I put the laptop down on the floor and lifted myself up. My head sang with pain.

"Sal," I called to him. "Hey."

He wouldn't look up.

I palmed the smooth stone I'd confiscated from Sal's pocket, sliding it off the table I'd place it, and bent down and put it at his feet.

"Sal."

When he finally looked up, he wasn't crying. Dried streams marked the hills of his cheeks. His bearded chin vibrated uncontrollably. I bent down and Sal scooted back, shocked, like I might hit him.

The torn paper towel roll lay scattered between us.

"Bro. It's alright."

There was nothing for him to say. I turned my radio down 'cept the fizzling kept on like bacon frying in the background.

"You – you really walk all the way here?"

"Yeah," he said hoarsely, nose to the floor.

I turned my head, hooked a finger under my jaw, scratched.

"Shit," I said. I knew I wanted to say more.

I looked at the laptop and studied the shot-to-hell café and gathered the scraps of paper. I didn't know what to do with them, so I just stuffed them under my Kevlar jacket. "Shit."

Sal didn't ask to be set free. He didn't beg or plead.

On the wall, to the right of the counter and partly on the tiled part of the wall, someone had hung a portrait of a father or grandfather – his Santa Claus beard and *keffiyeh* as white as paper – 'cept they'd hung it too high, and above the frame a second tiny hole in the plaster hadn't been painted over. Somehow, even after the firefight, the photo was still hanging. I stared at the portrait and thought. No thoughts came.

Quiet settled.

Aromas of ozone rode the breeze. Rain was coming. Rain brought good luck. We'd seen little of either.

Cracks of gunfire mixed with the radio's ambient breath. I stepped backward, crushing flakes of fallen ceiling. My boot heel hit the dimpled table we'd shot to shit.

"Okay," I said.

Lt. Jasper radioed they'd taken the tenement house – several dead and a few captured, small stockpiles of RPGs and other weapons. They'd hoarded coalition supplies: MREs, pallets of rice, sodas, cereal. They had a basement room with bomb-making supplies, schedules, and schematics. *We're evac'ing wounded, clear the surrounding area, over* – but the channel crackled as a helicopter chugged by, and Jasper ordered me to hold the café in case any insurgents doubled back. Ramirez was on his way to rendezvous. I strapped on my helmet, awkward with the bandage. I tightened the tourniquet, and told Sal to wait.

"Lemme see. Okay?" I said – like that meant anything at all – "*Lemme see.*"

Hands cuffed behind his back, Sal rocked in his seat and muttered. Maybe he was praying. I couldn't tell.

I stepped through what was left of the doorway. Curtains

freed themselves from rods and rolled down the block.

Gray billows consumed the street like rolling fog. Making sure it was clear, I radioed to Ramirez I'd meet him outside. I knelt on one knee, the loose magazine in my rifle chattering its teeth. Everyone was positioned at the intersection. Men screamed. They screamed at the heads of other men to turn their heads and keep their heads down, eyes down. I could barely see them. Smoke thickened and grew around their necks and screams. The street vibrated raw and resonated wrong through my bones and my molars and the whole wrecked steeple of my body. My elbow pads shook like the world shook – like the world was waiting on me to clamp my hands around it and stop its shaking.

I didn't want to move.

Headlights in the fog blinked on. I leveled my sights on the gray field above the right beam. Then the headlights shrank away, as slow as dying stars.

* * * * *

Probably Sal didn't bother to look up 'cause he thought it was me come back from the street. If he'd been listening to the radio too he'd know Ramirez would be there, and who knew what kinda crazy shit another soldier might do. His strangled wrists were purpled and probably stinging, and he could see on the laptop screen that I'd finished reading what he'd wrote. I'd set the laptop at that angle to prove it.

Sal listened.

Fruit flies gathered around the rim of the glass. Brave flies ventured into the pool, hit the tea, twitched in the cloudy grave. Used teabags of Nescafe sagged on the counter.

Someone was there.

He couldn't look up.

"Sal," the voice. "Salim."

Black Adedas blinked into view.

It was him.

It was Khalil laying a rifle on the shattered floor and saying, "We *have to hurry*." It was him snapping out the jack knife, the knife they'd carried all that way, and him trying not to slice Sal's wrists when he shimmied the blade under the tight plastic cuffs, turning the knife away from Sal's skin – bruised and bloated with blood – and freeing his friend's binds with a snap. He hugged Sal, wrangling his shoulders and kissing the top of his head.

It was him, and Sal couldn't believe it.

"Guess their mission got found out, huh, man?" Khalil asked. "*Shitty*."

Sal couldn't speak. Holding each wrist, inspecting them, he trembled so hard he couldn't see how deep the cuts were. Khalil said something and closed the laptop, unplugging it from the wall and handed it to Sal, whispered, "*We gotta go*."

"Are they dead?" Sal asked.

"C'mon," Khalil urged, yanking Sal by the shoulder, but he wouldn't budge.

"What did they make you do?"

"House-sit, man – c'mon, we gotta go."

"How'd you find me?"

Khalil walked over to the window, ducked, and made sure no one was coming. He muttered, "Anmar."

Sal brushed dust off the face of his laptop, smoothing his hand over the plastic like he was trying to erase what was inside its spinning drives. Khalil came back. He bobbed his head nervously, twisted the slack of his track pants, winding up his thigh.

They both eyed the rug. Its folds hid Anmar's dead friends from view, but they both knew who they were.

"Is *he* dead?" Sal paused. "Anmar?"

"I don't even know," Khalil blurted, teeth tight. He looked away, out the window. His eyes shifted around the room. He moved his hand to touch Sal's head one more time but fluttered away. Khalil picked up his rifle, the bayonet's tip scraping the floor, tip drawing a wispy thread of blood across the concrete. He walked over to the wall lined with shoes, kicking off his ragged Adedas.

Khalil found a pair of polished dress shoes. He slipped his toes into their open mouths, wiggling in. They were too tight. Lifting the rifle, he used the bayonet as a shoehorn, letting his heel slide against the cool steel, the blood dripping casually down the blade into the shoe. The rifle shook. It was awkward to hold. His mouth kinked with concentration. He did the same to the other, not bothering to lace the pair and he stood there with the rifle in his hands, facing the wall.

Khalil kicked the heels.

"Whose blood is that, Khalil?" Sal managed to say.

Khalil rocked back and forth, settling his feet, and when he did, the bayonet's tip tapped the tiled wall. "They fit good, huh?" he said.

"Whose is it?" Sal asked again.

Khalil rocked and wiggled his toes and tapped the pointed blade like a windup toy marching into a wall, unable to turn.

"Anmar's," he said, grimacing, smirking, his voice distilled.

His bayonet tapped and tapped.

Raindrops pelted car roofs, car hoods.

Concussions pounded the earth. White magnesium light made each wall tile crackle as brightly as sunlit windows. Sal and Khalil were showered in that light for a few failing seconds until the flapping afghans of fire waned. Khalil cringed. Sal watched him. The bayonet tapped again and again. Soaring fortresses roared overhead like stones sharpening the clouds, and their loud engines tore the blanket of the night in two and flew away invisibly. Khalil turned, heels on the baseboard.

"You know I'd never do it again, right?"

"I know, Khalil. I do."

Lifting the rifle, Khalil turned to Sal with renewed urgency.

"We must leave quickly," Sal said.

Dogs barked and dogs ran in the new rain.

Focused on the back door, Khalil didn't see me creep into the café until my own rifle was raised – the muzzle in his periphery. He cranked toward me, instinctually, like he had no choice or we had no choice and he didn't have time to react, and I was all reaction.

Five rounds unzipped his shoulder and chest. His face contorted, mesmerized and sleepy. He collapsed. His weapon slipped from his grip and cracked, bayonet down, on the cement, and his stomach fell on the stock where he balanced limp like a marionette and dropped, dead before hitting the floor.

He fell away from Sal.

I stood motionless.

Sal sat there with his hands on his laptop like the laptop was a shield against any bullet or bomb, and I lowered my rifle so that he knew I wouldn't shoot again. His peeled eyes told me, then, that I'd killed Khalil, I'd shot him – Khalil with black track suit, Khalil from the photo – and Sal couldn't move or make his mouth sound.

I couldn't move.

Dogs moaned in the strewn wreaths of the landfill. We wanted to moan like the dogs moaned 'cept we weren't free to.

I raised my left hand, fanning my fingers that shook like Sal shook. It was the only thing I could do.

And this is the way I've told it – and will tell it –'cause somewhere in the telling there's a peace waiting to be made.

I backed out of the café.

At the intersection, a Humvee pulled up from the direction

of the raided tenement, but I didn't recognize the men leaping out of its rattling shell 'cause I didn't care. They led a limping soldier into the passenger seat where he slumped in relief.

Grungy-faced men set about the street corner, one with a handheld radio, the others waiting anxiously for instruction. I walked to them.

SnackWell waited with Ramirez on the sidewalk, breathing hard. He asked, "Where is he?"

I shook my head.

"Ran off. Got away when I was patching myself up."

"Thought I heard shots."

"Missed 'em." I said.

SnackWell shrugged.

"Anything in his backpack?"

"No," I said. "Nothing."

We started walking where the platoon convened, patting backs and exchanging congratulations, all of us dazed. More vehicles – Bradleys, transport trucks, a confiscated Jeep – cordoned off each street, with Apaches chopping in broad circles, swirling dirt. The desert twisted its dusty fingers in our ears and in our nostrils and we coughed into the havoc.

"Took a mean crack on the head, man. Should have that looked at," SnackWell sniffed, reaching into his breast pocket for what I thought was a cookie.

"Yeah," I said.

He passed me a stick of gum.

I chewed it. Bruised auroras bloated above the tenement house – baked on the clouds.

There was a fire we had to let burn.

Justin Sirois is a writer living in Baltimore, Maryland. His books include *Secondary Sound* (BlazeVOX, 2007), *MLKNG SCKLS* (Publishing Genius, 2009), and *Falcons on the Floor* (Publishing Genius, 2012) written with Iraqi refugee Haneen Alshujairy. He also runs the Understanding Campaign with Haneen and co-directs Narrow House. Justin received several individual Maryland State Art Council grants and a Baker "b" grant in 2010.

Interview with Justin Sirois

Katherine Villarreal interviews *Falcons on the Floor* author Justin Sirois for *Dark Sky Magazine*. Their conversation is reproduced here with their permission.

Dark Sky Magazine: What are some of the books you've enjoyed or that have influenced/inspired you? Is there anything else besides books or authors?

Justin Sirois: Dahr Jamail's *Beyond the Green Zone* heavily influenced me to begin a project about Fallujah. His courageous, unembedded journalism was something I had never encountered before, and I knew, after reading his book, that there were stories to tell about the people involved in the conflict — specifically the sieges of Fallujah.

Bing West's *No True Glory* was another book I turned to for a much different perspective. The physicality of his reporting was extremely helpful in imagining the landscape.

I watched every film I could find on the Iraq war. Documentaries like *Iraq in Fragments* and *The Dream of Sparrows, Voices of Iraq, Operation Dreamland*, and *The War Tapes* were all extremely informative. Most of the Hollywood films about the war have been cliché or poorly produced. There was also nothing notable that was told primarily from an Iraqi perspective. Part of my motivation was to correct that problem — the lack of an Iraqi perspective in literature and art.

DSM: Was it difficult collaborating with someone on a project like this? Was the process easier or harder?

JS: It made the process much easier. Haneen Alshujairy acted as a creative consultant and editor on the novel. I wouldn't have had the courage to begin such a large project without her help. She's a brilliant woman and, thankfully, fluent in English. Out of the 60 or so Iraqis I solicited online, she was, by far, the easiest to communicate with. Also, her father is from Fallujah, and he was also a great help when we were stuck.

The entire writing process transpired over email. I have plans to visit her in Cairo for the first time in the fall.

DSM: Why did the scenes in *MLKNG SCKLS* get separated from *Falcons on the Floor*?

JS: *MLKNG SCKLS* came about after I finished the second draft of *Falcons*. I just couldn't get Salim and Khalil out of my head. I was/am in love with them. So I went back to my notes and drawings; post-it notes stuck to my wall contained seeds of anecdotes and stories that could be developed further. I keep a sketchbook where I actually draw characters and work out scenes, much like a movie storyboard. Ideas and themes that weren't developed in the larger manuscript started coming together. At first I just wrote very small vignettes or flash fiction pieces. Then I started working on short stories like the "uncooking" story.

Adam Robinson of Publishing Genius helped me shuffle them into a real concrete collection. In a way, *SCKLS* is a great teaser/trailer for the novel.

DSM: What is the meaning behind the title?

JS: I can't tell you that. I don't believe in revealing those particular meanings in the work. Sorry.

DSM: Have you ever been to Iraq?

JS: No. Not yet anyway. I could have flown to Iraq and spent way too much money on a fixer and accommodations, but it was terribly dangerous and still is. It would have been a waste of resources. Even the most talented and resourceful war journalists are frustrated that they cannot cover stories properly over there. It's a shame.

DSM: Often times when I was reading, I felt like I was reading a poem. Do you write poetry as well?

JS: I do come from a poetry background and have a book of poems that came out in 2007. My prose is lyrical at times, I have to admit. I try to keep it as subtle as I can. Composition and the sound of my language are very important to me. It has to fit in the mouth before it fits on the page.

DSM: There's no hidden political agenda in *MLKNG SCKLS*, is that the same case for *Falcons on the Floor*?

JS: I'm glad you said that. I agree, there is no political agenda or opinions in either of the stories. I'm not interested in opinions, really. Left or right, for me all that is boring inside literature. *Falcons on the Floor* is a novel about people struggling to maintain their identity in a time of great violence against their culture. It is not a typical war story. Ultimately, it's a novel about friendship and love and death.

DSM: How did the idea for this book come about?

JS: Interestingly enough, it had nothing to do with Iraq or two young men leaving Fallujah. I walked out of work one day and saw a man struggling to carry a child's car seat. There was no baby in it or anything. I just watched him heave this big thing across the parking lot and into the building — sweating and panting. Something about it struck me on a simple visual level. Then, all of a sudden, Salim was walking up the Euphrates. I know that's a big jump, from a man with a car seat to a young Iraqi man walking from Fallujah to Ramadi, but that's how it developed.

DSM: What are some print/online journals that you read regularly?

JS: Anywhere that pushes the envelope a bit. I typically end up on news sites, though. HTMLGiant's staff has been extremely generous to me so I go to their website often.

DSM: In a word, describe your writing.

JS: SCCNCT.

Haneen Alshujairy Interview

Publishing Genius Press's founding editor interviewed Haneen Alshujairy, an Iraqi refugee who consulted on the writing of *Falcons on the Floor* for HTMLGiant. Their conversation is reproduced here with permission.

HTMLGiant: How many English words do you know? From what I've heard on the radio, it seems like you are very fluent.

Haneen Alshujairy: Thank you! Well, I haven't counted them yet, but I'm sure the number of the ones I don't know is much more than the number of the ones I know. It does sound like a good idea to start counting though.

H: How much do you understand the culture of the US?

HA: My understanding of the U.S mostly comes from Hollywood, I've watched tons of movies since I was a kid, I also read a lot of books by American writers, and other than Justin I've made like 5 or 6 online friends who were Americans. But I gotta give the biggest credit to Hollywood.

H: What is it like in Cairo? Like, what's a typical day consist of?

HA: Well, my life is not very interesting. A typical day for me would be a 9 am - 4 pm school, a couple of hours at home with my family after that, then hang at my friend's apartment. We sometimes drive 30 minutes to go to Cairo – I live in 6 October City, so when we have enough energy left we go to one of the cafés that has a view on the Nile—awesome places in there! Or if a good movie was showing we'd skip that and go straight to the cinema.

H: What kind of music and stuff do you have over there?

What about Iraq? In MLKNG SCKLS there's a reference to the Monkees and I thought incorrectly that it was a mistake on Justin's part. So is American culture fairly popular in Iraq?

HA: Egyptian songs are very popular in all of the Arab world, Egyptian movies also, you find everything though, every taste, here or Iraq, you can find people who are obsessed with Egyptian music, Iraqi songs or English songs, Spanish, even the Turkish songs has its fans. In the novel though we tried to show that Salim's mom influenced his taste in general cause a typical Falluji won't probably know much about the Monkees.

H: Can you describe a football?

HA: A ball played by foot :)

H: Can people actually read Arabic? It seems bewildering.

HA: Oh, I can read AND write Arabic. It's not that hard.

H: How did you decide to be a dentist?

HA: That was more of a family decision—my parents thought I'd rock as a dentist. They kept talking me into it till I decided oh, what the heck, let's do it! Here the average you make in the last year of high school determines the type of college you can go to, so if you get a high score everyone around you will want you to be a doctor! For social status and such . . .

H: What is it like, not being able to live in your own country? Why did your family leave?

HA: I hate it, but I know us leaving was the best decision my parents ever made, 'cause it was getting worse by the second. I mean the situation over there. When I talk to my friends who are living there still and they describe the way they live, it makes me feel very grateful to be on the other side, the safe side, I mean. We left 'cause it wasn't safe anymore, the kidnapping in exchange for money was starting to be a trend, people were too scared to leave their homes, and my dad saw that it was only gonna get worse. So we went to Jordan. We thought it was only gonna last a couple of weeks and then we'll be able to go back, but just like my dad imagined it didn't. It's been 7 years now.

H: Do you resent American interference in Iraq?

HA: Yes.

H: In 1996, when asked about the hundreds of thousands of children suffering and dying under US-led sanctions during the Saddam regime, Madeleine Albright said, "We think the price is worth it." You were about 7 at the time, right? So she was talking about you. Do you know about this? Albright was our Secretary of State under a relatively respected President, Bill Clinton, so that was kind of our official opinion. So, what is it about the USA that you want to understand?

HA: I didn't know about that, I do remember my father cursing that lady a lot though. Now I can see why.

H: Why *don't* you hate us?

HA: Unfortunately, there are many of us who do hate you, but for me, I hate the bad actions that the governments did, same time I do believe there is good in the people, governments are not the people, and you just can't hate a whole country only judging by it's government's actions. I've talked to many, many Americans who have shown their love and support to Iraqis and helped many Iraqi families. I couldn't possibly hate that.

H: Are you a Sunni or Shiite?

HA: Sunni.

H: How much does this matter to you?

HA: It doesn't. Up until the war no one cared about that. But after the war people seemed to care, which I think is one of the very bad things that the war has brought to us.

H: I heard recently on public radio that literature is making a resurgence in Iraq, now that the Saddam regime is out. What plans does the Understanding Campaign have for literature there?

HA: We want to support Iraqi universities with reference books, which are very needed, and we also wish to make donation programs to support other libraries in Iraq that could use our help.

H: Thank you for that, and for sharing with us.

HA: Thank you.

Also from Publishing Genius Press

Meat Heart by Melissa Broder (poetry 2012)

The Disinformation Phase by Chris Toll (poetry 2011)

Fog Gorgeous Stag by Sean Lovelace (other 2011)

Sasquatch Stories by Mike Topp (other 2010)

We Are All Good if They Try Hard Enough by Mike Young
(poetry 2010)

Pee On Water by Rachel B. Glaser (fiction 2010)

The Best of (What's Left of) Heaven
by Mairéad Byrne (poetry 2010)

Words by Andy Devine & Michael Kimball (other 2010)

Easter Rabbit by Joseph Young (microfiction 2009)

MLKNG SCKLS by Justin Sirois (fiction 2009)

A Jello Horse by Matthew Simmons (fiction 2009)

Light Boxes by Shane Jones (fiction 2009)

The Origin of Paranoia as a Heated Mole Suit by
Rupert Wondolowski (poetry 2008)

these here separated to see how they standing alone by
Stephanie Barber (poetry/film 2008, 2010)

Six off 66 by David Daniel (fiction 2008)

and more

visit www.publishinggenius.com to order